Ezekiel's
passion

The Bluette Men Series
Book Two

BAILEY WEST

FROM BLUE'S BEAUTY

One day during one of our clothes swapping sessions in the bathroom, Zora informed me that she was leaving home as soon as high school was over. She'd received a scholarship to Columbia University in New York. She wanted to become an Oral Surgeon.

"I haven't told my parents because I don't want them to stop me."

"How are you going to pay for your ticket to get there? I have money if you need it."

"Thank you, but I've saved up enough money from babysitting those bad ass kids at church to pay for a one-way ticket. I am going to stay in the dorms, and my scholarship will cover my tuition, room, and board. I just have to maintain my grades."

"How will you get out of your house with your stuff?"

"I will bring stuff out slowly and keep it at your house. I don't have a lot there. Most of my stuff is at your house anyway. I just can't stay *here any longer Nette. I'm going to lose my mind if I have to continue to live with these people. It's just...I hate church. I hate church people. I hate church stuff, and they are always making me do it. I just want to be able to experience life without them ruining it."*

She let one tear fall and quickly wiped it away. She told me some things that she has experienced while living with her parents and she swore me to secrecy, so it's her story to tell...

1

"THE 4:45 am bus to New York City is now boarding at door number three," the muffled voice said over the intercom.

"Thank goodness," I said to myself as I stood to collect my bag. I followed the other waiting passengers and formed a line at door number three.

"Hey, Lil Momma," I heard a raspy voice say over my shoulder. I turned around hoping that it was not who I thought it was. It's him. He smiled at me displaying an open face gold tooth that was next to a spot in the front of his mouth where another tooth used to be. He looked like a Jack-o'-lantern.

I saw him when he first came into the bus station. He looked like he was fresh out of the pen...as in penitentiary. He had on some high waisted stone washed jeans that were rolled at the bottom and tucked into his white slouch socks. He had on a windbreaker jacket with earth tone colored paisley print. I'm figuring that was the style when he went up. No one told him that we have graduated from paisley jackets and stone washed jeans.

He sat across from me in the waiting area and kept looking at me. I made eye contact with him once, and he pulled his bottom lip between his teeth...well, tooth. I named him 'Toothless.' I always make up names for people when I don't know their names or don't care to know their names. I felt uncomfortable under his glare, so I moved and sat closer to the guard station. I don't know how much help the security guard would have actually been since he seemed fascinated by a crossword puzzle he was working.

After realizing Toothless was standing behind me in line to board the bus, I looked into my bag and pretended like I'd left something in my seat. I stood by my seat for a few minutes until I saw the line move then I stood back in line. I needed to make sure Toothless, and I wasn't sitting anywhere near each other.

The bus was somewhat full, but the seat directly behind the driver was still available. I chose that one. Toothless sat in the back of the bus.

The bus loaded its last passengers and pulled out of the station. The bus passed the Gateway Arch and crossed over the Mississippi River. I watched as we crossed the bridge into Illinois from Missouri indicating that I'd actually done it. I left Saint Louis. More like escaped Saint Louis. I walked across the stage at my high school graduation, celebrated with my best friend, Zanetta, then I snuck out of my house in the middle of the night. I walked a couple of blocks and then called a cab to take me to the bus terminal. I probably should be nervous or scared, but I'm not. I am just ready to be gone. In the last couple of weeks, things in my house had gone from bad to hell. I knew I had to leave.

No one knew my travel plans including Zanetta. I did tell her I was leaving but the less she knew, the better. I knew that Zanetta would be the first stop my parents made when they started looking for me. *If* they started looking for me. They may not care. Then again, they will look because they will want to save face in front of the church people. How bad would it look to the church folks if the Pastor and First Lady have no idea where their child is? It's all about image for them. They are only concerned with how things look. They could care less about how things really are.

I left a letter for my parents so they wouldn't think I was kidnapped.

Dear Mom and Dad,
I guess you know by now that I have left home. I couldn't stay any
longer, and I didn't feel like you would understand my need to leave. I
will be okay. I have a plan. God will protect me.

Love Zora

I didn't tell my parents that I was accepted to every college I had applied to. Nor did I announce that I had chosen Columbia University. I didn't think they would care, so I didn't share. I don't recall either of them asking me about my future plans. I believe that it was assumed I would stay in Saint Louis and find a job or go to a community college. How crazy is it that no one thought to ask me what my plans were? For a normal family it would be very crazy, but for my family, it was...what it was.

My dysfunctional family consists of my dad, mom, and my three older brothers; Countee, Amiri, and Langston. Yes, they are all named after famous poets or authors. So am I. At some point, my parents read something other than the Bible. I'm surprised my brother's names aren't: Moses, Noah, and Abraham. Then they would have named me Mary or Ruth. Thank goodness they stuck with the pattern and named me after a famous black author also. It never occurred to me to ask why they chose our names. Those weren't the types of conversations we had in my family. We really didn't have any types of conversations in my family. Outsiders probably looked at us and thought we were the Cleavers or the Huxtables. They had no idea what we were really like.

My dad is the Pastor of Pool of Siloam Church in Saint Louis, Missouri. When I tell you that his passion is that church, I mean it. I think he loves it more than he ever loved anything or anyone including his family. Certainly, more than he loved me. He spends all of his free time either at the church or doing church stuff like preparing his sermon, listening to church on the radio or watching church on TV. I don't ever remember a time when he was around long enough to actually know what was going on in my life. He wasn't at any of my honor roll award ceremonies or any of my parent/teacher conferences. Oh, but let Sister So-and-So from the church have an ingrown toenail! He would go to wherever she was, pleading the blood of Jesus over her raggedy ass feet, until she thought she felt better. Let Brother So-and-So be in the hospital, Reverend Chambers would be the first visitor on the list. He would show up with his Bible and his blessed oil all ready to grease that man's forehead. He cared for everyone else, but not for his family.

My mother was the one who was in charge of the house. I don't think she really likes me. She tolerated me, but I always felt like if given a choice, she would have chosen not to be my mother. How do you give birth to a child but have no patience or time for them? She never established a mother/daughter relationship with me. We didn't do anything together. If I needed clothes, she would shop for me and bring things back. If I needed my hair done, she would pay someone to do it. She never hugged or kissed me. She never said she loved me or empowered me as a woman. We never had conversations about boys or the birds and the bees. She never told me about her pregnancy or my birth. She did a fantastic job of ignoring me.

The good church folks thought she took care of me. She is a great actress. She would smile at me and hold my hand while people were around but as soon as they left, she would go back to completely ignoring me. People would give me compliments about my long, black 'good' hair or my blue eyes. My mother would always find a way to downplay their compliment. Someone would say, "Oh Zora, your hair is so long and pretty." My mother would respond, "Girl she so tender-headed, God should have given that hair to someone who would appreciate it and take care of it. It smells so bad by the time I get her to put some shampoo in it. It's a shame really." One time someone complimented me on my blue eyes. "Oh Zora, your eyes are so blue and beautiful." My mother responded, "You know blue eyes are not really blue. They are actually absent of color. You are complimenting her on a birth defect!". She kept up that type of behavior my whole life. Almost as if she was jealous of me but she created me! How can you be jealous of your own child? Most of the female traits that I have, I learned from Zanetta and her Aunt.

Auntie Elisa is the one that taught me how to cook, clean and how to take care of my body. She introduced me to scented body washes and taught me how to use maxi pads and tampons. I'd had my period for almost a year before my mother even knew.

I can't say that I hate my mother because honestly, I don't really know her. Hate is such a strong word. Let's say I am anti-Sheila Chambers. She could probably go missing, and I would be sad for my dad, but that's about it.

My feelings for my Dad are different than my feelings for my mother. I love my Dad, although I'm not sure if he loves me back. I think he got lost in *Religion Land* and there was no one around to direct him. That should have been the job of his wife, but she didn't. She watched him neglect me. She encouraged his complete immersion into the church instead of reminding him that he had a little girl that needed him at home. I really needed my Dad. I yearned for his love, attention, and protection. The church got those things from him, but I didn't. I would sit in church and watch him beam with pride at other kid's accomplishments. *Little Sally is on the honor roll two semesters in a row.* I stayed on the honor roll. There was not one semester my entire school career that I was not on the honor roll. *Little Buddy got a full ride scholarship to the local community college.* I got full ride scholarships to every single Ivy League school that I applied to. *'Little sort of smart person' scored a 19 on their ACT.* I scored a 35 on my ACT and 1500 on my SAT. I took the SAT just to be doing something. I knew I could go anywhere I wanted to go with my ACT score. My accomplishments were never celebrated. He celebrated those old raggedy ass mediocre church kids every chance he got.

I think my dad is the reason why I have such strong views of church and church people. I don't deal with any of those mouth foaming, hypocritical, Bible-thumping, hell raising, judgemental people that call themselves Christians. Well, except for one but she is none of those things. She is my best friend my A-1 from day one. My sister from another mister, my Sissy-Zanetta. I met her in elementary school. During our first conversation, I forced her to be my best friend. We have been close ever since. She is my biggest cheerleader. She is my support system and my confidant. She doesn't judge me even though we are very different. I don't like church, at all. She loves church. She can go every day and never get bored. If I had to go every day, I would stab myself in my eardrums with a dull butter knife. She's a fashionista. She has an eye for fashion. Me, not so much. I know if something is cute but I usually let her pick out my clothes. We are opposites, but that has never mattered to either of us. She just loves me for me, and I love her for being the one constant in my life. I know she has my back no matter what.

I stayed awake until Toothless got off the bus at his stop. I couldn't risk falling asleep and waking up to him seated next to me. So, I stayed up. After he got off the bus, I tucked all my belongings in close to me, and I slept until the bus arrived at a stop in New Jersey. The bus slowly made its way through the Lincoln tunnel into the hustle and bustle of New York City. When I first decided that I was going to leave home, I didn't know if it would actually happen. I thought somehow my parents would find out and try to stop me, but they didn't. I finally made it. I got off the bus at the Port Authority right in the middle of Manhattan. Things were moving so fast around me, but I was determined that I would learn this city. I *had* to learn this city. Failure was not an option. I couldn't go back to Saint Louis.

I got my small suitcase from the bottom of the bus. I sat down on a bench and thought, "I finally made it here. Now, what do I do?"

Where can I go to get help? I have seven hundred dollars. That money needs to last me until I can find employment or the semester starts. I need to go to my school, but it's Saturday. I know the offices are closed today and tomorrow. I have to figure something out. I asked for directions to the library and was directed to the largest library I had ever seen. I saw this library in movies. I waited to use the computers and Googled 'homeless shelters.' I found one that was for people under the age of twenty-one. I wrote down the address and asked the librarian for directions. I followed her directions and found myself standing in front of a nondescript building. It didn't have any special markings or signs. I knew this had to be the place based on the address. I stood outside the shelter contemplating everything that could go wrong. They could be full. They could call the police and report me as a runaway. Even worse they could call my parents. This was my only option. I had to go in.

I rang the bell. A short latin woman came to the door.

"Can I help you?"

"Hi, um...I just got in town, and I need somewhere to stay."

She smiled, then opened the door to let me in.

I explained my situation to the lady who turned out to be the director. Her name was Sylvi.

"We don't have any beds here, but I am going to send you to my friend who runs a group home. I know she has a bed available for you. That will be a better fit for you anyway."

She made a quick phone call. After she finished her conversation, she said, "Yes, she has a short-term bed for you. Follow these directions to her house. It's not too far from here. It's walking distance."

"Thank you."

I followed her directions to the address that looked like a regular house on the outside. I double checked the address before I knocked on the door.

The door was opened by a small woman.

"You must be Zora?"

"Yes, I'm Zora." I smiled.

"I'm Evelyn, come in."

She moved to the side and let me enter the house. I didn't know what I was expecting, but it was just a house.

"Sylvi explained everything to me. You are welcome to stay for a few days. Anything longer than a few days will force me to put you into the system. I'm sure that's not what you want."

"No, it's not."

"Good, follow me, I will show you to your room."

Evelyn showed me to the small room upstairs. There were two sets of bunk beds facing each other and a small desk between them. There was a girl on each bed except for one of the top bunks. There was nothing new or updated about the room, but it smelled like someone had recently wiped everything down with bleach and washed the linen.

"Here is a lock and a key. You can put your things in that locker against the wall for safe keeping. Keep this key on you. I wouldn't want to think that these young ladies would steal from you but you can't be too careful." Evelyn explained.

"Thank you," I said after taking the key and lock from her.

"Girls introduce yourselves to our new guest," Evelyn said before she left the room.

"You can take that top bunk, it's empty," one of the girls on the lower beds said. "I'm Martica," she pointed to herself. "This is Leeann," she pointed to the girl across from her. Then she pointed above her, "and Bethena."

"Zora."

"Dang girl where you from talking all country and shit?"Martica asked.

"I'm from Saint Louis."

"Saint Louis? Like that island where the Jamaicans be coming from?" Leeann asked.

"No dumb ass that's St. Lucia and Jamaicans come from Jamaica," Martica rolled her eyes.

"Saint Louis is south, right?" Bethena asked.

"Naw, man it's in Missouri. I got some family there," Martica answered. "How you get here?"

"I came here for school," I answered.

"*Hearr*," Martica tried to mimic my accent. "You country den a mug!"

I'm country, but you just said, '*den a mug*'...I thought to myself as I busied myself with putting my bag in the locker. I put the key around my neck.

"Aye man, for real. Keep your stuff locked up cause these chicks in here is some straight up thieves, man. Remember those red Nikes I had?"

"Yep, they came up missing one day. We never did figure out who took them." Bethena said.

"Aye, I think it was that one girl that ended up going back home."

"Oh yeah, I forgot all about her."

I left them to their conversation while I climbed up into my temporary bed. I listened to the girls talk and argue. I held on to my key as I laid in the bed formulating my plan.

I stayed at the shelter for the weekend. Monday morning Evelyn and I called Columbia University and spoke with a friend she had there. She explained my situation to them.

She wrote some information on a piece of paper and handed it to me.

"Go to your school and ask to speak with Mary in the residential life office. She will help you from there. Good Luck, Zora."

"Thank you," I responded. I took the paper from her and smiled as I left her office.

I found my way to my school, but not before getting on the subway going in the wrong direction. Then once I got on going the right direction, I missed my stop and had to walk back down the street to the school. I was frustrated, but failure was not an option. I had to learn this city.

I walked into the housing office and asked for Mary. I was escorted to her office.

"You must be Zora?"

"Yes, I'm Zora Chambers."

"Have a seat and let's see if we can't get this all figured out for you."

I sat and watched as Mary typed away at her computer and made a couple of phone calls.

"There are some summer jobs available that I can set you up with." She jotted something on a post-it pad. "In the meantime, take these numbers and contact some people that can help you with the other things."

I took the paper from her.

"Can you do this on your own? I can go with you if you need me to."

"No, I will be okay."

"You sure?"

"Yes, but thank you."

I left her office feeling hopeful for the very first time in my short life. I knew that if I could just survive these couple of summer months that Zanetta would be here and I wouldn't be alone.

I contacted the people that Mary told me to. They were also very helpful. Mary found me a job on campus working with the housing office. I stayed in one of the dorms. When the semester started, my goal was to be at the top of the class. I had something to prove to myself and to my family. Failure was not an option. I had to succeed or die trying.

Zora

I had been in New York for two years. My parents never did come looking for me. I thought that maybe one of my brothers would try to reach out to me, but they haven't either. Zanetta told me that my parents came to her house looking for me right after I left, but that was the extent of their search.

After having time to think about the choice I made to leave home, I realized that maybe I could have handled it differently. Maybe I could have at least told them that I planned on leaving instead of disappearing into the night. After my first year of school, I sent a letter home.

Hi Family,
I am in New York attending Columbia University. I am maintaining
all A's while taking 18 credit hours. I am hoping to finish undergrad at
least a semester early. I'm sorry that I left the way that I did. I felt like
I didn't have a choice. Please forgive me. It would mean a lot if we
could talk about it.
I love you all.
Zora

I don't know what I was expecting, but I did receive a letter back in my mother's handwriting. The letter said:

Zora,
I hope you did not contact us thinking that we owe you something or
that you would get anything from us. You thought you were grown by
leaving the house and moving to New York? Well, how about you stay
grown! Do not contact us again.

She didn't even sign her name. I could feel the hate through that letter. After reading it, I felt so alone. I had Nette but the reality set in that I would never have a relationship with my family again. I learned to push that whole experience to the very back of my mind and keep going. I promised myself that I would succeed and I plan on it.

"'Scuse me, miss?" I felt a tap on my shoulder.

I turned around ready to curse someone out. I was greeted with an enormous toothy grin from a handsome guy.

I looked him up and down with the meanest face I could muster.

"I am trying to find the number one subway?"

Someone was always stopping me and asking for directions. When I first arrived here, I'm sure I sent some people on wild goose chases with my directions, but now I know the subway system like the back of my hand.

"You have to walk across campus to the other gate. The subway entrance is right there."

He looked in the direction I pointed then turned back to me and said, "Thank you gorgeous."

"Gorgeous is a big word. Is that one of the new words you learned in your ESL class?"

"I tried to give you a compliment, and your response is that I'm some foreigner taking English as a second language class? Wow." His olive colored skin, dark hair and thick accent said that he was from somewhere else.

He put his hand on his chest covering his heart feigning offense. I gave him a fake smile and walked away. He was cute, but I only dealt with chocolate. Dark, milk, or even white, as long as it's chocolate. New York had an array of chocolate, all for the sampling. I was taught to abstain from sex until I was married. I always hated when they would talk to the females about saving yourself for marriage, but they never had those talks with the men. I don't think it's a good idea to wait. I mean what if the sex is whack and you've already married him. Then what? You're just stuck with terrible sex for the rest of your life? No ma'am, no sir! That's not going to be me! It's like getting one of those Valentine's day boxes of assorted chocolates. I would squeeze each piece to determine what type of chocolate it was. Only after sampling each piece did I decide which one I would eat. That's how I feel about sex. Sample, sample, sample.

I made the conscious choice to be sensual and sexual. If I wanted to have sex, then I was going to do it. No attachments, no relationships just really good sex. I always hated the double standard that was imposed on women. If a woman sleeps around with multiple men, then she is a whore, but when men do the exact same thing, it's normal. It's even celebrated. I decided not to care what people thought about me or my sex life.

Over the next couple of weeks, I kept running into the same guy that asked for directions.

"Are you following me?" I finally challenged one day.

"Yes," he replied. "I was hoping that you would tell me your name, Gorgeous."

"I didn't offend you enough the last time you called me Gorgeous?"

"I don't offend easily, Gorgeous."

"Well, I offend easily, so stop calling me that."

I think it's so disrespectful for men to call women pet names without their permission. Don't call me sugar, darling or any of those fake ass, annoying ass pet names.

"I don't give random strangers my name. Especially ones that can't take the hint when they are being brushed off."

He smiled.

"My name is Bahir. Now I'm not a stranger."

He was very persistent. I will give him that. The longer I looked at him I realized how cute he really was. He wore his hair in a low cut. His eyebrows were so thick that they were the most prominent thing on his face. He had soft brown animated eyes. His lips were thin but full enough to see them. He didn't have that no top lip syndrome that I hate. His looks were not going to stop me from giving him a hard time though.

"You could have made that name up," I challenged.

"If I wanted to make up a name, I would have said something way cooler like Michael Jackson or James Bond."

"Oh yeah, those are way cooler," I sarcastically responded.

"Let me buy you a cup of coffee, please?"

I thought about it for a minute before I relented and led him to the coffee shop around the corner.

We sat at a table near the window. He told me that he was originally from Lebanon but came to the states from France. He said that he was attending Columbia also. I drank my free coffee and let him tell me all about himself.

"So tell me something about you."

"That's not going to happen, Bahir. I don't know you from Santa Claus. Your story was very interesting, though."

"You have the most beautiful eyes."

"Thank you. I have to go now, so I won't be late to class. I will see you around."

I stood to leave.

"Okay Gorgeous. I will see you later."

"You're gonna keep calling me that even though I told you that I don't like it?"

"You won't tell me your name, so I have to call you something."

"Don't you usually like your women all covered up and stuff? It's too hot to be walking around here with only my eyes showing."

I was being ignorant on purpose, but he wasn't deterred.

"I like for my women to look just like you, Gorgeous."

He was getting on my nerves but was charming at the same time.

"Zora...my name is Zora."

"See you later, Zora."

Over the course of the next few weeks, I would see him on campus. Every time I saw him, he would ask me out. My standard reply was no.

"How many times do you need to hear no before you finally stop asking?" I was tired of having the same conversation with him.

"I'm a patient man. I want to get to know you, Zora."

"Fine, you know what? Let's go out. When do you want to go?"

He smiled brightly as he said, "What about Friday?"

"Friday is fine."

"Can I pick you up at your house?"

"Hell naw! You don't need to know where I live. We can meet somewhere."

"You don't trust me?"

"I don't know you so, no I don't trust you. Where do you want to meet?"

He chuckled.

"We can meet at the pizzeria on Carmine and Seventh. It's the West Houston stop on the one subway."

"Okay, I will find it."

We met after class on the following Friday and went to Spunto Pizzeria. As much as I didn't want to admit it, I had a good time with him. He got me to talk about myself by asking me questions that no one had ever asked before.

"If you could hop on a plane right now, money was not a concern, where would you go?"

I had gotten used to men saying just enough to get me in the bed, which the joke is on them because that was my goal as well.

"Hawaii, or anywhere warm. I love the ocean and the beach."

"Are you more of a TV person or do you like movies?"

"I'm a movie person. What about you?"

"I like movies too. What is your favorite movie?"

"Napolean Dynamite."

"I don't think I've ever seen that before."

"It's a cult classic! I remember the first time I saw it, I laughed so hard. I still laugh every time I watch it."

"I will have to watch it so we have something to talk about on our next date. That is, if you are willing to come out again with me."

"I might say yes, if you ask nicely."

He asked again, and I said yes.

Bahir and I started spending a lot of time together. I wasn't trying to be in a committed relationship, but he changed my mind. Sex with him was cool. It wasn't earth shattering, but he made up for it by treating me like a Queen. I didn't have to worry about anything when he was around. He paid for all of our dates. He opened doors and pulled out chairs. He was the perfect gentleman.

He and his family had a strained relationship just like mine, but he did have some cousins out of state that he would visit once a month. We talked about me meeting them but my class schedule was tight, and I didn't have a lot of time for travel. I appreciated the way Bahir didn't smother me. He let me be me. We could go days without seeing each other and be perfectly fine. That's what really endeared me to him.

I found out I was pregnant with our son right before I graduated from undergrad. Bahir and I used condoms, but one broke. I figured that I would be fine. I wasn't worried until Aunt Flow decided not to visit. Then I panicked. Leave it up to me to get pregnant the first time a condom breaks. I was terrified. I didn't know if I could be a good mother because my mother was such a terrible example. What if I ignored my kid the same way my mother ignored me? What if I didn't have it in me to be a mother? What if my kid was anti-me the same way I am with my mother? I was so scared.

I told Bahir about the pregnancy. He looked like he was going to be sick.

"You want to keep it? I will support whatever decision you make," he finally spoke after sitting for several minutes.

"Believe me, my first thought was to get rid of it, but I know that I can't do that so, yes, I want to keep it. I mean, I'm scared as hell. I didn't think this would happen...but yes, I want to keep it." I repeated myself a couple of times to convince myself. I know keeping it is the right thing to do.

I gave birth with Bahir on one side of my bed and Zanetta on the other side. As soon as the nurse put my baby on my chest, I fell in love. All of my fear about not being able to love him dissipated as soon as I held him. I knew at that moment that I would be my best for him. He would never feel the rejection that I felt from my parents. I am going to love this kid with my whole heart. If I can't give him anything else, he's going to feel my love. I named him Braeden James Chambers. We call him BJ. He reminds me so much of my father and brothers. He has my dad's eyes and big ears like my oldest brother Countee. I wish I could introduce him to them. He favors Bahir a little, but I think he looks like me.

Bahir and I worked out a schedule so I could continue with grad school. He would take care of BJ on Tuesdays and Thursdays while I attended evening classes. My classes started at six, so he would usually arrive by 4:30 if he hadn't spent the night. His sleepovers started to happen less and less. I wasn't really tripping off it because I was so busy with being a mom and a grad student. I needed the space. I appreciated the space.

One night when BJ was six months old, I was packing my bag getting ready to leave for class. I noticed that it was getting late and Bahir hadn't arrived yet. I called his phone. He didn't pick up. Maybe he was underground on the subway. I waited and waited...nothing. I started to worry, so I packed BJ up in his stroller and made the trip to Bahir's apartment. I knocked on the door to his apartment several times, and no one answered. I tried turning the door knob, it was unlocked. I walked in, and the sight in front of me took my breath away. I became lightheaded which prompted me to tighten my grip on BJ's stroller. I thought I was going to pass out. The entire apartment was empty. Unoccupied. Vacant. Without a speck a dust. I had just spoken to Bahir two days ago. He told me he would be busy studying, but would be over to watch BJ. I stood in the middle of the deserted apartment replaying our last conversation over and over in my head.

"Can I help you, Miss?"

I jumped at the voice coming from behind me. I didn't realize I'd left the front door open. I looked at the elderly man standing in the doorway.

"Ummm...how long has this apartment been empty?"

"At least a week. Was the door left open?"

"Yea...ummm...yes, it was. I thought someone I know lived here."

"Noone has lived here in about a week. This apartment is for rent."

"Okay, thank you."

I quickly turned on my heels and walked out as fast as I could while pushing BJ in his stroller.

I walked back to the subway deep in thought. "Why didn't Bahir tell me that he was moving out of his apartment? Where is he living now? Why hasn't he called me?"

The questions continued as a man helped me carry the stroller down the steps to the subway platform. "Did he tell me he was moving? Maybe he did, and I don't remember. I have been swamped with school. No, I would remember something that important."

I arrived back at my apartment. I fed BJ and put him down in his crib. I sat on the edge of my bed waiting for my phone to ring. Praying that my phone would ring. It didn't. When I didn't hear from him by that following Monday morning, I went to the police precinct. I wanted to file a missing person report, but they informed me that I could not. They said that since he is an adult and there were no signs of foul play, there was nothing they could do.

That's when I finally lost it. The dam broke, and the ugly cry commenced. One of the females that worked at the front desk of the precinct handed me a box of tissues and let me cry on her shoulder.

"It's okay honey, men are jerks. At least he left before he could ruin your life. I say good riddance!"

I didn't respond...

I didn't respond because I didn't agree. I needed Bahir's help with BJ. How was I supposed to finish school without his help? How was I supposed to raise a child in New York City by myself?

I got myself together and left the precinct. As soon as I got back into my apartment, I called Zanetta.

"He left me!" I yelled as soon as she answered the phone.

"Who, what are you talking about, Sissy. Calm down, please."

I ran down the sequence of events to her. I had to repeat myself a lot because I was crying so hard she couldn't understand me.

"I'm checking flights now, Sissy. I'm on my way."

"Okay," I continued to cry. I felt so alone. Having Bahir here made me feel like I had a family. After Nette left, he became my only support.

"I can be there tomorrow evening. I will fly into LaGuardia and get a cab..."

I flashed back to my first days in New York. I remembered how afraid I was. I also remembered the promise I made to myself; 'I am going to make it or die trying.'

"No, wait." I interrupted her. "Don't come."

"What?"

"Don't come here. I know that I am a mess right now, but I need to get through this on my own. I have to keep the promise I made to myself. I will call you if I need to talk but don't uproot yourself because of me."

"Uproot myself? Zora, what are you talking about? You're my sister. I will always be there when you need me."

"Nette, I need to do this on my own, please. Don't come here."

"Who's going to watch BJ while you're in class?"

"I don't know."

"What are you going to do when you need to study for a test?"

"I don't know."

"What's going to happen if..."

"I DON'T KNOW! OKAY? I DON'T KNOW!" I yelled.

I started crying again.

"Sissy, I'm not trying to upset you or make you cry. I'm showing you that you need me there."

"I do need you here, but I have to do this on my own. If something changes I will call you but for now, please let me do this on my own."

"This is the dumbest conversation we have ever had! Why wouldn't you want me there with you? Why would you want to go through this all on your own?"

"I have a son that will be looking to me when things get rough. I can't fold and call you every time life throws adversity my way. I promise if I can't figure this out, you will be the very first person that I call."

"I hear you, and I understand. Don't get mad if I call you twenty-four times a day. Once every hour."

We laughed.

I felt confident when I told Zanetta I could do this on my own, but a couple hours later, I wished she was here with me.

I stood over BJ's crib and watched him sleep. I watched the rise and fall of his little belly. I listened to his little snores like he'd had a hard day of work. I ran my fingers through his little mess of curls on the top of his head. Just when I thought that maybe I wasn't being punished for my decisions, this happens. Just when I thought I could breathe again, I'm once again holding my breath. I really didn't have any answers. I had no idea who would watch BJ while I attended class. I was clueless as to how I would study and care for him at the same time.

That night I had a dream. I was in a white room with all white furniture. There was a window where the sun's beams were shining through, illuminating the entire room. Red roses in a white vase added a pop of color. Standing in the middle of the room was a beautiful woman dressed in a long, white floor length sun dress. It flowed and moved like the fabric was being blown by the wind. She had long straight black hair that was pulled back away from her face and rested on her back. Her brown sugar colored skin was clear with a radiant glow. Her big, beautiful dimpled smile was enhanced by her full lips. She had blue eyes just like me. Big, clear, expressive blue eyes.

This was not the first time that I have dreamt about her. When I was a little girl, and I felt alone or scared, I would dream about her. She would let me lay my head on her lap while she stroked my hair and sang to me.

Hush a bye
Don't you cry
Go to sleep, my little baby
When you wake, you shall have all the pretty little horses...

I didn't know that what she sang was an actual lullaby until we learned it in choir class one year.

When I got pregnant with BJ, I dreamt of her again. This time I laid my head on her shoulder while she sang and rubbed my stomach.

She said, "We should name him Braeden James."

That's where BJ's name came from.

This time in my dream she said, "Don't give up. You and Braeden are going to be fine. You were born to succeed."

Then she rested my head on her shoulder and hummed a song. That dream gave me so much peace and strength. I knew that everything was going to be fine.

I didn't see Bahir again. A month after his disappearance, I received a letter in the mail with no return address. I almost threw it in the trash figuring it was some type of promotional material. I opened the letter and read:

Zora,

I guess by now you know that I am gone. I left without telling you because I didn't want to see the hurt in your eyes when I told you that I had to leave. I didn't have a choice. It would have never worked out between us. We are too different. Our lives are headed in two different directions. I'm not coming back. I wish you all of the success in the world.

Bahir

There were five checks included with the letter. Each certified check was for two thousand dollars. What I noticed was that he didn't mention anything about BJ in the letter. He didn't say I hope he is okay or I hope he dies. Nothing. Anything would have been better than nothing! I was so angry! This bitch ass muthafucka begged his way into my life. He BEGGED! I said no for months but he kept begging! He stayed long enough to knock me up and then left? What the hell! This is on me, though. I knew better. I had a plan, and I let someone come in and interrupt it. That's never going to happen again. The only good thing that came out of this was my baby.

Reading that letter was like reading his obituary because he was dead to me. Rest in Peace Bahir.

Ezekiel

"I will take one vanilla/chocolate double cone and one large chocolate dip cone with cherry dip on top."

I turned around and smiled at Zanetta.

"I got your order right, didn't I?"

She smiled and nodded her head. I could tell she was still sad about her confrontation with her ex-boyfriend at church. He came to church trying to apologize to her. I didn't hear the conversation but whatever she said caused him to walk away defeated. I'm proud of her for standing up for herself. If she hadn't stood up for herself, I would have. He hurt her and that isn't cool with me.

I met Zanetta through my parents. She was their fashion stylist, and she was attending our church while she was in college. I took to the role of big brother immediately. Not that I didn't think she was pretty because she was but I don't know, I just never saw her like that. I always saw her as my little sister. My bratty little sister.

I got our cones from the Mr. Softy truck. We walked to a nearby bench to sit down.

"So that was the guy, huh?"

I knew she was dating someone, but I'd never met him.

"Yeah, that was Antoine. I didn't think I would ever see him again. I haven't answered any of his calls, and when he came to my apartment, I didn't let him in. I just want to heal and move on, you know?"

"I can understand that. That's why I don't do relationships. They get too confusing, too much work and someone always gets hurt."

"That's a horrible outlook to have Zeke. Relationships are beautiful when they work. I think it just takes two people who are committed to making each other happy."

I had sworn off relationships since I was in high school.

IT TOOK me the entire first semester of my freshman year of high school to build up the courage to speak to her-Jameria Johnson.

Jameria Johnson was a Sophomore, and she was the prettiest girl in the school. She had smooth khaki-colored skin. She had high cheek bones that made it appear as if she was smiling even when she wasn't. She had one of those cute moles above her top lip. She wore her hair in box braids like Janet Jackson did in Poetic Justice. She even wore baggy clothes and boots like Janet. She was fly.

At that time, I thought that I was the settling down type. I wanted a girl to kick it with like my brother Blue. He was gone over a girl we knew from church named Michaela. I watched Jameria walking down the hall with her friends. Today she wore a black long-sleeved bodysuit with Tommy Hilfiger jeans and black boots. There was a wide black headband holding back her braids. I followed behind them waiting for an opportunity to speak with her alone. I practiced my speech for weeks. *"Hi, Jameria. I know you don't know me, but I'm Zeke Bluette. I think you are pretty and would like to get to know you better. The Valentine's Day dance is coming up, and I was wondering if you would go with me..."* no, I changed that to, *"be my date."* It was fool proof. I have been saving up my money from the paid gigs I have been taking as a drummer. I planned on buying our tickets and getting me an outfit. We can ride to the dance with my brothers. I know Blue is taking Michaela and Paxton hasn't said who he is taking, but the girls are lined up to be his date since he is the star defensive tackle on the football team.

I saw her break from the group and go to her locker. This is my chance. I have to go for it. I quickly walked up to her before she could get away.

I ran my hands down the front of my brand-new Karl Kani sweatshirt and jeans before I touched her shoulder. "Excuse me, Jameria?" She turned around and smiled down at me. I still hadn't hit my growth spurt, so she was a good six to seven inches taller than me.

"Yes?"

"I know you don't know me..."

"I know who you are," she interrupted.

I said, "Zeke Bluette."

At the same time, she was saying, "Paxton's little brother. You are so cute."

"Thank you!" I had recently started wearing my hair like Ginuwine with the curly top and slicked down baby hair. I thought I was cute too.

"So, I was wondering if..."

She interrupted again, "Can you give Paxton this note?"

She shoved a folded piece of paper in my hand.

"Thank you, little Bluette brother," she quickly said as she closed her locker and walked down the hall.

I stood frozen in the same spot for a few minutes. I looked down at the paper and then down the hall at her walking away without even looking back.

I was in a slump for the rest of the day. She was the only girl I had eyes for. Blue made it seem easy when he got with Michaela.

After school, I sat in my bedroom listening to R. Kelly's *I Can't Sleep Baby* on repeat. I was devastated.

I waited for Paxton to get home from weight lifting to give him the note that Jameria had given to me.

"What's up? Why you in here looking all sad?"

I handed him the note.

"What is this?" He asked after taking it from me.

"It's a letter for you," I said unenthused.

"Where did it come from?"

I ran down the whole story to Paxton. He let me tell him the whole thing from me seeing her my first day of school to receiving the note today. He didn't interrupt me. He nodded at the appropriate time and let me get it all off my chest.

"So, let me see if I understand. You have liked this girl since the first day of school. You finally get up the courage to ask her to the dance, and she hands you a note to give to me?"

"Yeah..."

He tore up the paper into small pieces.

"I don't want to read anything from her. Bros before hoes little brother. I always have your back. Don't worry. I will find you a date for the dance. She will be ten times prettier than what's her name, okay?"

"It's just that you and Blue are so tall. I haven't grown yet. I think that girls like guys that are taller."

"Zeke, don't worry either you will grow in height or in personality. Probably both. Either way, by your sophomore year, you won't be able to keep the chicks off you. You're a Bluette man, you don't have a choice."

He was correct. The summer after my freshman year, I sprouted almost six inches. I slowly started to notice the females paying more attention to me. They would talk about my 'good hair' or my pretty eyes. By the second semester of my sophomore year, the ladies was feeling ya boy! I decided with so many choices, why would a man choose just one?

"SPEAKING OF RELATIONSHIPS, did you tell Rose that you are leaving to go on the world tour with Lyrica?"

Lyrica Stansfield is the new pop 'it girl.' After singing background for her mother for years, she recently released her first solo album. It went platinum almost overnight. I laid some drum tracks on her record, and I have been playing at all her shows. Lyrica is also a talented percussionist. She and I did an instrumental together on her CD. She is going on her first world tour, and I have been hired as the drummer for the band.

"Rose is not my girlfriend, Nette. I don't owe her any explanation for the moves that I make."

"You say she's not your girlfriend, but she thinks she *is* your girlfriend."

"I never told her that she was, so I don't know why she thinks that. She's not the only female I kick it with."

"Maybe because you spend so much time with her, but most importantly you haven't told her that she isn't. Your words and your actions are contradictory."

"Spell it."

"Shut-up Zeke. I'm serious. Be honest about your intentions with Rose and with any other female that you deal with. Tell them from the beginning that they are not going to be your girlfriend. Make sure your actions line up with your words. Look at me. Antoine hurt me. If he would have just said, Look Nette, I'm not feeling this anymore. Then I would have been hurt but not nearly as hurt as I am right now. I would have respected his decision to move on to greener pastures or whatever. But no! He had to try to be slick and sneak around behind my back. Then he has the nerve to want a second chance."

"He doesn't deserve a second chance."

"Neither will you Zeke if you don't talk to Rose and be truthful with her."

I thought about what Nette said. It bothered me to see her hurt over some worthless clown. She's a good girl. He shouldn't have hurt her like that. I didn't want to inflict that same pain on someone, so I decided to have a conversation with Rose.

ROSE AND I HAD BEEN KICKIN' it for a few months. Kickin it is not the best term to use. I guess it's more like spending time together. She had integrated herself into my life before I'd realized it. She did things without me asking like picking up my dry cleaning or organizing my small office. She'd find inexpensive flights when I needed to travel and she would coordinate my transportation to the airport.

She was helpful so I sorta got used to her, but it was never my plan to make her my girl. I don't know why I let her assume that she was my girlfriend. I should have corrected her a long time ago, but I didn't. She is not my girlfriend. If I chose a girl, which I wouldn't, I can honestly say that I would not choose her. She is nice enough, but she's...sweet. My agenda doesn't fit well with sweet girls. I think that's why I haven't corrected her assumption about our relationship status. Sweet girls get hurt too easily. After speaking to Zanetta, I realized that it was only fair to tell Rose that I was leaving.

"Hi, Ezekiel."

I stood to greet her while the Maître D' pulled out her seat and she sat down.

"Thanks for meeting me, Rose."

"There's no other place I would rather be," she smiled.

We looked over our menus. We settled on what to order. I waved the waiter over, and he wrote down our food choices. We made small talk until our food came. After we finished our meal, I felt like it was time to talk to her.

"Rose, I asked you out to dinner because I want to talk to you about something important."

"Okay," she smiled.

I decided it was best to just snatch off the proverbial band-aid and be completely honest with her.

"I am going on tour with Lyrica. I will be gone for a year, basically."

"Wow Ezekiel that is amazing! Congratulations."

"Thanks. I am telling you because I don't want to lead you on. We are not a couple. You are not my girlfriend, and I am not your boyfriend. I never should have let this go so long without correcting you, but I wanted to be clear with you before I left."

She looked at me for several minutes before she responded.

"So that's why you invited me to this public location? So you could just spew all of those terrible things at me and hope that I wouldn't cuss your black ass out? You thought that telling me this in public would stop me from showing out and embarrassing your stupid ass?"

"I didn't plan out anything," I calmly said. "I just wanted, to be honest with you. I wasn't going to tell you at first, but then I thought about it and realized that I should say something."

"Am I supposed to thank you for being so considerate?"

"I'm not asking you to..."

She interrupted, "That's what's wrong with you worthless black men. You have something perfect in front of you, but you are too stupid to see it. I knew you were no good when I started talking to you. I said all he needs is a good woman to change him. I showed you all of the attention that you needed. I did everything that I was supposed to do in this relationship, but you are still saying it's not enough."

Bubble bursting time...

I kept my voice even as I spoke, "I'm not going to be too many more worthless' or stupids, straight up. Don't call me names. That's disrespectful, and I don't have a tolerance for disrespect." I looked at her to make sure she understood me. Once I saw that she did, I continued, "I never told you that we were in a relationship. As a matter of fact, I told you that I was not looking for a relationship. You thought you could change my mind, but you didn't. Let me give you some advice for the next man that you meet. A man will not change unless he wants to. No matter how much you are around cooking, cleaning, or sexing. We change because we want to change. I don't want to change. I'm satisfied with myself. You did things for me , yes, but I never asked nor did I want it or you."

She stood to her feet. Picked up her glass and threw the contents of it in my face. What is it with chicks and throwing drinks?

"I hope you die a painful and tragic death you bastard."

She stormed out of the restaurant.

"That went well," I said to myself while I wiped my face.

AFTER MY FIRST taste of life on the road, I fell in love with it. I loved going to different cities every night. I enjoyed the energy of the crowd, and I enjoyed the women. Lots and lots of women. I enjoyed being constantly on the go, not letting grass grow under my feet.

I took a short break from touring after my sister Michaela died from cancer. Our entire family took her death very hard but my brother Roman, her husband, took it the hardest. I slowed down to make sure that I could check in on him. I wanted to stop altogether until I had a conversation about it with Paxton.

Paxton and I were sitting in my parent's living room.

"Man, this has been the hardest time of my life. I knew we were going to lose Kay, but I didn't think it would feel like this."

"Yeah, it's been tougher than I expected," Paxton sat back on the couch and closed his eyes. "You would think that since we knew she was going, it would make it easier but its just as hard as if she'd died suddenly."

"I'm thinking about canceling everything that I have coming up for awhile to make sure Rome is taken care of. I'm worried about him."

Paxton sat up and looked at me, "There is no way I am going to let you pass up the opportunity to travel the world. If Blue heard you say that you wanted to quit something because of him, he would flip. I know that it looks bad right now. He's drinking and acting entirely out of character, but he has to walk through this. He's going to be okay."

"I know," I stood to my feet and started pacing, "but I can't be gone all the time knowing my brother is suffering like this."

"What can you do if you stay? No one can make him better until he is ready to be better. Live your life. Isn't that what Kay told you the last time you spoke to her?"

My eyes watered thinking about the last conversation I had with Michaela.

KAY MADE everyone leave the room so she could speak to me privately. She was bed bound and was on oxygen. She removed the oxygen mask from her face.

"No Kay, don't take that off," I moved to put the mask back on her.

She waved me away and said, "You know it's okay to cry. I'm an awesome person. I know you are going to miss me!"

I laughed, but I did go ahead and let the tears fall. I had been trying to be strong for her and Blue. I appreciated this moment to let it out. She held my hand while I tried to stop myself from crying. I thought that if I just let a couple tears fall, that would be enough to relieve some of the pressure, but they wouldn't stop falling. This hurt like hell.

"Let them out, Zeke. Tears are important. The water helps wash things away like grief and disappointment while the salt from the tears helps heal the wounds those things leave behind."

We sat quietly for a few minutes until I got myself together.

"This is my prayer journal," she said hoarsely. She pulled a book from under her pillow. "I write down my prayers or visions that I have. Can I read what I wrote in here about you?"

I nodded, "Only if it's good stuff."

She laughed, "It's good." She softly read, "Thank you, God for my brother Ezekiel. I know that he was created to impact the world not only in music but in business. I pray that you will guide him to make the best decisions. Always remind him of who he is and who you created him to be. I know that you will have to speak a little louder when it comes to women." She chuckled and continued, "I know he's my brother and not my child but I feel so proud to have assisted in helping him become the man that he is now. Protect him. Lead him. Teach him. Bless him. My golden drummer boy." She placed the oxygen mask back on her face and took a deep breath.

"Kay, what are we going to do without you?" My heart was breaking, and I didn't know what to do. I didn't know how to reconcile that I would be without her.

She removed the mask again, "You are going to live. Live for me. Live for yourself. Create memories. Tour, travel and love someone. Let her love you back. Make babies and be happy."

We lost her a couple weeks later.

"WHAT WOULD she say if she heard you talking about not going after your dreams?"

"Yeah..."

"I'm here now. I am going to make sure Blue is okay."

"I'm worried about you too! You haven't been back from overseas for that long. You haven't talked about it much, but I know that you went through some bad stuff over there."

Paxton joined the Army right after high school. He had been deployed to Iraq for twelve months. Army units are supposed to take a year off before they re-deploy, but his didn't. He was back in the States for six months before he was deployed to Afghanistan for eighteen more months. He didn't call home or send letters very often, but when he did, they were like gold to us. We worried all the time.

My mother always said, "He's okay. If something were wrong, the Army would let us know."

He's told me a story or two about some things that happened while he was deployed. He lost two of his good friends while he was there. He never detailed their deaths, but it hurt him deeply. I looked into his eyes when he came home, and I knew that he wasn't the same person we sent over there. He'd changed a lot. We sent a guy over there with a sense of humor, a guy who smiled all the time. Now it's a rarity to see him smile. He still has a sense of humor but not like he did before he deployed.

One time we were riding down the street right after he came back from Afghanistan. Blue was driving, and Paxton was sitting in the passenger seat. I was in the back seat. We pulled up alongside a regular looking van with tinted windows. The driver side window started to roll down. Maybe because the driver was hot or was about to throw something out of the window, I don't know. Paxton saw the window lowering. He yelled, "Situation! Situation, get down." He managed to throw himself over Blue while grabbing my neck and forcing me down into the back seat.

Nothing happened, I don't even think the person in the van saw the commotion that was happening in our car. When I was able to sit back up, the van was gone.

"Pax," Blue said calmly, "It's good. We are good."

He kept saying it until Paxton finally made eye contact with him and nodded his head. Cars backfiring, doors slamming or random groups of people. We never knew what would make him panic.

"I'm okay." Paxton continued our conversation pulling me from my trip down memory lane. "I've been going to therapy at the VA hospital, and there is an on-campus support group at my school. I know it's easier said than done but worry about chasing your dreams, don't worry about us.Things here will be fine. Okay?"

"Okay."

I agreed, but it was still so hard to leave them to return to touring. I paid for a chef to come and cook dinner for Blue. I also hired a maid and a lawn service to keep his house up. Paxton would go over and check on him frequently, so I had some peace of mind while I was on the road.

I poured my heart and soul into my craft. I wanted to do well so that my family, including Kay, would be proud of me.

2

Zora

"DOCTOR CHAMBERS."

I looked up from the textbook I was reading to see one of my former professors, Doctor Miller, standing in front of me. I was sitting in the library on the campus of my alma mater trying to stay up on my skills. I had one more year of my residency before I could take the test to become a board certified Oral Surgeon.

"Doctor Miller," I smiled as I closed the textbook and stood to greet him. I extended my hand, and he accepted.

"I wanted to speak to you about something. Would you have a minute to come to my office?"

"Sure."

I packed my textbooks into my backpack and followed Doctor Miller out of the library. We made small talk while traveling across the campus to the building that housed his office. He opened the door to let me in first then followed behind me and closed the door.

"Have a seat."

I chose the most comfortable chair closest to his desk. I was very familiar with Doctor Miller's office. I had come here on more than one occasion seeking advice or getting help with some class work that seemed to be impossible to figure out. Doctor Miller has an ability to explain things in a way that made perfect sense and helped me to comprehend. I have taken every class that he's taught while I was enrolled at Columbia.

"There are a group of doctors that are starting a practice in Houston, Texas. A general dentist, a pediatric dentist, orthodontist, endodontist and a periodontist. They have asked me to come on as the Oral Surgeon. As you know, I am retiring from teaching at the end of this school year. I didn't plan on going back into a practice, but I felt like this was an opportunity I could not pass up. I told them that I would take the position under one condition. That condition is that I get to bring along a protégé-someone who would take over for me after I retire."

"A protégé? That's going to be amazing for someone," I smiled thinking about how great it would be if I had the opportunity to be his protégé.

"I think so too which is why I called you into my office. We have the chance to work with one of the local hospitals and offer an oral surgery residency. I want you to come to Houston. Complete your residency at the practice and the hospital with me. Once I retire, you would take over the position as the head Oral Surgeon."

I tilted my head to the side trying to make sure I was hearing him correctly. Did he just say that he wants me to move to Houston to complete my residency?

"Doctor Miller...I..."

He interrupted me. "Don't answer now. Give it some thought. After you've made a decision, then we can talk about salary and what a partnership will mean for you. Can you give it some thought for me?"

I nodded my head.

"Oh, Zora." I turned to look back at him, "You know my wife loves BJ so having him close in Houston would be the icing on the cake for her."

I smiled.

"I will give it some thought Doctor Miller. I will let you know."

I DIDN'T KNOW Doctor Miller the first time I knocked on his office door. He was the head of the dental department. I was going to his office to inform him of my decision to drop out of school.

"Come in."

I entered the small office and stood in place until he motioned for me to have a seat. Doctor Miller was a handsome older man. He had a head full of white hair that he kept longer in the top and low on the sides. He had beautiful green eyes and a permanent tan. He kept his body right, so it was impossible to tell that he was nearing sixty years old. I'm sure he had the women lined up at his door when he was younger. It might be some outside the door now.

I looked around his office at all of the dental books that littered his desk and the bookshelves. I examined the old-school chart on the wall that illustrated the teeth numbers. I didn't think I would ever learn the teeth by number. Now I know number three is the first molar on the maxilla. Number twenty-two is the cuspid on the left side of the mandible. Number sixteen is the...

"Can I help you?"

I looked from the chart to meet Doctor Miller's questioning eyes.

"Yes, I wanted to inform you that I will not be continuing with the Dental program. I have too much responsibility. I have a baby who needs my attention, my boyfriend disappeared into thin air, my best friend, who is my rock, moved back to Saint Louis where we are from. I thought I could handle this, but it's too much. Oh, I'm Zora Chambers," I said without taking a breath.

Doctor Miller leaned back in his chair and tented his fingers in front of him. He stared at me for a moment before he spoke.

"I know who you are, Ms. Chambers. I make it a practice to know all of the students in the Dental program. I would really like it if you would reconsider leaving the program. Do you know how rare it is for a female to chose the dental profession? I read that you want to continue on to specialize in Oral and Maxillofacial surgery? You're not just a female but you are a black female. You are like a unicorn in a snowstorm in Florida. I really would like for you to reconsider leaving the program."

"So...you want me to stay because I check some affirmative action box?" I tilted my head to the side.

"No, I want you to stay because you tested higher on your Dental Admissions Test than anyone in the program. I want you to stay because you graduated from an Ivy League school, a year and a half early, with an almost perfect GPA. I know that you will be an asset to this field."

It was true. Since I didn't go back home, I went to school year round which gave me the opportunity to graduate undergrad early and start grad school right away. School always came easy to me but going to school and raising a child, that was another story.

"Doctor Miller, I can't. I'm so stressed out. I've never been a mom before. When I had BJ, I thought that I would always have someone around to help me. If not my friend then at least his father. Right now I don't have either. Sometimes, I am up all night because I can't figure out why he won't stop crying. If I do sleep, I'm up at five in the morning to get us both ready and out of the door by six. I have to ride the subway to Brooklyn because that's the only daycare I could find that has extended hours. I need the longer hours so I can go to class and get some studying in before I have to pick him back up. I get home. I feed and bathe him. I spend a little time with him before I put him down then the cycle starts all over again the next day. I'm exhausted."

"What if we could come up with a way to simplify your life for you. Would you consider staying in school?"

This is not how I thought this conversation would go. I thought I would walk in here and tell him I was leaving. He would say don't let the door hit you where the good Lord split you and I would be on my way. Instead, he is trying to talk me out of leaving. Ain't this about a bish?

"Yes, it's always been my dream to become an Oral Surgeon, but we have to play the cards that we are dealt. Looking at my hand, I have *Go Fish* cards in a poker game. Like everyone else is placing their bets, and when it becomes my turn I ask, 'Does anyone have a frog?'"

He chuckled, "Let me look into a couple of things and get back to you. Can you give me until the end of the week?"

I said yes, knowing that he wasn't going to be able to come up with anything. He fooled me! By the end of the week, I had a daycare provider that was right around the corner from my apartment and Doctor Miller's wife volunteered to pick up BJ on the days that I would have to study late. I wasn't trying to let just anyone around my son, but Hannah is a sweet person. Doctor Miller and Hannah saved me. I wouldn't have made it through school without them.

I PICKED BJ up from daycare, fixed him dinner, gave him a bath and put him to sleep all while thinking about moving to Houston. I believe that it would be a great opportunity for me and BJ. I could work with top tier doctors while still learning. BJ can grow up outside of the city with grass and trees. I don't know why I'm thinking about it so hard! I'm going to take Doctor Miller up on his offer and move to Houston.

Ezekiel

"When will I see you again, Ezekiel? I hope soon."

"I can't make any promises. You know that."

"I know, but I enjoy our time together."

I looked up from tying my shoes to make eye contact with this ebony goddess standing in front of me. Her skin was smooth and dark. Just like I like it. She was posed in front of me in the terry cloth robe the hotel provides.

"You know how I move Layna. I told you that I'm not trying to wife anybody. I just want to have some fun. You agreed to that, right?"

"I did, and I still do agree, but I wish that we could do something together outside of the bedroom," she poked out her lips.

See this is how most females move. I tell them up front that I'm not in the market for a main chick, side chick, wife or baby momma. Hell, I'm not even looking for a friend. I'm an eternal bachelor. They all agree to it at first, and then they decide that they want more. They try to change my mind. I can see it in her eyes, Rose had that same look, which is why I'm moving quickly to get the hell up outta this hotel room.

I stood to leave, and she dropped her robe exposing her perfectly proportioned breast, her pierced navel on her flat stomach and her lush thighs that when opened revealed a sweet secret. I blew out a breath knowing in my mind that I had to get out of here, but my body responded immediately. She slowly walked over to me and wrapped her arms around my waist.

"We have the room a few more hours. Are you sure you have to leave?"

"Naw, I got moves to make."

After that little conversation, I knew that I wouldn't be calling her anymore. I didn't do attachments. If they start to get too clingy, then I must move on.

I looked around making sure that I had retrieved all my belongings. I made sure the condoms were flushed, and my cell phone and wallet were in my pocket. You can never be too careful.

"I will see you around," I called over my shoulder as I closed the hotel room door behind me.

I had successfully avoided relationships by being honest and upfront with women. Some couldn't handle the way I rolled while others played like they didn't mind. Those are the ones you have to watch. They will roll with you at first then they try to start switching things up.

They say things like: "When am I going to meet your family?"

"Never," is usually my response.

Or: "Do you ever think you are going to settle down and raise a family?"

"Nope," is my standard answer to that question.

I'm not here to hold anyone back. If a woman wants those things, then she is wasting her time with me. I say be free little cheesy bread. Fly...fly. Straight up.

I don't want those things. I want to be free to enjoy life. I'm not against marriage. It's just not for me.

MY BROTHERS and I relocated to Houston, Texas from New York a couple years after Michaela died. My father is the Pastor of Abundant Blessings Church in New York. He decided to branch out and open another church. He chose Houston for the location of the new church and appointed Roman as the Pastor. Paxton and I moved to support him. I love New York, but I thought moving south would give me more bang for my buck. Houston is growing and thriving. The music scene is growing. It's been a good move for all of us. Both of my brothers are doing well mentally. Roman bounced back from Michaela's death, and Paxton's PTSD is under control.

I prayed for them a lot. Most people hear me say that I prayed and automatically assume that I couldn't be a Christian based on my lifestyle or their perception of my lifestyle, but I am. It's just that my ideas of Christianity compared to other's ideas are different. Most people would call me a rebel because I'm not a traditional Christian. I don't carry a bible around and say, "Praise the Lord" to everyone that I encounter. I don't quote Bible scriptures for every occasion, but I love God. Do I mess up? Hell yeah. All the time, but I know that He still loves me. I'm not perfect. I don't pretend to be perfect, I don't want to be perfect. I think some people believe that if you are a Christian, you are supposed to be this super human, no mistake-making individual. That is so far from the truth! I can't stand when Christians put on that façade like they are not subject to the exact same struggles and difficulties as everyone else. I struggle! I have difficulties! I like real people. Real people are the ones that can admit that they are somewhat dysfunctional but they are trying. I would much rather be around those types of people than those that feel like they have to front based on their beliefs. I'm sure that was not the idea when Jesus came to earth. He didn't say, "Hey everyone that wants to follow me, pick up a mask and come on. Don't let people see the real you. Be fake and phony my children." No, he said follow me, period.

I believe in having a relationship with God and allowing him to be my judge. Not people. I cannot stand a person that will pass judgment on someone else knowing good, and well they have their struggles too. Don't point out my flaws if you can't address your own. People will impose impossible rules and guidelines on you and then condemn you to hell when you can't follow them all. I choose not to follow the crowd. I'm a Christian, but I'm human.

"Now keep in mind that whatever changes you want to make, we will make them. Not only are you endorsing these kits but we want you to be satisfied with the finished product," Mister Ellis, the CEO of the drum company stated.

Roman, Paxton and I were at the factory of the drum company that was producing my signature drum kit. They had been working with them for months trying to get them just right. This was my first time seeing all the completed pieces together.

"Can I try them out?"

"Please!" Mister Ellis replied.

One of the men standing with him handed me a pair of drumsticks. I walked around to the back of the set and sat down on the stool. It was a basic set that consisted of the bass, snare and three toms. I placed my feet on the pedals to the bass and the snare and tried out each piece.

I have been playing the drums since I was six or seven. My father started me out on the piano, like my older brother Roman. The piano was cool, but it was more Roman's speed than mine. The drums didn't interest me either until my dad took us to hear live music, and I experienced the legendary Tony Williams. Tony Williams is arguably one of the best drummers of all time. He just happened to be sitting in on the set of a local band. They recognized him in the audience and asked him to come up on stage. He sat down at those drums and changed my life forever. Initially, I thought that I wanted to be just like him and play jazz but as my skill grew so did my genre of music. I play rock, pop, R&B and gospel. I can play any genre, but those are my favorites. Roman would go around the country learning from the best piano teachers while I traveled learning from the best drummers and percussionists.

I finished testing each piece.

"I can hear the potential, but they are not there yet. The bass sounds a little muffled, and the snare is tight. When will the cymbals be ready?"

"Our testers said the same thing about the bass. We are tweaking the painting process so that we can fix that. We will look at the snare again. The cymbals will be ready next month. Each piece will be complete with your signature and logo."

"And the tenor drums and cymbals for the marching bands?"

"We are on target to have those done at the same time as the kit."

"Great. The contest that we have for high schools and colleges to determine which one we will donate drums to is doing well, correct?"

"Yes, we've had thousands of entries. We are going through the videos now to narrow them down. We will inform you of the finalist then you can choose."

"Cool! I've watched some of them on my social media pages. They are very creative."

"Yes, and very talented."

When the drum company approached me to do a signature drum kit with them, one of my stipulations was that they would have to donate a complete kit to one college and two high schools. We came up with a competition to determine who would get them. Each school had to submit a video explaining why they should receive the set. It's been a very successful campaign.

I turned to my brothers.

"What do you think?"

"I agree with your assessment of the sound," Paxton answered.

Most people know that my brother Roman and I are musicians. What they don't know is that Paxton is also a skilled musician. He can play almost any instrument, but his instrument of choice is the lead guitar. He also has an incredible singing voice. He just chooses not to do anything with music. It may have something to do with my Uncle Nigel, his father. Paxton is our cousin by birth, but we were raised as brothers. Uncle Nigel was also a talented musician and taught Paxton most of what he knows.

"Yeah, it's going to be great once it's all put together correctly," Roman added. "Plus, that donation to the schools will be amazing. It will possibly save a music program."

This signature drum kit was another project that would get me one step closer to my empire. My goal is to create as many streams of income that I possibly can. I want Golden Drummer drum kits, sticks, music books and music schools. I'm not limiting myself to music. My brothers and I have invested in real estate, we've built a state of the art recording studio, and we've started an accounting firm. My brothers are the best business partners. We work well together.

"We leave to meet dad in Saint Louis on Sunday. He's excited about all of us being there to see him get his award," Paxton explained.

"Yeah, I know. I wanted to fly out with you after church, but I have a meeting that I can't miss so I will meet you there."

My family was going to spend the week in Saint Louis at our church organization's convocation. I haven't attended a convocation since I was a teenager. My father is receiving an Excellence in Ministry Award, and we will all be there for him. I haven't seen my

Lil Sis Zanetta in several years. She lives in Saint Louis now, so it will be great to see her.

Zora

After speaking with Doctor Miller and telling him that I would take him up on his offer, I got excited. It was such an adult decision, but I felt it would be great for my career. I looked forward to BJ having trees to climb and grass to play in. I can't believe that my time in New York is coming to an end. I sat thinking back to my first day here and how afraid, but determined I was to make it work. I did it! Not without huge bumps and potholes but I did it.

I was conferenced into a video call with the other dental partners.

"Doctor Chambers," Doctor Miller smiled from the other end of my computer screen. He introduced the other doctors seated around the table. I spoke to everyone by name as he introduced them. "We are all ecstatic that you have taken us up on our invitation to join our practice here in Houston."

"I am too. Thank you so much."

We sat for the next hour discussing how the practice would run. Everyone had useful input. When I spoke or gave my opinion, they all listened. I felt like I was a real part of the group. One of my concerns was not only being the youngest in the group but also being the only African-American and the only woman in the group. None of that seemed to matter to any of the other doctors. That eased my mind tremendously.

"Doctor Chambers, have you found a place to live yet?" Doctor Gaer, the endodontist, asked me.

"I have been looking on some websites, but I haven't locked anything down yet."

"I own several properties here in the area. You and your son are more than welcome to live in one of them. I can send you pictures. I will also give you the name of a great realtor."

"That would be terrific, thank you."

"Have you researched a school for your son?" Doctor Nerison, the Pediatric dentist, inquired. "My wife has some suggestions for you. I will have her email them to you."

By the conclusion of the meeting, I had a potential place to live, school suggestions for BJ, a car dealer's number and a realtor's information. I was even more excited about my move. As a part of my relocation package, the doctors paid for my entire move. All I had to do was find the moving company, and they would handle the rest.

A FEW OF the dental students that I'd been tutoring helped me pack up my apartment. It only took the movers a few hours to get everything loaded onto the truck. I got a little teary eyed as I loaded BJ into the Uber that was taking us to the airport. Leaving New York was bittersweet. I had a lot of great memories and some not so great ones. I came here to get away from my life and created a whole new one. I created a person here! I will always have love in my heart for this city, but I am ready for bigger and better.

BJ and I flew out of LaGuardia airport to Bush International in Houston. It was BJ's first time on an airplane. I hadn't been on a plane since I was a little girl. The captain let BJ see the cockpit and gave him some plastic wings. The flight attendants treated him like he was a superstar. He loved the attention.

Doctor Miller and Hannah met us at the airport. We went straight to the car dealership to pick up my car. I had purchased a 2001 BMW 325i. It's old, but it's in great condition, and I don't have to worry about a car note. After picking up my car, I went to meet with the realtor. My initial plan was to stay in the house that one of the doctors offered me, but after doing some research, I realized that I could afford my own home. I went through the process and was approved for a home loan. I was surprised by the property values in Houston. I could afford ten times the space I had in New York and would be paying less per month for something that I own. I wasn't making a ton of money yet, but I had money saved up that helped with this transition. My realtor sent me a lot of listings to look at while I was still in New York. We narrowed them down to five that we would walk through in hopes that one of them would be my home.

The first three were a no-go. One looked like it should have been in the desert. The realtor called it Pueblo Revival style. It looked like it was made of clay...by hand. The other two were those gingerbread looking houses. The correct term is cottage, according to the realtor. They were not my style plus they were too far from the office. I knew the fourth one was my house as soon as I pulled into the driveway. It was a two-story brick house with a two-car garage attached to the side. It was on a cul-de-sac that was very quiet.

We walked into the house, and I knew, I knew this was the one. I didn't even need to look around.

"Hester, please tell me this is in my price range," I turned to my realtor.

"Actually, it was just reduced by seven thousand, so the price is below your budget," she smiled.

We walked through the formal dining room, living room and updated kitchen. There were three bedrooms upstairs and the master bedroom.

"I love it. Let's make an offer."

"You don't want to look at the other house?"

"No, this is the one!"

It was large, but I couldn't pass it up, I wanted it. I'm hoping Zanetta will stay in one of the extra rooms.

I offered the full asking price. The sellers were motivated because they'd purchased another home and had already moved into that one. They accepted my offer and let me move in as soon as I wanted. Closing on the house was a breeze since the loan was already approved.

I found BJ an excellent school that he could attend from preschool through eighth grade. It came highly recommended by one of the doctor's wives. BJ and I qualified for one of the scholarships the school offers. Things were really coming together for me.

The night before my first day at the practice, I could not sleep. I was nervous and excited at the same time.

I dreamt of her again. She didn't sing this time. She let me rest my head on her shoulder while she rubbed my back. She didn't say anything. She hummed a song and let me rest next to her. I woke with such a feeling of peace.

I had a text from Nette:

I didn't call you because I know that you are preparing for your destiny. I am so proud of you. I prayed for you this morning. This is the scripture that I was given: Habbakuk 3:19 The Lord God is my strength, my source of courage, my invincible army; He has made my feet steady and sure like hinds' feet And makes me walk forward with spiritual confidence on my high places of challenge and responsibility.

That means you are built to be on top. You were designed by God for this moment. I love you. Now go and shine! - Sissy

Love you!

She always knows what to say.

I arrived early and was met by my two dental assistants; Susan and Liz. Susan, a bubbly blonde, had been a Dental Assistant for ten years. Liz, a caramel colored sister with a short natural cut, had just graduated from dental assisting school and was brand new. She's very laid back but eager to learn. They are total opposites.

The office has a modern design. They used a lot of muted greens and yellows in the décor. They were going for a peaceful ambiance. It works. All the equipment is new and state of the art. My office was bare, but I'm sure Zanetta will be decorating it since she will be in Houston. She called me with the wonderful news that she is moving to Houston for a job. I am so excited about her being here. I was able to put someone else on my son's emergency contact list at school other than me. She has no idea how happy I am to have her around for me and BJ.

Ezekiel

The Saint Louis trip was a success. Blue and I got to rock out with the church band one night. That was fun. We celebrated my dad receiving an Excellence in Ministry Award. I admire my Dad. He always calls my brothers and me his heroes, but he is mine. It had been a long time since my whole family had spent a week together. My mother was happy to be surrounded by all her boys.

It was good to see Zanetta again. She has become such a beautiful woman. Blue couldn't keep his eyes off her. He didn't even try to keep his eyes off her. It's cool to see him interested in someone. If I had known that he would fall all over himself for Nette, I would have introduced them sooner. I like them together. She already had him doing fun things like riding a motorcycle again. I hadn't seen him on a bike since before Kay passed. He needs someone in his life to bring some fun back into it. He is so into her that he offered her a position at the church in Houston and she accepted. He smiled the whole plane ride back to Houston.

I have watched my brother fall in love once, and I think I'm about to watch him fall again. He finds a woman, makes up his mind she is the one then that's it for him. Me on the other hand, I've never been in love. After my try with Jameria when I was a freshman in high school, I haven't tried again. I don't know if love is something that I want. Something Zanetta said jokingly has been on repeat in my head: "The day is coming where you are going to meet a woman that is going to match your wit and temperament and give you a run for your money."

I don't know why it's on repeat, but it is. Maybe it's because for the last few sexual encounters that I've had, there has been an empty feeling. Like something is missing, but I can't put my finger on what it is. When I first experienced it, I blamed it on my partner. She was a little closed off. She was cool but not the best I'd ever had. Then while I was in Saint Louis, it happened again. I hooked up with an old acquaintance while I was there. She was a freak, just like I like it but I still didn't feel accomplished. I felt...underwhelmed. I came back to Houston and hooked up with a standby. Again, I was under-whelmed, almost bored. I mean I did what I was supposed to do. I made sure she was satisfied. Afterwards, I felt like I could have spent my time in the studio or hanging out with my brothers. Maybe I'm getting older. I don't know. I'm trying hard to push Zanetta's words to the back of my mind; to the dark recesses of my memory. I am an eternal bachelor, always have been and always will be.

"What's up Percy?"

"Morning, Zeke."

Percy is my assistant. I hired him after my brothers and I formed our companies. I needed help keeping up with everything and Percy was the man for the job. I had a few females come to interview for the position, but I didn't have time for a sexual harassment lawsuit, so I hired a male...a heterosexual male.

"What do we have going on today?" I asked while I checked my social media sites. I'd lost a bet to Zanetta while I was in Saint Louis. I bet her that her football team, the Cowboys, would lose. They didn't. I had to post about how much I like the Cowboys for an entire week on my social media sites. Some of my followers were honestly upset. They called me a bandwagon fan and said that I was only cheering for them because they were winning. It killed me to endure that for an entire week, but a deal is a deal. I couldn't tell anyone why I was posting about the Cowboys until the end of the week. I was finally able to tell them I lost a bet. Things are back to normal now.

"Mr. Isaiah Noble wants to schedule a meeting with you about a collaboration with Noble Naturals. They are looking for someone with a strong social media presence to represent their new re-vamped brand," Percy said.

"Isaiah and I go way back. He's a talented musician and producer."

"Well, now he is the head of the Noble Naturals company."

"That's what's up! It will be good catching up with him."

"After that, we have to look at some of the videos for the drum donation campaign. Then we have to meet with Lyrica about the concert. You also need to get back into the studio to finish the drum tracks that you started."

"Did you look into getting my bike shipped here from New York yet?"

After my ride in Saint Louis with Nette and her friends, I realized I was missing out not having my bike here with me.

"That's on my to-do list."

"Cool, sounds like a full day. Let's get started."

3

Zora

BJ and I met Zanetta at her apartment early Saturday morning. I hadn't been over yet, but she had given me a tour on Facetime.

The front desk called up to her apartment before giving me access to the elevators. This building is beautiful. We rode up to her floor and found her standing outside her door.

"Tee-Tee!" BJ yelled as he ran to meet her.

"Hey! My most favorite person in the whole wide world!"

They hugged. Zanetta and I hugged as I entered her apartment.

"Sissy, this is even more beautiful in person. I love this apartment!"

"Thank you. I love it too. I have space for BJ to come over and spend time with me. We can have our sleepovers like we used to, remember?"

"Yea, that's going to be so much fun. Have you given any more thought about staying here permanently? Don't have me and BJ get used to you being here only for you to leave and abandon us."

"Way to lay on the guilt, Sissy. I've been thinking about it, but I haven't decided yet. I really do like it here so far."

"Good, then maybe you will stay. How are the church folks treating you in your new position?"

"Everyone is nice except for Roman's secretary, Jocelynn."

"She did something to you?"

I was ready to go to that church and let anyone have it that thought they could cross my sister.

"No, she's just like a little dog, nippy. You know she does little petty stuff like not speaking to me but will speak to everyone else."

"You need to check that witch before I come up there and do it for you. Does she want Roman or something?"

"I don't know. I don't think it's that. I think she feels threatened by me. I don't know. It's not a big deal. I will talk to her about it at some point."

"Yeah tell her you have a sister that don't care nothing about church or church protocol. I will come up there and drag her ass."

"Okay, thanks, Rocky. I will let her know," she laughed.

"Anyway, let's get to these stores. I want to take BJ to the park for a little while to wear him out."

"WHO WILL BE at your apartment tomorrow?"

Zanetta and I were sitting at the park watching BJ play. We had just left some home stores and furniture stores shopping for decorations for my house and office.

"Ezekiel, Paxton, and Roman. Zeke and Paxton are Roman's brothers."

"So, I am going to spend my Sunday with a bunch of church boys? Sounds like so much fun." I exhaled sharply and rolled my eyes. I was being completely sarcastic. I really didn't gel well with church people. They were usually uptight, judgmental and always could see what you were doing wrong but was blind to all the things they were doing wrong.

"Yes, church boys but I think you will like them. Be on your best behavior."

"Best behavior? I am not a heathen, Nette. I know how to act... most of the time."

"I didn't call you a heathen. Describing you as a heathen would be like calling an anaconda an earthworm. Heathen is way too mild."

I yanked her braid.

"Ouch, stop!" She pushed my shoulder. "I'm serious. No talk about penises, sex, disgusting dental surgeries gone wrong...I know how you do when you are around people you don't necessarily care for. You have no filter."

"Fine, you want me to sit there mute. I will," I folded my arms across my chest.

"Zora, if you come to my house tomorrow and act crazy, I am going to pinch you so hard that it's going to leave a bruise for weeks."

"Okay! Dang, your pinches hurt. I won't start nothing..." She glared at me. "I won't end nothing either, dang."

I would be at Nette's apartment for dinner because she is one of the best cooks that I know. I wouldn't deprive myself of the opportunity to eat her food on the strength of avoiding church people. Now the best behavior part...I can't promise anything. However, after being threatened with one of her pinches, I will try my best. She will surprise you with a pinch that you will never forget. If she's threatening with pinches, she's pulling out the big guns which means this is important to her.

I GOT BJ up the next morning and got him prepared to go see his Tee Tee and spend the day with the church boys. I am not looking forward to this at all. Best behavior...best behavior. I keep repeating those words to myself.

I put on my distressed jeans with a black and white striped t-shirt. I wore my long red cardigan over it. I chose to wear my red low top converse so I would be comfortable.

I arrived at Zanetta's building and parked in one of the visitor's parking spaces.

I grabbed BJ by the hand and entered the building. The man at the front desk informed me that Zanetta had added me to the list so I could go up without being announced. We rode the elevator up to the 12th floor. I rang her doorbell. I could hear her talking to someone on the other side of the door, but I couldn't make out exactly what was being said. She opened the door.

"Hey, Sissy."

We hugged as BJ, and I entered the apartment.

"Roman, Paxton and Ezekiel this is my best friend Zora and my little godson, BJ."

Roman and Paxton said hello. Each man giving a genuine smile. Ezekiel didn't say anything, but he nodded. I nodded back.

"Hi everyone."

BJ pried his hand away from mine and walked over to where Ezekiel was sitting.

"Up," he lifted his arms in the air indicating he wanted to be picked up.

Ezekiel looked down at BJ with his arms extended in the air. He didn't hesitate to pick him up and sit him on his lap.

BJ speaks in full sentences. Why he chose that one word, I'm not sure. I was shocked at first, but I quickly recovered and said, "I'm sorry." I reached to get BJ off Ezekiel's lap, but BJ pushed my hands away. That has never happened.

"No, he's fine," Ezekiel caught me off guard with his golden eyes. They are beautiful.

"Are you sure?"

"I'm sure," he smiled. He is beautiful.

I looked at BJ again just to be sure. He didn't even glance over at me.

"Okay," I shrugged and followed Zanetta into the kitchen.

"That was weird, right?" Zanetta asked as soon as we were out of earshot.

"Yes," I nodded, "He usually doesn't take to strangers like that."

"I know! He didn't even speak to me!" Zanetta said with an attitude.

We laughed.

I turned around and snuck a peek at each man. "Dayum Sissy, this is your group of friends now? Those men are all delicious!"

"Shh!"

"No for real. Any one of them could get it. Well except Roman cause y'all already booed up. Any way they wanted it. Any time they wanted it. Front, back, side-"

"Zora!" she whispered interrupting me. "Stop it."

"Especially the one holding BJ," I fanned with my hand.

"Zora!"

"Okay, dang. I'm just saying. Church boy or not, those men in there are fine!"

"Help me finish up, please."

"Come on Sissy! You know I'm on a self-imposed sexual sabbatical. I can't have a little fun?"

I hadn't been kicking it with men since giving birth to BJ. I'd had a little bit here and there, but it was important for me to keep BJ first. I didn't trust people with him, so I didn't date.

"No, not tonight!"

Nette tried to put on her stern voice, but she knew it was true. Those men in the other room were delicious versions of chocolate. Like a chocolate spectrum. No, like a chocolate rainbow; each one unique but each one delicious in their own way. I wonder if they melt in your mouth or in your hand?

Roman is the darkest of the three. He is dark like coffee without creamer...which is my favorite way to drink coffee-strong and black. All his features are dark except for his eyes. They are the color of worn pennies. I can see why Zanetta is attracted to him.

Ezekiel's caramel colored skin is complemented by his dark

brown dreadlocks and golden eyes. Paxton is the lightest of the three. He has sand colored skin with auburn hair. I love red heads. He has freckles too.

"Which one is the oldest?" I asked Zanetta while we were finishing the meal.

"Roman is the oldest, he and Paxton are the same age. Ezekiel is two years younger than they are."

"How are they the same age? Their papa was a rolling stone?"

She laughed, "No, actually Paxton is their cousin, but they were raised as brothers."

"They look like brothers. I wouldn't have been able to tell that Paxton has different parents."

"Ezekiel told me a little of the story back when I was in New York. I believe that Paxton's father and Bishop are brothers, but Paxton calls Bishop and First Lady; mom and dad."

"That's a black family for you. We can be confused on the titles, but the love is undeniable."

"That's for sure."

We both peeked out of the kitchen from time to time to check on BJ. He was content sitting on Ezekiel's lap and watching the game on TV with the men. I could hear him holding a conversation with them from time to time.

"Dinner is served," Zanetta called into the living room.

All three men got up and came to the table. I didn't realize how tall they were since they were sitting. Each man was easily over six feet tall. I love a tall man. Since I am five-foot-nine, I am taller than a lot of men once I put my heels on. Not these men. They are giants!

I tried to take BJ from Ezekiel, but BJ was not going for it. So, he ended up in the seat between Ezekiel and me. I can't believe he is playing me for a stranger!

Roman blessed the food, and we all began eating. Once everyone had a little to eat the conversations started. I was pleasantly surprised by the topics during dinner. I figured with them just coming from church they would want to recap the service or

ask me what church I attended. That's how it always went at the
dinner table when I was growing up. These men were different. I
talked about my new job and the practice. Ezekiel is a musician.
He plays the drums. He talked about his upcoming tour. Paxton
added to the conversation here and there. He is more of an
observer and not a talker. That's cool. He did mention that he is an
accountant. Roman talked about *EZ Blue Sounds*, the new
recording studio he and Ezekiel built. Nette talked about her
ministry at the church. We had great conversation. I quickly forgot
that they were church boys. They were completely down to earth
and very relatable. They weren't preachy and judgmental, and I
appreciated that.

We all cleaned up and then watched the last of the football
games that were on and caught some of the highlights.

"Zora, you're not a Cowgirls fan like Zanetta are you?" Ezekiel
asked me while still holding BJ.

"Cowgirls! I bet she gets indignant when you call them that,
doesn't she?"

He laughed.

"She does. I've pretty much mastered the ability to push her
buttons."

We both laughed.

"To answer your question, no, I'm a Giants fan through and
through. Aren't you?"

"I'm an Eagles fan."

"An Eagles fan! What in the entire world? How in the heck did
that happen?"

"I like the Giants and the Jets too, but the Eagles are my team. I
became an Eagles fan because I followed Donovan McNabb's career
since he played for Syracuse. When he was drafted to the team, I
followed him there, and I haven't left."

"I'm going to give you a pass because he was a great quarterback
and he is black. Outside of that...you trippin'!"

"I'm a Knicks fan. Does that help?"

"It would help if the Knicks had won anything in the last decade. But since they haven't..."

We laughed.

He laughed and showcased his beautiful white teeth. They were straight and cavity free from what I could assess. His gums were healthy too. That means he's a flosser. That's one of the downfalls of working in the dental profession. The first things I notice about people are their teeth. In just a quick glance I can tell if they brush and floss regularly. Nasty mouths are a turn-off. I checked out all three men's teeth. They have very pretty teeth and healthy pink gums.

Eventually, BJ fell asleep on Ezekiel's lap. I was able to get him away from Ezekiel and lay him down in the guest room.

I came back out and sat on the couch next to Ezekiel.

"I'm sorry he was so clingy with you. He's usually not like that," I explained.

"It's no problem. He's a cool Lil dude. He said he likes the drums. I could show him some of my drum sets one day if his father wouldn't mind."

"His father is long gone."

"Well, your significant other."

"BJ is my significant other."

I felt like he was fishing for information. I wasn't just going to give it away that easily. Besides, Sissy asked me to be on my best behavior, and so far, I was doing a great job.

I turned around to say something to Zanetta, but she and Roman were in the kitchen together. That man is so into her. I love the way that he looks at her. It's a look of adoration mixed with curiosity. He likes her but tries to figure her out at the same time. She deserves someone that looks at her that way. I turned back around to give them some privacy.

"How long have you known Zanetta?" Ezekiel questioned.

"I met her when we were in elementary school. During our first conversation, I forced her to be my best friend. She can't get away from me. We went to the same college, and now we are living in the same state again."

"You went to college in New York?"

"Yes, we both attended Columbia."

"Did you ever come to church with her? I'm sure I would have remembered you."

"Hell, no. I'm allergic to church. I break out in hives and everything."

We laughed.

"Oh yeah?"

"Yep. I keep Calamine lotion stocked just in case someone mentions it to me. I'm itching now," I scratched my arm for dramatic effect.

"Calamine lotion! That thick pink crap that was like putting Pepto-Bismol on your skin? You couldn't just wipe it off, you needed soap and water. You're not old enough to remember calamine lotion."

That's interesting how he switched topics. Most church people that hear that I don't go to church try to get me saved and back in church. He didn't even dwell on it.

"I'm twenty-six and yes I do remember it. My parents kept that crap in the house. My brothers and I always got into poison ivy or something that would make us itch."

"I remember Calamine lotion because Blue, Pax and I all had chicken pox at the same time. Blue came home one day from school. I think I was about eight so he was ten. He said, "I think I'm going through puberty because I have a pimple." We had just watched that film about growing pubic hair and getting acne. You know the one they made us watch in health class."

"Yes, I remember," I laughed.

"Well, Blue said he was going to pop the pimple. Me being the ever-helpful little brother, I volunteered to assist."

I listened to his story while observing his full lips, outlined in a perfectly manicured mustache and goatee. His eyes are so hazel that they take on a golden hue. His locs are braided, and the length of the braid is resting on his back. I nodded as he continued.

"Paxton and I watched him take a needle and pop that pimple not realizing it was his first chicken pox. By the next morning, he had them everywhere! Paxton and I had them also. We all had to sleep in the same room to 'contain the outbreak,'" he used his quotation fingers. "The only thing we had on were our underwear, and each of us had our own bottle of calamine lotion. We sat for days itching to death and using that stupid lotion."

I laughed so hard at his story.

"That's a funny story. I don't remember having chicken pox."

"Maybe you were lucky enough not to get them. That was a hard few days for us!"

I threw my head back laughing. I stopped laughing and noticed he was smiling and staring at me.

"How often do people ask you if you're wearing contacts?" Ezekiel asked.

"All the time. How often do they ask you?"

"Not nearly as much as they ask you, I would assume."

"How do you know they aren't contacts?"

"I peeped your vibe. I know your eyes, your hair and everything else is real."

He looked at me from head to toe then back up to my eyes.

"Oh yeah?"

"Yeah."

I leaned in, "Is that one of your standard pick-up lines?"

He leaned in too. I could smell his cologne. It wasn't overpowering. It was pleasant and created a small puddle between my legs. It's been too long since I've had sex if this Lil church boy is making me wet.

"No, I created a new one just for you," he winked.

"Zeke, you ready to go?" Roman was walking out of the kitchen holding Zanetta's hand.

Ezekiel looked at me for a minute before he answered, "Yeah, I'm ready." He stood from his seat, "It was nice meeting you, Doctor Chambers."

"It was interesting meeting you, Mr. Bluette."

He smiled.

They collected a sleeping Paxton and left the apartment.

"Did you see how BJ was with him? I have never seen him act like that. He didn't even want to be with his Tee Tee. That was weird, huh?" I looked at Zanetta.

"It was weird."

BJ has never reacted to anyone the way he reacted to Ezekiel. He is usually very clingy to me when we are around people that he doesn't know. I couldn't get him away from Ezekiel the entire evening. Once he fell asleep and I had a chance to talk to Ezekiel, I could see why BJ didn't want to leave him. He's a charmer for sure.

"What did you think of the church boys?" Nette asked after sitting next to me on the couch.

"They were all really cool and down to earth. Paxton doesn't talk much, but he said enough. Roman was too busy watching you, but when he took breaks from staring you down, he was a great conversationalist."

"Girl get on somewhere, he was not staring at me like that."

"Yes, he was, and the other two men must be used to it because they didn't say anything about it."

"Or maybe it was because Zeke was too busy watching you."

"He can watch all he wants. He is absolutely gorgeous, but I can tell he is a flirt. No telling how many women he has lined up to spend time with him. Those hazel eyes, long locs, and all of that swag, he probably has at least two baby mommas."

"Nope. No baby mommas. No girlfriend either."

"That's interesting."

I stayed the night at Nette's house since BJ had already fallen asleep. We sat up laughing and talking.

"Oh, Ezekiel asked me to give you his information."

"His information?"

"Yeah, his contact information. He sent me a text while I was texting Roman."

"Why didn't he give me his information while he was here if he wanted me to have it?"

"I asked the same thing. I don't know but do you want it?"

"You can text it to me, but I don't have time to be playing around with some church dude that thinks he's a playboy."

"Playboy? Wait...hello?" Nette put her phone to her ear. "It's 1980, they want their word back." We laughed.

"I can't speak for the man that Zeke is now, but when I lived in New York, and we were around each other, one thing I can say about him is that he's honest. No one can ever say that he lied because he's going to tell you the truth. Even if it hurts your feelings. I haven't been around him in a while, but I can't imagine he's changed that much. I'm going to text you his number. Use it or not. It's up to you."

"Okay, whatever."

Zora

After finishing decorating the offices at the church, Zanetta came to the practice and decorated my office. She made it very feminine with crème colored walls and white furniture. She accented it with gold and silver accessories. All the other doctors were talking about using her for their offices as well. The practice has been well received in the community. My schedule has stayed full of patients either at the office or at the hospital. I am so glad I made the choice to come here.

I was actively trying not to use Ezekiel's number. It was almost impossible not to use his number because my son would not stop talking about him. Ezekiel really made a lasting impression on him. BJ asks me every day if we can call Zeke. I make up an excuse every time he asks. I'm about to run out of them. I'm not trying to get mixed up with anyone, but especially Zanetta's friend. I don't want things to go bad, and then I'd have to be around him all the time because of Zanetta and Roman. I know I'm overthinking things, but I can't help it. Things are finally going well, and I don't want to mess that up.

We had dinner with Zanetta again on Sunday. Ezekiel was out of town, so he didn't come. I was disappointed, but I tried to play like it didn't faze me. Why am I disappointed when all I have to do is call him? BJ likes Roman and Paxton also, but he was looking for Ezekiel the same way I was.

I pulled up to BJ's school to pick him up. One of his teachers, Lucy, escorted him to the car. She helped him into his car seat before I thanked her and pulled off.

"Mommy."

"Yes, baby?"

"Can we call Zeke now? He said I could come over and see his drums. I want to see his drums mommy."

"I know baby, I'm sure he's busy, though. Maybe another time?"

"Please, mommy. I want to talk to my friend. He said I could come over. I want to play the drums. I told my class that I was going to see a real drum set. Please mommy, he said I could call!"

I had to stop making excuses as to why I didn't want to call him. I can't tell my son that I am hyper-attracted to this man. I can't say that I want to jump his bones in front of everyone. I can't say that if I call him, it's a possibility that I will be breaking my own rules. Okay Zora, woman-up and give him a call. What's the worst that can happen?

"Okay, baby. As soon as we get settled in the house, I will call him for you, okay?"

"Yay!"

The smile that spread across my son's face was worth every ounce of discomfort I am about to feel when I dial this number.

4

Ezekiel

"THANK you to Thomas for hosting me and thank you to all of you for coming out. You can follow me on social media. All my names are the same, golden drummer. Let me know you were at this clinic if you have any questions and I will get back at 'cha. Again, thank you all."

I wiped the sweat from my face as I stood from my drum kit to shake hands. I had just completed a Master Class for drummers at a small music school in Houston. I love doing stuff like this. It gives me the ability to reach back, pull up a young drummer, to help him, or her reach their potential. I do several of these classes a year. I don't charge the smaller schools or shop owners because I know that it's hard for them to bring in big talent due to their operating budgets.

As the last person was filing out of the room, Thomas, the school's owner came up to shake my hand.

"Ezekiel, thanks so much man. These couple of hours that you spent with these kids has changed their trajectory. It's always cool when they can interact with someone who is doing the work they aspire to."

"Man, I love this kind of stuff. It always surprises me that people actually listen to me!" We laughed.

"You are one of the coldest Cats out here when it comes to the drums so yeah, we are listening and taking notes. Maybe one day we can get you and your brother to come and do a demonstration for us."

"That's something I can mention to Blue. You know he is busy with his church and everything, but I think he will be down for that."

"Well thanks again, man."

"No worries."

"Zeke, everything is all packed up," Percy informed me.

"Alright cool."

I headed out to the Sprinter checking my phone to see if I had missed any calls while I had it muted during the class. I sat in the passenger seat while Percy drove.

Nothing.

It had been almost three weeks since I asked Nette to give Zora my information. She hasn't called yet. I don't know why I am sweating it, but I am. I have been checking my phone since I sent the text message to Nette. When Zora walked in the apartment, the first thing I noticed was her height. I'm a sucker for a woman with some height. Her skin is a cocoa brown color, and her eyes are the brightest blue color I have ever seen. She has full lips that she covered with a matted brown color lipstick. Her hair is up in a bun on the top of her head and her body...I could see that she takes superb care of herself. I would guess that she was or maybe still is an athlete.

Her son BJ is a cool Lil dude, and I don't even like kids. I think that he is the first kid that has ever sat on my lap. I haven't held any babies either. There aren't any in our family, and I'm not that dude to be smiling all up in people's faces to hold their offspring. I'm cool on that. I won't kick it with a woman that has kids. That's one of my rules. I don't have time for the drama that comes along with baby daddies and baby mommas. Although, I didn't mind BJ sitting on my lap. He communicates very well for a three, almost four-year-old (that's what he told me when I asked his age). Well, I guess he does. I don't think I have ever been around a three-year-old. His mother tried several times to get him away from me. He didn't want to leave, and I was cool with him hanging out with my brothers and me. There is something about the kid that drew me to him, the same way he was drawn to me. He looks like his mom, but his skin is several shades lighter. He didn't get her blue eyes, but he has big brown expressive eyes. She keeps his dark hair cut in a wavy low fade.

I looked down at my buzzing phone. It was a 718-area code. This was my personal line, so I'm sure whoever it was got the number from me.

"Hello?"

"Hi, Ezekiel? This is Zora, Zanetta's friend."

Finally.

I smiled, "Hi, Zora. How are you?"

"I'm great and you?"

"I can't complain."

"I am calling because my son won't stop talking about seeing your drum set. He has talked about you and your drums non-stop since we met you."

"Oh yeah?"

"Yes, so I was wondering if we could set up a time for him to see your drums so that he can give my ears a break."

I laughed, "I think I can make that happen."

"Great! My sche...I'm sorry Ezekiel. One second."

I could hear Zora speaking to someone in the background.

"Yes, sweetheart... I know...I'm asking now...can you give mommy a minute...please..."

She came back onto the phone and said, "Would you mind if Braeden says hello to you? He won't leave me alone until he does."

I laughed, "Of course he can."

"Hi, Zeke!" BJ enthusiastically said into the phone.

"What's up, man! I'm happy you called me!"

"My mommy called you for me cause I want to come and see your drums."

"You like drums, huh?"

"Uhn huh. When I am at school, and we sing, my teacher lets us pick a instrument to play, and I pick the drums cause the drums are cool."

"They sure are. What other instruments do you have in your class?"

"We have drums and tambourines and recorders and bells and xyl...xyla..."

I heard Zora say, "Xylophone."

"Yeah and Xylospones."

I smiled at his mispronunciation.

"Wow, that's a lot of instruments!"

"Yeah and at my school...huh, Mommy?"

Zora was saying something in the background.

"Okay, I have to go now, Zeke. I will see you when I come over to see your drums."

"Alright, Lil man. I look forward to it."

I didn't realize that I smiled through the whole conversation. I actually settled into my seat to listen to him tell me about the instruments in his class.

"Ezekiel?"

"Yeah."

"I'm sorry, if I didn't stop him he would have talked your ears off. He would have switched from subject to subject seamlessly," she chuckled.

"It's all good. I don't mind talking to him."

"So, back to the reason for my call. Can you look at your schedule and let me know a good time for you?"

"I'm pretty much free right now. I have a couple of weeks before I start rehearsals for the next tour. My days will mostly consist of me taking care of business at the studio. What time do you get off work?"

"I'm usually finished by six."

"What about tomorrow evening. Would that work for you?"

"Yes, that's perfect. If we go any longer than that, I will have to put this kid outside because he won't stop talking about you or your drums," she laughed as she finished.

"So, tomorrow around 7:30?"

"7:30 is perfect. Will we be coming to the studio?"

"No, my house. I will text you the information."

"Okay, thank you so much."

"Not a problem. Make sure you bring your appetite. I will have dinner prepared."

"Wow, dinner. Will it be edible?"

"Ahhh, you're a comedian?"

"No, I'm a mom who doesn't want to feed poison to her son."

We laughed.

"Mrs. Grace Bluette would not let any of her sons leave out of her house without knowing how to cook well enough to feed ourselves. What does BJ like to eat?"

"He likes french fries and chicken nuggets. Those are his favorites."

"Then that's what we will be having for dinner."

"I look forward to it. If for nothing else than to get this little person off my back!"

"I'm looking forward to it too."

"Ezekiel, save my number just in case you need to cancel or change or whatever. I will understand."

"I'm going to save your number I but definitely won't be using it for any of the reasons you just gave."

"Bye, Ezekiel."

"Bye, Zora."

We disconnected the call. It's so strange because not only am I looking forward to entertaining a woman at my house, which I've never done, I'm also looking forward to entertaining her kid. I'm breaking all sorts of rules with this, but it feels right, so I'm going with it.

I arrived home and settled in before calling my mom.

"Hey, beautiful lady!"

"Hi Baby," my mother responded after answering the phone.

"How are you?"

"I'm doing good baby. How are you? You are getting ready to be on the road again soon, correct?"

"Yes, ma'am. I start rehearsals in a couple of weeks. Momma, I need a recipe for chicken nuggets."

"Chicken nuggets?"

"Yes, ma'am."

"Ezekiel, why would you need a recipe for chicken nuggets? You dating someone that young?"

"Momma you know I don't date. I smas..."

"Ezekiel Levi Bluette, I will come through this phone and throat chop you!"

I laughed, "I'm just messing with you. If you must know nosey lady, I have company coming over tomorrow. My new friend BJ and his mom, Zora. BJ wants to see my drum kits, so I invited him over, and I am going to cook dinner. Zora said that his favorite foods are chicken nuggets and fries, so that's what we are going to have."

"New friend, huh?"

"Yep. He's Nette's godson. I met him the other day at her apartment."

"Is his mom Zanetta's friend that she always speaks so highly of? The doctor?"

"Yes. That's her."

"Ezekiel, I don't have to tell you that when you are trying to date a woman with a child, it's a different ballgame. You can't introduce yourself into the child's life with the intentions of smashing his momma."

"Momma, smash...really?"

"I know that's what you were about to say. I watch all sorts of reality TV shows. I know all the slang. Like I was saying, it's a delicate situation because you don't want to hurt a child."

"I'm not befriending him to smash his momma. Although, I wouldn't mind..."

"I'm warning you, Ezekiel!"

"I'm kidding," I laughed.

That's one of the cool things about my mother. She allows me to be myself. I can tell her anything. Not too many details but enough where she gets a clear picture of what's really going on.

"For real, I like him. It's odd because he sorta chose me. You know I thought I didn't like kids, but BJ is different. I'm not going to pretend like his momma is not the most beautiful woman that I have ever laid my eyes on, next to you of course, but I'm not going through BJ to get to her, I promise."

"Well, let's make sure you have some good tasting chicken nuggets for your new friend and his mom."

Zora

It took me forever to get BJ to calm down after I told him that we would be going over to Ezekiel's house tomorrow. He is so excited.

I went on Ezekiel's social media sites and saw how active he is on them. I didn't see any pictures of him with any females aside from the platonic pics that he took with fans. People seem to really like him. His posts are usually about music, of course. He posted a short video of him showing his mom and dad how to use Instagram. It was really cute. There were also some photos that he was tagged in from his appearance on the cover of Sticks magazine. It's a magazine that targets the interest of drummers and percussionists. The cover of the magazine showed him behind an enormous set of drums, shirtless. His chest was intricately carved like he spent hours in the gym. He had a tattoo of sheet music that covered his right pectoral and extended down his entire arm. In the interview, he said that tattoo was the sheet music to the first song he'd written. His locs were twisted up into a bun on the top of his head. There was one photo that was a close-up showcasing his beautiful golden eyes, carved facial features and luscious lips. The comments that were left by women and men under that picture were borderline pornographic. I don't blame them, though. I wanted to leave a comment too.

Now I'm trying to decide what to put on to take my son on a playdate with him. I left work early so that I could pick up BJ, and come home to change my clothes. Should I do a full face of make-up? No, right? We are just going over so BJ can finally see the drums. It's not like it's a date or anything. I had been talking to myself the entire day. There was a level of nervousness for some reason. Maybe because I hadn't been in such close proximity to a male who wasn't old enough to be my dad in a long time. All the doctors that I work with are old and white.

"Mommy, I'm ready to go. Can we call Zeke and tell him we are on our way?"

"No, baby. He knows we are on our way."

"I'm going to tell him about my drums at school today, and then I am going to tell him about..."

I tuned BJ out as we headed to the car. I strapped him into his car seat. I put the address into my GPS and followed the voice prompts.

After a thirty-minute drive, I pulled up to an ultra-modern house. It was slate gray with black trimmed windows. I pulled up next to his black G-Wagen and put my car in park. I looked back, BJ was already busy unhooking himself from his car seat. I took a deep breath and mumbled, "here we go."

5

I LOOKED at my watch as I walked to my door to open it. She is punctual. I opened the door and saw Zora standing on the other side holding BJ's hand. I smiled at BJ, and he ran in to hug me. I couldn't help but pick him up. Seeing his little face light up when he saw me did something to me on the inside. It warmed me and made me feel like the most important person in the world. He wrapped his little arms around my neck and laid his head on my shoulder. I've had hugs from all sorts of people in my lifetime, but this hug is the best that I've ever experienced.

"Hi, Zeke!"

"Hi, BJ! I'm so happy you are here!"

"Thank you! I'm happy to be here too. My mommy brung me here."

"Hey Zora, come in."

"Hi Ezekiel, thank you."

I stepped out of the way so that she could enter while still holding BJ. She stepped into my house smelling amazing. She has a scent that I noticed when she sat next to me a Nette's house. It's a mix of coconut and jasmine.

"Welcome to my home. Let me take your jackets."

I put BJ down and helped him take off his jacket while Zora handed me hers. I put them in the coat closet and walked back over to my guests.

Zora was wearing a black t-shirt with faded denim jeans and a red and black plaid shirt tied around her waist. She had on some peep-toe booties that showed off her neon pink toenail polish. She had BJ in a gray and black Nike sweatsuit with matching tennis shoes.

"So, are you ready to see my drums?"

"YES!" BJ screamed.

His excitement was contagious. I took his hand, and Zora followed as we walked through the kitchen of the house out the sliding door, past my pool to my music house.

"Oh, a pool!" BJ commented as we passed by my pool.

"Do you like pools?"

"Yes, my mommy takes me to the pool to swim and play."

"There is a pool by your house?" I looked back to ask Zora.

"No, he's talking about when we lived in New York. We haven't been to a pool since we've been here."

My music house was originally my guest house, but I had it soundproofed. Now I use it as a studio and practice space. I keep all my instruments in it, and there is a small studio that I use when I have epiphanies in the middle of the night that need to be recorded before I forget.

I opened the door and let Zora enter then BJ, and I walked in.

"This is my music house. I keep all my drum kits here." I walked them over to the first kit. "This is the very first kit that I ever owned. My dad purchased this kit for me when I was a little older than you, BJ."

"He did?"

"Yes, before this set, I would create my own set with anything in the house that made the noise that I needed to include books, skillets, and boxes."

"Don't give him any ideas," Zora laughed.

"Have you ever seen a full drum set, BJ?"

"No, just the drum in my classroom."

"I bet it looks like this one, right?" I pointed to the snare drum.

"Yes, but it's littler."

"Smaller, BJ. Not littler," Zora corrected.

"It's smaller," BJ amended.

"This is called the kick drum. This is the most important piece in this whole set."

"It is?"

"Yes, it is. This is the piece that provides the rhythm. It helps you to feel the music."

I tapped the pedal of the kick drum a couple time. "See, you can feel that bass?"

BJ nodded.

"These are called Toms, and these..." I continued to name each piece in the kit. BJ listened intently to everything that I said. We walked further into the house. I showed him my travel kit, and then I stopped at my show kit, my custom set that I used for touring.

"There are a lot more pieces in this kit than in the others," Zora observed.

"Yes, this is the one I use on tour. I used to keep it all bagged up and stored until it was time for me to go on tour again but now I keep it set up that way I can practice on it."

"It's really nice."

"Thank you. It's all custom made. I am in the process of creating a signature set that will incorporate some of these pieces into it. BJ, would you like to try these out?"

"Oh no, Ezekiel. I don't think that's a good idea. I wouldn't want him to break anything."

"It's okay. Everything is replaceable. Besides, I will show him how to use them correctly. What do you say, man?"

"YES!" BJ screamed.

"Alright, first let me get you your own set of sticks," I went into my storage room and grabbed a pair of brand new sticks. "These will be your own personal sticks, okay?"

BJ nodded vigorously.

"Let's get your stool all set up, and we will be ready to go."

I lowered the stool and helped BJ on to it. I pulled up a stool next to his and started with the drum basics.

We played around for about forty-five minutes. Zora sat close. She cheered BJ and encourage him as we played.

"Your mother told me that you like chicken nuggets and French fries, is that true?"

"Yes. I love chicken nuggets." He smiled still holding on to his sticks.

"Let's go into the house, and get dinner ready, okay?"

He nodded, and we moved back into the main house.

"BJ can you take your mom down the hall to the bathroom on the right to wash your hands, and I will get the food ready. How does that sound?"

"Okay, come on mommy."

He took Zora's hand, and they walked to the bathroom while I started working on the food. They returned to the kitchen.

"BJ, do you know how to cook?"

"Yes, my mommy lets me help her in the kitchen. I can't do anything in the kitchen without a grown up because it's dangerous."

"That's true. Would you like to help me make dinner?"

He smiled and nodded.

"It's going to get a little messy. Is that okay?"

He nodded again.

I looked over to Zora just to make sure she was okay with it. She smiled, so I continued. I've never interacted with a kid, and I thought that I would be bored or nervous, but this kid is keeping me thoroughly entertained. I don't know if all kids are cool like this, but I'm digging BJ.

His job was to dip the sliced chicken breast into the egg wash and then into the flour. I showed him how to use one hand for the dry ingredients and the other hand for the wet. He mastered the technique immediately.

He told me about his school and all his friends that he named one by one. It seems like the whole school is his friend. I didn't mind. His conversation was great. Zora was right he could switch from topic to topic seamlessly.

"Zora, what do you do when you are not creating smiles?"

"You have been watching too many dentist commercials," she chuckled.

"You don't create smiles?"

She smiled, and her eyes brightened, "I'm not *that* dentist. I do more of the foundational work. The general dentist, prosthodontist or orthodontist create smiles. When I'm not working, I enjoy playing sports. I play basketball..."

"Basketball?"

"Yes, basketball. I grew up with three older brothers. I had to know how to play basketball if I wanted to hang out with them. I'm nice on the court, son."

I busted out laughing at her trying to use a New York accent.

"I will have to see you on the court one day then."

"Let me know the time and the place," she smirked. "I also play tennis, but I recently joined a kickball team."

"Kickball? For adults?"

"Yes."

"That sounds like fun."

"It is. One of the doctor's wives told me about the team. I've played about five games with them so far. It is a blast."

"I didn't know that adults played kickball. Is it in a league?"

"Yeah, it's a league. It's so much fun. You should come and check it out."

"I just might."

"What about you? What do you like to do when you're not playing music?"

"I make pottery."

"Oh, okay...that's cool." She looked around the kitchen without making eye contact with me.

I looked at her and laughed, "I don't make pottery! You must think I'm a lame! You just accepted it and didn't even challenge it. You think I'm a lame, Doctor Chambers?"

She laughed, "I mean, I've never met a man that was into pottery, but there's a first for everything."

We laughed.

"Your facial expression was priceless! You were probably thinking, 'I got my son around this lame that makes pottery!'"

"That is not what I was thinking!"

"Yes, it is! I saw it all over your face!"

"You're playing and didn't answer the question," she laughed.

"Music is my fun, straight up. When I'm not playing, I'm producing or writing. Music is my career and my hobby."

"I like music too," BJ chimed in.

We finished preparing dinner and sat down to eat. I bowed my head and said a quick prayer over my food before digging in.

"BJ these are some of the best chicken nuggets I have ever eaten. You did a great job cooking," Zora commented.

"Thank you, Mommy. Zeke helped too."

"You did a great job cooking also Ezekiel," she smiled.

"Thank you, Zora. I couldn't have done it without my Lil dude. I hope you saved some room for dessert."

"Dessert! Yay!" BJ cheered.

I left the table and returned with vanilla ice cream and three bowls.

"When I was a little boy there was an ice cream truck that had the best ice cream. I would always get the chocolate dip cone. Do you know what that is BJ?"

"No, I just usually get bamilla."

I smirked at his pronunciation of vanilla. "Let me show you."

I put two scoops of ice cream into a bowl.

"Look, this is the fun part."

I opened the top of the magic shell topping and poured it on top of the ice cream. I pushed the bowl toward him.

"Touch the chocolate. It's not soft is it?"

BJ touched it. He snatched his finger back and smiled.

"It's hard!"

"Yep, that's why it's magic."

BJ was fascinated by the magic shell topping.

I made a bowl for Zora and then one for myself. We kept up our conversation until we finished our dessert. I picked up the bowls and cleaned off the table. Zora and BJ followed me into the kitchen.

"Ezekiel, can we help you clean the kitchen?"

"No, I don't need any help."

Zora looked around the kitchen and back at me.

"Really?" She asked with one eyebrow raised.

I looked around too. I have a maid that comes in, but that wouldn't be until tomorrow morning. The kitchen was destroyed.

"Well, I guess you can help."

We cleaned the kitchen together. I washed and rinsed. BJ dried, and Zora put them away. They are the first real guest that I've had in my house, and I enjoyed them immensely.

"Ezekiel, thank you for having us. I need to get this little guy home so he can get into bed."

They followed me to the closet where I retrieved their jackets. I helped BJ with his.

"Thank you for letting me come over Zeke," BJ sang while yawning.

I got down on my knee to talk to him.

"Thank you for helping me cook tonight. You are welcome to visit anytime, okay?"

"Okay!"

He threw his little arms around my neck. I hugged him back, fighting off the feeling I was having being around this little guy. I picked him up and followed Zora out of my house to her car. She strapped him in and closed his door.

"Thank you for your hospitality, Ezekiel. This has made his week."

"I meant what I said. He is welcome anytime."

I opened my arms to hug her. This was my first time touching her. I like the way she feels. She's almost my height, so I don't have to bend over to hug her. I like the way she smells. Her hair brushed against my nose. I got another whiff of the coconuts and jasmine; fresh and sweet. I let her go and opened her car door. I waved at BJ as they pulled away.

I walked into my house.

"Did I just have a date with a three-year-old and his mom? If I did, I hit that one out of the park!"

Zora

"Okay, man give me these sticks and go and get in the shower."

"Mommy, can I take them with me into the shower?"

"No, baby. I will put them right here on your nightstand. I promise they will be here when you get out of the shower, okay?"

"Okay."

I watched BJ go into his bathroom and close the door. I put his pajamas out on his bed and put the sticks on his nightstand. Sometimes I let BJ go into the bathroom on his own and take a shower. When he comes out, I check to make sure he cleaned all the important areas. He is getting to the age where he wants to do everything on his own. I am trying to let him be independent, but it's hard.

I sat in the chair in his room and waited for him to complete his shower. I thought back to the evening we had with Ezekiel. I watched his interaction with BJ. He was patient and fun but always maintained his role as the adult. He answered all of BJ's questions and didn't ever appear to be overwhelmed with the million questions BJ asked. He explained things to BJ in a way that he could understand and didn't mind repeating himself. I didn't peg him for the type to like kids. He was great with BJ, though. BJ loves him. On the way home BJ talked about Zeke's drums, then he talked about Zeke's cooking, Zeke's magic ice cream, Zeke, Zeke, Zeke. My son has his first man crush. I don't blame him. I might have a little one myself.

I kept stealing glances at Ezekiel while he was working with Braeden. I've never been a fan of locs, but on Ezekiel, I loved them. His locs were long and well kept. He knows he's fine, but when he interacted with BJ, he didn't show any signs of arrogance. He showed my son a good time, and I appreciated it.

I reached into my pocket to retrieve my ringing phone. I saw Ezekiel's name on the screen.

"Hello."

"Hey, Zora."

"Hey, Ezekiel."

"I was calling to make sure you made it home okay. You didn't get lost in the neighborhood, did you?"

His voice was husky and sensual like he was completely relaxed.

"No, it was easy to get out of the neighborhood. We made it home fine. BJ talked about you the entire ride back to our house. I had to tell him not to take his sticks into the shower with him. He doesn't want to put them down."

He laughed, "I'm glad he likes them. Thank you for bringing him by. I enjoyed my evening with him."

"Thank you for having him."

"Is he still awake? I would like to say goodnight if you don't mind."

"I don't mind. He should be coming out of the shower any minute."

"What does he do to stay busy? Do you have him in any sports or anything?"

"No, I don't know if he wants to play sports."

"Do you think that he may want to learn how to play some instruments?"

"I've never thought about it, but as much as he likes the drums, he would probably like to learn."

"We can set up some time for him to come over and start learning the basics."

"That would be wonderful, but I don't want you to have to do that, though. I know your time is precious. I can find something for Braeden to do."

"It's not a problem. I think he will excel with instruments because he's so fascinated with them. That's usually how it begins. I will look at my schedule and see when we can set something up if that's alright with you?"

"I would like that," I smiled.

BJ came out the bathroom with his towel draped around his little shoulders. I put the phone on speaker while I helped him dry off and get into his pajamas.

"BJ, Ezekiel is on the phone. He wants to say good night."

"Hi Zeke," BJ spoke while I was helping him into his pajamas.

"Hey, BJ. I wanted to call and tell you that I had a good time. Thanks for hanging out with me tonight."

"You're welcome. I will come over again if my mommy brings me, okay?"

"Okay, that will be nice. Are you going to bed now?"

"Yes. Are you going to bed now too?"

"Yeah, I am. I just needed to tell your mommy one one more thing. Good night, man. I will see you soon."

"Goodnight, Zeke."

I turned off the speaker and spoke back into the phone.

"You needed something else, Ezekiel?"

"Yeah, I wanted to tell you that I enjoyed my evening with you too."

I smiled so hard.

I kissed BJ on the cheek, "Goodnight baby."

"Goodnight, Mommy."

I closed Bj's door and turned my attention back to my phone conversation.

"Is that right, Mr. Bluette?"

"It is, Doctor Chambers."

"So, I'm invited back again too?"

"You are always welcome as well."

"Maybe you can teach me pottery."

"There are some things I'm sure I can teach you, but pottery isn't one of them."

"Really?"

"Really."

"Goodnight, Mr. Bluette."

"Sleep tight, Doctor Chambers."

6

ZORA and I have started having regular conversations. BJ and I usually begin the conversation then Zora and I end it. Talking to them has become a bright spot in my day. Our conversations aren't long, and they aren't every day, but when they do happen, I usually hang up the phone smiling. I haven't seen them since they visited my house because I have been traveling.

I was in Sweet Rapids, Nevada for a meeting with Noble Naturals to discuss me coming on as a brand ambassador for their hair care line. I sat down with Isaiah Noble and his team. We discussed their plan to use me and my social media presence to promote their products that I already use on my locs. The pitch was well thought out and would be easy to accomplish. I requested to use Zanetta as my stylist for any events and photos. Isaiah agreed. I believe this will be a great collaboration.

After my meeting with Isaiah, I met a couple of my old band mates at a local bar. Warren, a keyboard player, and Dru, a lead guitarist, were both on the first tour with Lyrica. We were together so much, we became family.

"Warren, what's up?"

We dapped each other up before I did the same with Dru.

"Ain't nothing much over here Mr. MD!"

Lyrica's camp had recently announced that I was chosen as the Music Director for her next tour.

"Yeah man, it's a brand-new level of responsibility. I'm ready for it, though," I said.

"Will you still be playing with the band or are you going to hire someone else?"

"I'm not sure yet. I've been thinking about giving someone else the chance to..."

I felt my phone vibrating and took a quick look to see who it was. It was an incoming FaceTime call from Zora.

"Excuse me one minute," I quickly answered.

BJ's little face filled the screen.

"Zeke!" He smiled brightly.

"What's up big man?"

I smiled. I was happy to see him.

"I called you all by myself!"

"You did? Where is your Mommy?"

"Her...she in the other room." He pointed behind him then turned back to the phone.

"Did you have a good day today?"

"Yes. I got to show my class my drumsticks and they all..."

"BJ!" Zora came into view behind him. "What are you...Zeke?"

"Hey, Zora," I smiled. She looked cute in her cut off jogging pants and ribbed t-shirt. Her breasts were displayed nicely in her t-shirt.

"I called Zeke all by myself Mommy," BJ said proudly.

"Baby, I told you Zeke was busy."

"It's okay," I interjected. I was happy to hear from him...them.

"Zeke, I'm so sorry! I didn't even know he knew how to do this."

"He's a genius," I chuckled. "Hey big man, I'm glad you had a good day, and I'm also glad you called me but remember, you should always ask permission before using your mommy's things, okay?"

"Okay," he nodded while looking sad. "I'm sorry, mommy. I just wanted to say hi to my Zeke."

I don't know when he added the 'my' to my name when referring to me, but it made me feel unique and special.

"It's fine baby, you just know for next time," she soothed.

"Hey BJ, I will see you when I get back in town, okay? We will do something together if it's okay with your mommy."

I looked at Zora. She smiled.

"Okay!" BJ smiled brightly.

"Sorry again," Zora apologized.

"It's not a problem. I will talk to you soon."

"Bye, Zeke."

"Bye Doctor Chambers. Bye B."

I disconnected the called and looked up to find Warren and Dru staring at me with confused looks on their faces.

"What?" I looked between them both.

"Did we miss something? Like a wedding or birth announcement?" Warren asked.

I chuckled. "No, she's a friend, and he's my Lil dude."

"Friend?" Dru asked.

"Lil dude? The Zeke that I know would have never, ever dated a woman with a child," Warren added.

"She must have platinum in between those thighs!" Dru laughed while slapping high five with Warren.

I shrugged my shoulders, "I wouldn't know."

"WHAT!" they both said at the same time.

"Say it ain't so Zeke!" Dru laughed.

"I can't say what it is yet, but things are changing."

HEY, **I'm back in town. I wanted to know if you and BJ wanted to come over to swim this weekend. If you're not busy.**

Zora and I had a conversation about my pool and how underused it had been. I've been so busy that I don't have a whole lot of time to enjoy it. When BJ was over, he commented on the pool. I thought it would be a good way to see them again.

We don't have plans. I'm sure BJ will be siked to come and play in the pool. - Zora

Cool. I missed my little friend while I was away.

He missed you too. - Zora

Is he the only one that missed me?

Yep. Oh wait, I'm sure your brothers missed you as well. <wink> - Zora

Whatever, Z. I will see you bright and early on Saturday?

Yep. We will be there. - Zora

"Percy," I yelled.

He appeared in the doorway of my office.

"What's up?"

"I need for you to find all of those little safety things that kids use at a pool; those noodle things, floating vest and what-not. I need it by Saturday. Also, call the pool company and see if any adjustments need to be made to my pool for a young child to enjoy it. BJ is coming over, and I want to make sure it's all cool."

"I got you. You're digging Lil Dude, huh?"

"I am," I smiled.

"That's what's up. He's a cool lil kid."

"He is."

Percy had met Zora and BJ during Sunday dinner at Nette's house while I was away.

"His Momma is fine too."

I laughed, "Yep, she is."

"You think she would like an up and coming musician like myself?"

I stopped what I was doing on my phone to give Percy my full attention.

"Percy, don't get your ass fired in here."

He laughed and backed out of my office door after the doorbell rang.

"I'm just messing with you, Zeke. That must be Lyrica and Obasi."

"Yeah go and let them in before I murder you," I laughed.

Obasi is Lyrica's fiancé. He's a supermodel. He is originally from Mozambique. When I first heard about them dating, I thought that he would be one of those pretty, superficial dudes that were after her for her fame. I was wrong. He cares for her and protects her like he's her bodyguard instead of the 300-pound dude named Brick that follows her around everywhere.

I stood to greet them as they came into my office.

"Zeke," Lyrica walked into my embrace. I gave her a tight squeeze before releasing her and shaking Obasi's hand.

They both sat down. I didn't notice it at first, but the right side of Obasi's face was swollen.

My facial expression must have given it away.

"You see it too?" Lyrica commented. "I told you it's swollen baby. You need to go to the dentist."

"Absolutely not. My mother told me to chew on some garlic cloves. It will make the pain go away," Obasi answered her with his thick accent.

"No baby, all that's doing is making your breath smell terrible! Zeke, please tell him he needs to see a dentist. Your face shouldn't be swollen like that," Lyrica pleaded.

I had a thought.

"I have a good friend who is a dentist. I can ask her if we can come by her office so she can take a look at it."

"No," Obasi answered without giving it any thought.

"How about this: If you don't go and get your tooth looked at, you will never look at anything else on me," Lyrica tilted her head to the side waiting on Obasi's answer.

I averted my eyes from them and waited for Obasi to respond to the ultimatum that Lyrica had just delivered.

"Fine! Call your friend, Zeke," Obasi relented.

I picked up my cell phone and dialed Zora's number. She answered immediately.

"Hey, Zora."

"Hey, Ezekiel, What's up?"

"I have a huge favor to ask you. I will owe you one if you can help me with this."

"I'm listening."

"My friend Obasi..."

"Obasi as in fine ass Obasi, the model?"

I cleared my throat, "Yeah. He and Lyrica are here with me now and..."

"Lyrica as in his fiancé Lyrica with the amazing voice?"

"Yeah...Obasi's face is swollen, and he is having some tooth pain. I was wondering if we could come to your office so you can take a look at him. He doesn't like dentists, but I told him I know one whose beauty will take his mind off the pain."

"Whatever, Zeke."

"No for real though, he's in pain."

"Yeah bring him over. I will take a look. If I can't help him one of my partners will be able to. When you arrive, park in the garage and let me know you are down there. I will have one of the assistants take you through a back way, so people aren't in here 'fanning out.'"

"Thanks, Z. See you soon."

We arrived at Zora's office building. I rode with Lyrica and Obasi in her truck. Obasi sat stewing the entire ride. I sent Zora a text.

We are in the garage.

That was fast. My assistant is coming down. She will direct you to the private entrance. She has on Hello Kitty scrubs. – Zora

Cool.

We waited for about five minutes. A small female appeared from behind a door that is not readily visible from the outside. We all filed out of the truck and followed behind Brick.

"Hi, I'm Susan, Doctor Chambers' assistant. Please follow me."

We followed Susan through the hidden door to a set of elevators. She punched in a code. The elevator doors closed and then opened to a plush office area. We followed her past several doors with name-plates listing the doctor's names. We stopped at the door that read: Zora N. Chambers, DDS. Susan knocked before opening it.

"Doctor Chambers, your guests have arrived. Should I set them up in Operatory six?"

Zora appeared in the doorway wearing her dark blue scrubs and a white lab coat over them. She smiled at everyone. She had her hair pulled back into a ponytail and didn't have on much makeup. She was still gorgeous.

"Hi, I'm Zora Chambers. She extended her hand to Obasi and then to Lyrica. Susan will show you to the room, and I will be right in."

Lyrica, Obasi, and Brick moved through the office and disappeared behind a door down the hall. I moved in to give her a hug. She moved into my embrace.

"Thank you for doing this for me."

"I get a chance to meet two superstars? Please! My pleasure. Let me go and see what's happening in his mouth."

I followed her down the hall.

Zora

I walked into the operatory. Obasi was seated in the patient chair. Lyrica stood beside him while the giant bodyguard stood in the corner quietly observing.

"Mr. Babtunde, how long has your face been swollen?"

I looked from his dark almost black eyes to his beautiful dark skin. I've seen him on countless magazine covers, and I've seen him walking in fashion shows. He is even more handsome in person. I couldn't ogle him too much because he was in pain. The right side of his handsome face was visibly swollen.

"He woke up like this," Lyrica answered for him. "I told him that he needed to see a dentist as soon as the pain started but he wouldn't listen to me."

I smiled at Lyrica then turned back to Obasi.

"You've had problems in the past with dentists, Mr. Babatunde?"

"I hate you guys," he rolled his eyes.

"Obi," Lyrica hissed.

I chuckled, "I'm not offended. If I had a nickel for every time I heard that, I would be a billionaire."

I moved to the small sink in the room and washed my hands.

I looked at Susan, "No allergies, correct?" I didn't see any unique markings on his dental folder that would inform me that he was allergic to anything.

"Correct," she confirmed.

I put on a fresh mask and covered my eyes with my glasses then I donned a pair of fresh latex gloves.

"Is it okay if I rest my hand on your face? I just want to see how the swelling feels."

He took a deep breath and nodded.

I lightly placed my hand on his cheek.

"It's warm. That means that there is some infection present. Can you determine if it's the upper tooth or the lower tooth?"

He nodded, "I just know that it hurts. I don't know where it's coming from."

"Can you open for me?"

He slowly opened his mouth.

"I'm going to recline your chair some for a better view."

I used the foot pedal to recline his chair. I used the mouth mirror to look around in his mouth to determine where the swelling was coming from. I saw his bottom wisdom tooth peeking through his gums, but it was erupting horizontally instead of vertically.

"First things first, let try to relieve some of this discomfort."

"I hate needles," he replied.

"Most people do. I'm going to put something on here to numb your gums so we can get an x-ray, okay?"

While I was talking, I reached behind the chair to retrieve the syringe. I was going to attempt to give Obasi an injection without him knowing.

"Does it hurt when I pull back on your cheek like this?" I used the first finger of my left hand to pull his cheek back.

"No," came out a little muffled since I was pulling his cheek back.

"What about when I wiggle it like this?" I wiggled his cheek while simultaneously giving him an injection of Lidocaine. I pulled back, and Susan went right in with the suction.

I went behind him, refilled my syringe with another cartridge and pushed another dose without him realizing what was happening.

Susan suctioned him again.

"Baby! You did so well," Lyrica cheered.

"What?" Obasi was confused.

"You just got a shot, and you didn't even flinch!"

"A shot? No, I didn't. She just put that jelly stuff on me."

"No, Obi, she gave you two shots!" She held up two fingers.

"I didn't feel any needle. Doctor, did you give me a shot?"

"Technically, I gave you two injections of Lidocaine to numb the back area of your mouth."

I removed my gloves and went back to the sink to wash my hands.

"No, way!"

He looked at Brick and Ezekiel who both shook their heads.

"Yeah dude, she numbed you up," Ezekiel confirmed.

"But I didn't feel anything!" Obasi continued.

I spoke to him while I wrote notes in his record, "Dentistry has come a long way. It doesn't have to hurt. We are developing new techniques all the time to reduce the pain. Susan is going to place a device in your mouth that you shouldn't feel at this point. She will take an x-ray so we can accurately diagnose you. Then I will be back, okay?" I smiled and touched his shoulder. "Susan, dim the lights in here for a few minutes and give the anesthesia time to work. Then get me a panoramic x-ray."

I went back to my office and waited for the x-rays to populate on my computer screen before I went back into the operatory with them.

"Mr. Babatunde, you have an abscess on your wisdom tooth at the bottom. It's trying to erupt, but it's coming in horizontally instead of vertically. It has some decay that has gone down to the pulp of the tooth and caused the infection. That tooth needs to be extracted along with your other three wisdom teeth. Do you have a dentist in California?"

"No, I don't. Can you do it?" Obasi asked with his eyes slightly closed.

"Yes, I can, but we would need to wait for about a week. First, I am going to write you a prescription for Penicillin. It's an antibiotic that will treat the infection. Also, I am giving you a prescription for eight hundred milligrams of ibuprofen. Take both of these as soon as you pick them up from the pharmacy. This will help you stay ahead of the pain once the numbing medication wears off. We have to treat that abscess before we can safely perform any dental surgery."

"Okay, then we will come back in a week," Obasi answered. He was much more pleasant now that he was out of pain.

I went to the computer and pulled up my schedule for the next week.

"I have space. Susan, can you go up front and confirm a time for Mr. Babatunde? Use the name Ezekiel Bluette, please. I don't want everyone knowing they are here."

Susan handed me my prescription pad and left the room.

"Doctor Chambers, after he has the teeth removed, can he get a regular exam and cleaning?" Lyrica asked.

"Yes, but we are going to give him a few weeks to heal from the extractions then we can look at getting his mouth into optimal shape."

Obasi was still reclined in the dental chair dozing off.

"He hasn't slept because of this pain," Lyrica whispered.

"Dental pain can change your whole personality. We try to get them out of pain before they start making decisions on dental treatments. If we don't take care of the pain first, then everyone's answer would be to extract their teeth, just so the pain would go away. We don't want to do that because teeth are important."

Susan came back with one of my business cards with the date and time for Obasi's next appointment.

"Here you go," I handed the card to Lyrica along with Obasi's prescription.

She smiled and moved in to hug me. We embraced.

"Thank you so much!"

Brick helped Obasi out of the chair.

"We need to get one of these at the house!" Obasi pointed to the dental chair. "Thank you, Doctor Chambers. I will see you next week."

We shook hands.

"Susan will direct you back out the way you came."

"I will be out in a minute," Zeke called to them.

They all left the room leaving Zeke and me by ourselves.

"Zora, thank you. You were amazing. I just knew he was going to be flopping all around like a fish out of water when you gave him that sho...I mean injection."

I smiled. He listened when I explained what I did to Obasi. "We don't like to call them shots because that frightens people and they are already afraid of my profession as a whole. You notice I didn't say I needed to pull his teeth. I said extract."

"I noticed. That's dope," he smiled.

I didn't realize how much I missed seeing him until now.

"So, I will see you and my Lil Dude on Saturday, right?"

"Right," I smiled.

We hugged. It felt good to feel his arms around me. He kissed my cheek.

"Susan will take you down the elevator."

"Bye, Doctor Chambers."

"Bye, Mr. Bluette."

Ezekiel

I came out of the room and saw Susan waiting on me. I followed her back down the hall and onto the elevator.

I was so proud watching Zora do her thing with Obasi. She was extremely professional and knowledgeable. She put the whole room at ease. I couldn't take my eyes off her. She was in her element, and I loved watching her.

I emerged from the secret door and hopped into the SUV.

"So, Doctor Zora is your friend, huh?" Lyrica asked as soon as I fastened my seat belt.

"I thought she was your meal from the way you were looking at her," Obasi commented.

"Oh, someone is feeling better," Lyrica said.

"Much better, thanks."

"Yeah, she's my friend," I smiled.

"Well, she is gorgeous. Those blue eyes are mesmerizing," Lyrica stated.

"I told you her beauty would take your mind off the pain."

"It almost did, bruh...it almost did," Obasi laughed.

When I walked into Zora's office and saw her, it was like I started breathing again. Like these few days that I was away, I had been holding my breath. I didn't realize that I missed seeing her until I saw her. Then I realized that I missed her a lot. When we hugged, I didn't want to let her go.

I WAS all prepared to spend the day with my Lil Dude and Zora. I had the pool checked. According to the pool company, I had all the safety equipment needed for a child. Percy stocked up on floatation devices and pool toys. Chef Leilani was coming over to prepare lunch and dinner for us. I was all set.

Zora and BJ arrived at ten o'clock. I opened the front door and was greeted by BJ running into my arms.

"Zeke!"

I picked him up and gave him a hug.

"Hey man! I missed you!"

"I missed you too," he returned excitedly.

I turned to Zora. She smiled and walked to me. I hugged her with my free arm. I was still holding BJ.

I put him down.

"Let me look at these cool swim trunks you have on." He was wearing a little red swim shirt with blue and red Spiderman swim trunks. He had on some Nike slides. "You look cool."

"Thank you," he replied.

Zora had a large bag on her shoulder.

I took the bag from her shoulder and said, "Follow me."

I grabbed BJ's hand and led them through the house to the pool.

"I wasn't sure of his skill level, so I have some floaties and stuff."

"He swims like a fish. I put him in water as soon as I could."

"The deep end and everything?" I wanted to be sure.

"Yep, everything."

"Can I get in Mommy?" BJ asked while jumping up and down.

She looked at me.

"That's why you're here. Let's get in." I followed BJ to the pool.

Sure enough, he dived into the deep end and came right up swimming. I jumped in and joined him. I turned around to ask Zora if she was getting in and saw her pulling her white cover-up over her head. She had on a black two-piece swimming suit. The top tied around her neck and the bottoms looked like they tied on each side. She had a small tattoo of a dream catcher on a string in the valley between her breast. She also has a tattoo of a trail of roses that started right underneath her left breast that got smaller in size as they continue down her side and disappeared into her bikini bottom.

I would love to see where that ends. Her breasts are the perfect size, a handful. Her stomach is flat. She does crunches or planks...probably both. I can tell she does squats by how round her butt is. Her legs...

"Mommy, are you getting in?" BJ's little voice forced me to close my mouth.

"I'm coming!" She responded while putting her hair up in a bun on the top of her head. She finished and jumped into the pool with us.

BJ and I raced from one end of the pool to next. I had a basketball hoop set up over the pool. We played that for awhile. BJ wanted to see who could hold their breath the longest underwater. He won. We swam and played for a couple of hours before we got out to eat the food that Leilani prepared.

"What are your plans? Are you going to stay a partner at the dental practice or open your own?"

I was becoming more and more interested in Zora. Her past, present, and future.

"I think I will stay with the partners for awhile. My dream is to open a free clinic where low-income people or people who don't have insurance can get quality dental care. I remember volunteering at the free clinic in Saint Louis. It was the most disgusting place I'd ever seen. I was scared to touch the equipment out of fear that I would catch some communicable disease. The clientele was poor but just because they were poor shouldn't mean that the facilities were not kept up. I want to provide a clean place for them to come and feel taken care of. I don't want to just focus on pulling teeth but overall dental health."

"That's cool."

"I want it to be a charitable organization and have 501(c)-(3) status so that the time the doctors donate to the clinic will be a tax write-off for them."

"My dad's secretary is a lawyer. She knows all about not for profit stuff. I could connect you with her."

"That would be nice. I don't really know where to start, I just know that I want to see it happen."

"She can help you think through the process and get some things on paper."

"Thank you, Zeke. I know that it won't happen overnight, but I'm willing to work to see it happen."

"That's what's up!"

Zora and I were talking at the table when I noticed that BJ had gotten quiet. I looked over at him to find his head resting on the table. He was sound asleep with a hot dog in one hand and a barbecued chicken leg in the other.

"I guess he wore himself out," I chuckled.

"Yeah, he doesn't fight his sleep. When he gets sleepy, he goes to sleep."

"No matter what he is doing, apparently."

"Right!"

Zora removed the food from his hands while I collected him in my arms.

"He can take a nap in my guest room."

Zora followed me through the house to one of my guest rooms. It had a sliding door out to the pool, so when he wakes up, he will be able to find us.

I laid him on the bed after Zora put down a couple of towels to protect the bedding from his wet swim trunks. I opened the sliding door, and we went to sit back by the pool.

"Oh, Blue asked me to call him while you were over here. He needed to talk to you about something."

"Talk to me? Is he going to propose to my sister?"

"I think he is sooner rather than later but I don't think that's what he wants to talk to you about, though."

"Okay, call him."

Zora

"What up Big Bro. I have Zora here with me," Ezekiel spoke into the phone. "Yeah, let me put you on speaker."

"Hey, Zora. How are you?" Roman's voice came through the phone.

"I'm good, Roman. How are you?"

"I'm great. Look, I'm out of town. I asked Zanetta if she would speak at both services tomorrow and she said that she would. I have a couple of favors to ask you."

"Okay," I sat up in my seat to listen.

"Well, first Chef Leilani is going to cook dinner for Nette tomorrow. I don't want her to preach and then come home and have to cook. So, can we set up the Sunday dinner at your house instead of Nette's apartment?"

"Sure!"

"Cool, Chef will give you all the details. The next thing is that I know it would mean a lot to Nette if you could be there when she ministers for the first time at my church."

My stomach dropped.

I took a deep breath and said, "Roman, you know how I feel about church."

"I know but hear me out. I can't be there. Pax is here with me. We are her family, and I want for her to have as much support as possible. Zeke will be there but the more family support, the better."

"Roman..." I wasn't feeling this request at all. I will support my sister in any way possible, but this request felt a little over the top.

"What if we can set it up where you can be there but you don't have to sit in the sanctuary, would that work?" Roman asked.

"Where would I sit?" I questioned looking at Ezekiel.

"You can sit in the sound booth," Ezekiel interjected. You can see and hear, but you don't have to go into the sanctuary. I can make sure she gets to the booth, Blue."

"Please, Zora. This would mean a lot to Nette and in turn, mean a lot to me."

Roman knew I wasn't going to be able to say no to him and Ezekiel. He set me up. I'm surprised Paxton isn't in the background to seal the deal. These men have quickly become my family. They have been supportive and caring. There is no way I can say no.

"Okay, fine. I will do it," I relented.

"Great. Let's make this a surprise. Don't let her know you are coming."

"Okay."

"Be safe Bro, see you when you get back," Ezekiel said.

"You too, Bro. Thanks for everything. I will see you when I return."

"One."

Ezekiel disconnected the call.

"I guess I will see you at church tomorrow," I rested my back against the back of the lounger.

"I guess so," Ezekiel smiled.

Zeke's phone rang. He looked at the screen. His eyebrows knitted together before he pressed the button to connect the call.

"Zeke!" I heard a female voice come through the phone.

I know he is not talking to another female while I am here with him. Then again, I guess I can't say anything about him talking to someone since we are not dating. It is rude though.

"What's up? Is something wrong?" Zeke responded.

I'm not going to even look over there to see what she looks like. This is ridiculous. I am going to get my son and get out of here. I mean, I only really came over because BJ wanted to come anyway. I sat forward about to get up to start collecting my things.

"No, nothing is wrong. I wanted to know if I can get Doctor Zora's number so we can call and thank her."

I turned my attention to the phone. Is that Lyrica?

"Well, you are in luck. She's right here."

He turned the phone so that I could see Lyrica's beautiful face on the screen. My attitude change immediately. I relaxed and smiled.

"Doctor Zora! Look, baby, she's with Zeke."

Obasi came into view next to Lyrica.

"What's up Zeke?"

"What up Obi?"

"Man, cover up that pre-pubescent chest don't nobody want to see that," Obi scrunched his face up.

"Whatever, man I saw you wipe that drool out of the corner of your mouth when you saw me."

They both laughed.

"I see your face isn't still all distorted and swollen," Ezekiel commented.

"No, I feel much better thanks to Doctor Zora."

I smiled.

"Doctor Zora, I wanted to thank you and apologize for my rude behavior at your office the other day. I am taking my medicine, and I feel much better." Obasi's face was back to its normal state. The swelling had gone down. His smile was back also.

"You don't have to apologize. I totally understand."

I've dealt with so many patients that are in such severe dental pain that they are coarse when they normally aren't. I don't take it personally.

"Oh, yes he does! You went out of your way to help us, and we appreciate it. We don't get to come across a lot of genuine people. So, thank you," Lyrica chimed in.

"Thank you for saying that. You're welcome. It was my pleasure to help," I smiled.

"Zeke, you're lucky I'm with this beautiful creature next to me because if I weren't, I would take your girl."

I smiled waiting for Zeke to say something like she isn't my girl or we are not together.

"You can barely speak English. You can't take anything from me,"

Zeke countered. "Shouldn't you be out chasing lions or preparing for the village ritual?"

"Oh, only if you're about to go to Baby Gap to find a shirt to cover your skinny chest."

"You wish you..."

"Boys!" Lyrica yelled cutting them off. "Stop it. She's too good and smart for either one of you! Doctor Zora, do you see what I have to deal with all the time?"

We all laughed.

"Anyway, Doctor Zora, thank you again. We will see you next week," Lyrica smiled.

"Zeke, we will have our meeting next week while we are in town," Obasi added.

"Yep," Zeke responded.

"Bye," I waved at the phone.

Zeke disconnected the call and powered off his phone.

"I answered the phone because she never calls me like that anymore. I thought something was wrong."

"You are pretty close to her?"

"Yeah, she's like a sister to me. She had a dude in the past that was an ass clown. He was always doing something stupid like trying to put his hands on her. He would play cruel mind games on her so she would call one of our other friends or me. I honestly thought that he was going to kill her at one point."

"Wow. I'm glad she got out of that."

"Yeah, Obasi is a good dude. I trust him with her."

I sat back in my lounge chair feeling a lot better since realizing that he answered his phone for his friend. I smiled thinking about his response to Obasi when he called me his girl. I mean I don't know if I want to be his girl, but I am feeling this Lil church dude.

Ezekiel

"Where is BJ's father?"

I was resting in my lounge chair next to Zora after getting off the phone with Lyrica and Obasi. I've wanted to ask where he was since I met her.

"Bahir? I have absolutely no idea. One day he was around and the next he wasn't," she shrugged.

"So, BJ is not his nickname because he's a junior?"

"No, it's his first name and middle name; Braeden James. Thank God he's not a junior, especially with Bahir not being around."

"Was the responsibility too much for him?"

"I don't know. Literally, one day he was there and the next he was not. When BJ was six months, I was waiting for Bahir to come and watch him so that I could go to school and he never showed up. I went to his apartment, and it was cleaned out. He just disappeared."

"You haven't heard from him since?"

"No. Well, yes. I received a letter from him about a month after he disappeared. It didn't have a return address. It was a few short words to tell me to move on with my life and forget him. He didn't mention BJ at all. He gave me some checks totaling ten thousand dollars. That's actually how I was able to purchase my house and my car. I deposited the checks into my account one at a time over the period of several months then I moved it over to a savings account. I didn't need the money because I had a full scholarship to school and my grants were refunded to me, so I always had enough money to do what needed to be done. Not to mention food stamps and WIC. Doctor Miller taught me how to invest, so a little of it grew. He also taught me how to take care of my credit."

"Ten thousand dollars? Was he into something illegal?"

"Not that I ever saw."

"Have you thought about trying to find him?"

"I went to the police station when he first disappeared. They couldn't help. I had a connect in the registrar's office at our university.

I asked her to see if there was another address on file for him. There wasn't. After I received that letter from him, I stopped trying to find him. I mourned the relationship and then I had to focus on taking care of my son and finishing school."

"So, you finished graduate school as a single mother by yourself?"

"Yes, I did. I really didn't have a choice. My family and I are estranged...that's a whole other story for another time and Nette was back in Saint Louis. Even though she kept trying to come back and help me, I wouldn't let her. I had to complete school to prove to myself that I could."

I admired her drive to be independent and take care of herself. I was thinking that maybe she and BJ's father were not on speaking terms due to a bad break-up or something. He just left. That's crazy.

"Tell me about life on the road."

I let her change the subject even though I wanted to know more. My respect for her had gone to another level after hearing that she has raised BJ all by herself his whole life.

"I know the main artist has groupies, but I'm sure you have them too, right? They take one look at those golden eyes and long ass locs... they are climbing the walls to get to you, huh? How long have you been growing them?"

"I started right before my big Sis passed."

"Oh, Roman's wife?"

"Yeah, Michaela. I really didn't plan on letting it get so long, but after she lost her hair, she told me to hold on to mine. So I did. Now they are a part of me. I think about cutting them off sometimes, but I'm going to keep them for a while longer."

"I like them a lot. That's saying something because I've never been one for a dread head," she smiled.

"Oh, but now you are?"

She seemed flustered for a second, but that look was quickly replaced with a smile, "So groupies?"

I let her off the hook...for now.

"I've had my fair share, maybe a little more than fair."

"I've heard that chicks will sneak into your hotel room and everything."

"Yeah, usually security will do a sweep of all the hotel rooms before we get there and then they will lock the floor, so no one has access unless we want them to. There was one band member, cold as hell percussionist named Busta, he didn't want security to do a sweep of his room. He didn't feel it was necessary. One night we arrived back to the hotel and Busta met a chick that he brought back to his room. Well, little did he know that another chick from a city that we were in previously had snuck into his room to surprise him. Ole' girl jumped out the closet on that fool with the new chick, and all hell ensued. The girls started fighting, and Busta's dumb ass tried to break it up. Rule number one: never, ever try to break up a girl on girl fight by yourself. They are way rowdier than men. He learned that lesson that night. Those girls kicked and scratched and slapped the hell outta him trying to get to each other. This fool had to call security to come and break up the fight. We clowned him for weeks afterward. The makeup artist had to work her magic for about a week to cover up all of the scratches and bruising on his face. Needless to say, we all learned a lesson that night. Make sure your room is secure before entering it," I chuckled.

She leaned forward laughing at my story. She wiped the tears from her eyes and said, "Has anyone ever gotten past security and snuck into your room?"

"Once, but the way she wobbled out, I bet she never did that again."

Zora burst out laughing again.

"She couldn't handle the D, huh?"

"Naw, when I saw her in there all laid up in my bed, I said to myself; I'm about to teach her a nice, long, hard lesson."

She laughed again. Her laugh is contagious. She made me laugh along with her.

"How is it that you've been all over the world touring and don't have any kids? Or do you?" She raised one eyebrow and looked at me.

"That's easy, I always strap up. Every single time. I use my own. If I don't have one of my own, then it's not going down. I don't get my condoms from anyone else and I sure as hell won't use one supplied by a female."

"Really? So you could be in the heat of the moment, realize you don't have a condom and just stop?"

"Yes, but you have to realize there never really is a heat of the moment. When I was younger, and it was a fantasy to have all the women falling at my feet then maybe, but now these broads are just helping me blow a load so I can think straight. No connection, just sex. If I'm in the heat of the moment, as you put it, and I don't have one, either she will wait until I go and get a rubber or she will have to get back in line and wait her turn."

"Dayum...It's like that, Zeke?"

"Fa sho."

"They usually wait, huh?"

"Yeah, they wait." We laughed again.

"So, you've never had sex without a condom?"

"Never."

"Really?" she gave me a skeptical look.

"For real. When we were teenagers, Paxton had a pregnancy scare."

"Paxton?"

"Yeah, Paxton was the man in high school. He was the star of the football team. He would be kicking it with a few girls at a time, and none of them would ever find out. See people think he's just quiet to be quiet, but he's not. He's quiet because he's very calculated and sneaky as hell. It wasn't just a scare. She really was pregnant, but she ended up losing it like a month or two into the pregnancy. Her parents came over to the house and sat down with our parents to hash out how they were going to handle it and everything. It was a whole big to do. After that, my dad established the condom account. It was a drawer in our bathroom where he would keep condoms stocked and money to buy condoms. Then he went out and got those stupid baby dolls that act like real babies. You know they cry and everything. He made each of us take one of those things and care for it for an entire weekend. He made us name them too."

"What did you name yours?"

"I named mine Pearl."

"Pearl? Why Pearl?"

"After my drum kit. Pearl was the brand name. Blue named his Ebony Ivory Bluette. He was all excited to do it. He wanted kids and a family so he thought it would be good practice. Paxton named his Trojan."

"Trojan, after the condoms?"

"Yeah," I laughed.

"You all were very creative with those names," she laughed.

"Those damn things cried and peed and peed and cried, and they didn't sleep through the night. My mother wouldn't come and help us because we were supposed to be learning a lesson, so we were all sitting in Blue's room with babies, trying to get them to go to sleep. We even had to take them to church with us. I learned my lesson. I knew I didn't want to go through that, so I strap up every single time."

Zora is mad easy to talk to. I am enjoying our conversation. My personal life has always been off-limits to women, she's different. It feels natural to share with her.

"So what about you? I'm sure those other doctors at the hospital and your patients are jonesing over those bright blue eyes. Where is your boyfriend?"

"I don't date patients or my colleagues. My rule is: Don't make your honey where you make your money."

That was cute.

"I went through my whore stage. Well more like my hoe stage. I'm not going to lie. I was getting it in on a regular basis. After I had Braeden, I had to make smarter choices because I had a son watching me. I don't want him to marginalize women because his momma is a hoe. So, it's been awhile. He's never seen me around a man because I haven't dated since he's been alive. Don't get me wrong, like you said, there is a basic need that has to be met. Backup is a real thing. I think it's almost leaking out of my ears at this point."

"It's been that long, for real?"

"Yeah, it's been that long. I'm getting used to thinking through the haze, but it would be nice to have a good release. You know just really good, back breaking, stomach dropping, fantasy making sex."

I was completely hard listening to her talk. I sat up on my lounger and turned to face her.

"I could help you with that."

"Help me with what?" She sat up in her chair and turned to me.

"Your backup problem. I wouldn't want it leaking out of your ears. Other people would find out. It would be a whole big thing at the hospital. People would be talking about Doctor Chambers has cum leaking out of her ears. It would get around the dental community and be a huge scandal. I can save you from all of that. I can alleviate your problem."

"That sounds like a good idea, but I couldn't do that to you."

"Do what to me?"

"Give you a taste. I don't know if you can handle that. Countries have gone to war over the thought of it."

I threw my head back laughing at her silly comment.

"You don't think I can handle it?"

"Nope," she popped her lips when she pronounced the p.

I moved in towards her and stopped right before I kissed her. I saw her breathing increase. I licked my lips while looking her in the eyes.

"I can handle it, and I will handle it if that's what you want. If I'm what you want."

She moved in closer. Our lips were slightly touching.

"I want it and you."

She used her tongue to outline both my lips and then sucked the bottom one into her mouth. She caressed it for a second before releasing it. I held on to my man card by not releasing the moan that threatened the back of my throat.

I grabbed her by the back of the head as I claimed her lips. I prompted her to part her lips with my tongue. She opened and gave me complete access to the sweetness of her mouth. I had never tasted anything like her. My mind started racing wondering what the rest of her tasted like. I reluctantly pulled away.

She opened her eyes and looked at me with those beautiful blue eyes. I had so many erotic thoughts pass through my mind looking at her. I was having visions of her thighs on my shoulder and my face between her legs. I pulled her closer to me and was about to kiss her again.

"Mommy," BJ called from my guest room.

I smiled, "Looks like my friend is awake."

"I see," Zora looked down at my erection that had tented my swim trunks as she stood to go and retrieve Braeden.

I watched her walk away trying to figure out how I was going to get her to myself to finish what we started.

The rest of the evening was just as nice as the beginning. We changed from our swim clothes and watched a couple of movies that BJ chose. We had dinner that Chef prepared then BJ and I went to the music house while Zora sat in my media room reading a book. After BJ and I played around for awhile, we went back to the house to find Zora peacefully sleeping on one of my recliners. I didn't want to wake her up, but she must have felt us come in because she woke up on her own. I wouldn't have minded if she and BJ had stayed the night with me. I wouldn't have even tried to relieve her tonight. I would have been content just having them close to me.

Wait...what? Where did that thought come from?

"I guess we better get going. We have to get up for church in the morning," Zora stretched as she stood from the chair.

"I will make sure you have a parking space. Just call me when you're on your way."

I helped her collect all of her and BJ's things and followed her out to her car. I placed everything in the trunk while she put BJ into his seat.

I pulled her into a hug knowing we were in front of BJ, I made it quick even though I wanted to taste every inch of her body. I kissed her cheek even though I wanted to kiss her like we kissed next to the pool.

I opened her car door.

"I will see you in the morning. Let me know you made it home."

"I will."

She got into her car and pulled off as I waved to BJ.

I have never wanted to be close to a woman the way I want to be close to her. The feelings that I am experiencing are actually scaring me a little. It's like they came from nowhere and are getting stronger. They are getting harder to mask or ignore.

When was the last time a woman had me this aroused? I don't think this has ever happened. I know not to this extent. I can't control the feelings I am having for Zora, and I don't like it.

"This is some bull," I said out loud while pulling my phone from my pocket. I was preparing to call Kailee an old standby. Maybe if I let her entertain me tonight, it will take my mind off Zora. She is always up for my company. I unlocked my phone, and the first thing I saw was a picture I had taken earlier of Zora sitting in her lounge chair by my pool laughing with BJ. I was doing something on my phone when I looked up and saw them together. He looked so cute in his swim attire, and she takes such good care of him, I snapped the picture. I exhaled and locked my phone.

"I got it bad."

7

MADE IT.

I sent a text to Zeke letting him know we made it home.

I chuckled thinking about our interaction today. Watching him walk around in his black swim trunks and no shirt, had me hot all day. He exudes swagger and sex appeal. His strides are confident as he moves around on his bowed legs. His waist is small but his thighs are thick, and his calves are muscular. His body is unbelievable. I watched the muscles in his chest move and ripple as he played in the water with BJ. Even his back is sculpted. I kept trying to imagine where that V in the front of his swim trunks led to. He makes me feel comfortable, so our conversations always get personal even though I don't mean for them to. He's easy to talk to.

I didn't plan on kissing him, but I am so glad I did. Kissing him had me wanting to jump his bones. I knew BJ was going to be waking up soon, but if he hadn't, I was going to experience him.

Cool. I will see you in the morning? - Zeke

Yes even though it is going to be so weird and uncomfortable. I will be there for Sissy.

You have your own special seat. I will sit in there with you if it makes you feel better. – Zeke

No. I will be okay. I will do anything for Nette. If she needs me there, then I just have to put my big girl panties on and make it happen.

Big girl panties? What do those look like? – Zeke

You will see when you do what you told me you would do.

Oh yeah? – Zeke

"I CAN'T BELIEVE I let Roman talk me into this."

I stood in the full-length mirror in my room trying to decide what I would wear. I had to dig deep in my closet to find something that was suitable to wear to church. Church! I can't believe I'm doing this. I haven't been to church since I left Saint Louis almost ten years ago. This is going to be weird, but I have to do it for Nette.

I found a hunter green pleated midi skirt. I put on my white sleeveless t-shirt and my nude leather moto jacket. I put on my nude pumps and gold accessories. Nette is going to be proud of me for putting this outfit together without her. She still picks out my clothes. She has been dressing me since we were in high school. I threw my hair up in a messy bun. I dressed BJ in a white button-down shirt with his khaki pants and brown saddle shoes.

I let Chef into my house before I left so that she could prepare Sunday dinner. Roman made sure that all of Nette's favorites were being served.

I pulled into the church parking lot and told the attendant my name. He directed me to a parking space next to Zanetta's car.

I got out of the car and opened BJ's door to let him out. I was met at the side door by Ezekiel. He was killing it in a blue double-breasted blazer with white buttons and small white polka dots. He paired it with blue pants, a red striped bowtie, and a white shirt. He finished his outfit with blue loafers.

"You look nice Zeke." More like delicious, but I chose to say nice instead.

"Thank you, so do you. What's up man?" Zeke bent down to talk to BJ.

"What is this called?" BJ pointed to Zeke's bowtie.

"It's called a bowtie. Do you like it?"

"Yes, I want to wear a bow tie to church, Zeke."

"I will make sure you have one for next time, okay?"

"Okay," BJ smiled and hugged Zeke.

Zeke stood and took BJ's hand in his. I followed them into the church. We went past some offices and straight into the control room. There were two men working back there. One was controlling the sound while the other directed the cameras.

"Have a seat. I'm going to take BJ to children's church. If you don't mind."

"I don't mind."

I honestly did not mind. I've never trusted anyone with my baby, but with Zeke, it's different. I know that he won't hurt BJ.

"Bye baby. I will see you in a little while," I waved.

"Bye, Mommy."

BJ and Zeke left the control room. He was right. I could see everything from here. It was like watching it on TV. The next time I saw Zeke, he was coming out onto the stage with the band. He got on the drums.

This is my first time hearing him play live, except for the couple of times that he has shown BJ how to play on his set at his house. I have watched a few videos of him on YouTube conducting drum clinics. I couldn't take my eyes off him. After the devotion service, they collected one offering. One! When I was in church, they would take up at least two offerings. After offering they introduced Zanetta. I'm not used to church being this concise. I thought after the devotion service (which I found out they now call praise and worship) the choir would come out and they would sing two songs (an A&B selection). Then somebody would get happy, and everyone would yell, scream and run around the church for about thirty minutes. We would be in church all day. Not here though, they called Zanetta right up.

Zanetta came to the podium looking beautiful in her black wide leg pants. She wore black suspenders with the pants. Her shirt was white, and she wore a houndstooth bow tie. She had on black and white spectator high heel booties. I didn't know people were dressing all stylish at church nowadays. Go, Sissy!

I felt the tears stinging my eyes as soon as Zanetta opened her mouth. The tears started flowing freely when she started singing. Sam, the sound guy, handed me a box of tissues. Her voice is beautiful! I have never heard her sing! The audience sang along with her. I didn't know the song, but when I find out the name of it, I will have it on repeat.

"What song is this?" I asked Sam.

"It's called *Rain on Us*. A couple of people have recorded it, but she is singing the version by Sha Simpson."

"Is it a new song?"

"No, it's been out for a while. She's singing the crap out of it though."

"Yeah, she is."

I cried the entire time she spoke. I am so proud of her! She did such a wonderful job. I kept up with what she was saying, and I could relate to every word that she spoke.

That's my Sissy!

Ezekiel

Zanetta did an amazing job. I'd never heard her preach or sing. She kept everyone's attention including mine. Roman is going to be pleased when he sees the recording of this service.

Our girl did an amazing job.

I sent a text to Paxton.

I knew she would. – Pax

Everything good there?

Yeah. Rome is about to get up in a few. I will let you know when we are headed back. – Pax

I took a picture of Nette while she was preaching. I posted it to my Instagram page with the caption: ***Lil Sis big audience. #ABCHouston #theygonelearntoday***

I went and picked BJ up from children's church. I signed him out and held his hand as we went to get Zora.

"Did you have fun, BJ?"

"Yes. I had a lot of fun! I have a new friend named Cullen and another new friend named Kerry."

"Oh yeah?"

"Yeah, and I have another new friend named Jesus, but you can't see him 'cause he lives in Heaven, which is in the sky."

I smiled down at him.

"Jesus is my friend too."

"He is?"

"Yep. He's been my friend for a long time."

"He's going to be my friend for a long time too."

"That's what's up."

I love this Lil dude. It's cool to see things through his eyes. How could anyone not want to be around this kid? He is smart, funny and intelligent. I would be proud if he was mine. His father is a clown for walking out on him and Zora. I'm not glad that he hurt Zora, but I am glad that I have the opportunity to get to know them both.

I sat up last night after they left thinking a lot about my life and the next moves that I need to make. I thought my life was good, no...I thought my life was great. I have money, businesses, I travel, I have women at my beck and call, and I have my music. I thought all of those things filled me and kept me content. Then I met Zora and Braeden, and I realized those things are great but at the end of the day I was lonely and I don't want to be alone anymore. I enjoy their company. I love the way my house felt yesterday with them in it. I decided that my approach to

Zora and BJ would change. I want to be a role model for my Lil dude and honestly...I can't believe I am saying this but...I want to be Zora's man.

BJ and I picked up Zora from the control room, and I took them back to Zanetta's office. While Zora and Nette were talking, I called to make sure Chef had everything prepared at Zora's house. She was waiting for us to arrive. We ate dinner together then Nette went home.

"So, how did you like the service today?" I asked Zora while we were chilling on her living room couch.

"I enjoyed Zanetta's message. I liked the way the service flowed. It wasn't a whole bunch of extra like I remember. I'm glad Roman asked me, and I'm glad I went."

"I'm glad you came too. BJ was sad when he had to leave the children's church."

"He was?"

"Yeah. I think between me, Lil Sis and my brothers, we could get him there every Sunday."

"I don't know about that."

"Why? We are all together every Sunday anyway. I don't mind taking him in with me. Sometimes I have to stay for both services, but I usually don't. Either way, he would be fine."

"Mommy!" BJ called from the back of the house. "I pooped, and now I'm clean!"

"He likes to announce that for some strange reason," She laughed. "I'm going to go and put him down."

"Is it okay if I come along?"

"Sure."

I watched Zora's routine with Braeden. She let him go into the bathroom by himself and undress after she turns the shower on the make sure the water is the right temperature. Braeden washes and then comes out for Zora to check him and help him into his night clothes. I wanted to learn his routine because I plan on helping. I want BJ, and I want his momma.

BJ climbed into bed.

"Zeke."

"Yeah, buddy?"

"At kid church, they told me that I should pray before I go to bed. They said I should thank my new friend Jesus. They said he will listen to me when I pray cause he's in Heaven."

"You learned all of that today?" Zora asked.

"Yes, I learned it with my new friends at church."

"Sure, man. I will help you. Come down here with me."

I got on my knees and folded my hands in front of me. BJ mimicked my actions.

"Now you tell Jesus what you want him to know. My dad taught me to first tell God that you love Him. Close your eyes."

He closed his eyes and said, "Hi Jesus. It's me BJ. I love you and thank you for being my new friend." He looked at me and said, "Will he speak back?"

"No, not usually but that doesn't mean He's not listening. You know how sometimes you can tell your mommy a story. She may not respond, but you know that she heard you?"

"Yes."

"It's the same thing with Jesus. He always hears you no matter what time of day it is or where you are."

"Wow, that's cool."

"I know. Next, you ask Him to forgive you for any wrong choices you made today. After you ask him to forgive you, He forgets you did it."

"He does?"

"Yeah, he completely forgets!"

"Wow. I wish my teacher forgot. Sometimes when I make a wrong choice, my apple gets moved down the tree. If your apple hits the ground, then you miss playtime outside."

I wanted to laugh, but I didn't. My apple would have stayed on the ground when I was his age. My apple stays on the ground now!

"Well, Jesus forgets, so remember to always ask for forgiveness, okay?"

"Okay."

"You can just say please forgive me for all of my wrong choices."

He repeated after me.

"Now you thank Him for whatever you want. You can thank Him for things like your family and friends."

"Okay, Thank you, Jesus, for my mommy, my Tee Tee, my teacher, my friends and my Zeke. That's all."

He included me on the list with his Mom and Nette? I swallowed hard so my voice wouldn't crack when I spoke again.

"Now you can ask him to keep you safe while you sleep or ask for whatever you want. It's up to you. You talk to Him like you talk to me."

"Okay." BJ thought for a moment before he continued. "I want to be a good boy for my mommy and my teachers. I want to learn to play the drums real good like my Zeke. That's all."

"When you are finished, you say amen," I instructed. "Amen means you have finished praying. It's like saying 'the end' when you are done reading a book."

"Amen."

"Good job!"

We both got off our knees, and I helped him climb into bed.

Zora came over and kissed him on the forehead. "Goodnight baby."

"Good night, Mommy. I told my friend Jesus about you."

"I heard you baby, thank you."

"Good night, Lil man," I kissed him on the cheek.

"Good night, Zeke."

Zora

I pulled the door closed behind me as Zeke and I left out of Braeden's room. I watched as Zeke got down on his knees with my son and taught him how to pray. I was speechless...and turned on. I probably shouldn't be turned on by a man praying with my son, but I was. I mean like squeezing my thighs together, fanning myself, turned on. I've never seen a man interact with a boy in such a nurturing way. I feel the genuine care, and concern Zeke has for my son. I also see the genuine reverence and respect my son has for Zeke.

"Thank you for teaching him, Zeke. I really appreciate it."

"It's my pleasure."

I moved in front of him and stopped him by putting my hand on his chest.

"I mean it, Zeke. I have a dad and brothers, but none of them are in his life. You have become his role model. I can't teach him to be a man. So, when I say thank you, I mean it. Thank you."

He covered my hand that was resting on his chest with his hand. I could feel the callouses and the roughness of his hand, but his touch was gentle. He moved my hand to his mouth and kissed it.

"It's my pleasure, Doctor Chambers."

He kissed my hand again before moving around me to go back into the living room.

"Zeke, do you want something to drink? I have water, and I think I have some wine."

"Water is fine. I don't like wine."

I handed him a bottle of water while asking, "You don't like wine? That's blasphemy! The people in the Bible drank wine all the time."

"It has nothing to do with my Christianity. I'm not against drinking, but I would prefer a cognac or brandy. Nothing clear and certainly not wine. Wine is nasty, and it gives me a headache."

"You just haven't had the right bottle. I prefer a dry red wine. I don't like sweet wine at all. Semi-sweet is cool."

"You are probably the hundredth person that has told me that I haven't tried the right kind of wine. I've had cheap bottles here in the states to very expensive rare bottles overseas and guess what? Every single one is nasty, and all of them; dry, sweet and semi-sweet gives me a headache."

I laughed at him.

"You're silly."

"You know what's good though?"

"What?"

"Kool-Aid. You get the right person that knows how to mix them flavors together and then add just the right amount of sugar! Kool-Aid has been and still is my most favorite drink. Blue makes the best Kool-Aid. Not that fake Flavor-aid or Wyler's. I'm talking about Kool-Aid with the dancing Kool-man pitcher on the package."

"I thought I was the only one who could tell the difference between them."

"Naw, don't nothing else taste like Kool-Aid. The other ones have an after taste no matter how much sugar you add to them."

"I know! I've had this conversation with people in the past, and they swear up and down that there isn't a difference."

"That's because they don't know Kool-Aid!"

"Exactly! What's your favorite flavor?"

"Cherry. Grape is a close second. You thought I was going to say red, didn't you? I know how to talk to smart people, Doctor Chambers."

He tapped the tip of my nose with his pointer finger.

"Shut up Ezekiel!" I laughed. "Besides, for people that really know Kool-Aid, they know that red is actually a flavor."

We both laughed.

"Are you going to tell me about your family?"

I knew he was going to ask about my family again. It's not that I don't want to share with him, but I can get so emotional when I talk about them. I have to think while I talk to make sure to leave out certain parts because there are some things I'm just not ready to talk about. I don't know if I will ever be ready to talk about them.

"I am the youngest of four children. I have three older brothers: Countee, Amiri, and Langston. The boys are all close in age. Countee and Amiri are Irish twins; they were born about nine months apart. They are the same age for three months before Countee's birthday comes again. Langston was born the next year. There are six years between Langston and me.

My dad is a pastor, and my mother is the ever loving first lady. My mother and I never got along. Well, I can't say we never got along. She didn't deal with me, and I learned how to cope. I was never disrespectful to her or anything like that but she never took an interest in me. The church monopolized my dad's time, so he wasn't around either. My brothers got old enough, and they all left and didn't come back. I would see them maybe once every couple of months after they left home. I left home without anyone's knowledge. I left Saint Louis by myself the night I graduated from high school, and I haven't been back since. I wrote a letter to my parents apologizing and asking them if we could talk about it but my mother responded with a *Fuck you go play in traffic* letter."

"She said that to you?"

"Not in so many words. She said you thought you were grown so stay grown and don't contact us again. So..." I paused to fight back the tears I felt building. "I've been on my own."

"And your brothers?"

"I haven't heard from them. I don't even know where to look for them. I thought that one of them would have come looking for me by now, but they haven't."

Ezekiel sat silent for a few minutes before he said, "Now I'm even more impressed with you Doctor Chambers. You've created a great life for you and BJ all on your own. I don't know if this means anything to you, but I'm proud of you."

Queue the tears...

"Thank you, Ezekiel, that means so much to me."

Ezekiel

After Zora told me the story of her family, I was so impressed. I mean, I was feeling her already, but her strength is remarkable. Her life could have easily gone another way, but she fought hard to make sure it didn't. That's what's up. That made me want to help her even more.

BJ likes to call me and tell me about his day at school or whatever new thing he has discovered. I look forward to our conversations. I asked Zora if I could spend some time with BJ. I wanted to build my own relationship with him. At first, she was a little reluctant which I understood. She'd been taking care of him and making sure he was safe his entire life. She eventually let me take him out for dinner. From there we started having regular outings together. Sometimes we would invite Zora and sometimes it would be just me and BJ. My goal for spending time with BJ was not only to build our relationship but give Zora some time alone. I'm sure she doesn't get much of that.

I want to be around Zora all the time which is why I am following the directions she gave me to the park where her kickball game was being held. She invited me to play the first time they came to my house. I finally had time in my schedule to participate.

I parked my truck and got out to look through the crowd of people for Zora. I found her standing next to some square looking dude all cheezed up in her face. She had on some black leggings with the sheer panels on the sides, a black sports bra, but she covered it with a sleeveless white t-shirt and some black Nike Huarache tennis shoes. Her hair was pulled up into a top bun, like mine.

"My Zeke!" BJ ran to greet me as I approached Zora and Mr. Squarepants.

I was happy to see him. His smile always makes my day. I had been traveling for the past week, so I hadn't seen him.

"What's up man!" I picked him up and continued over to Zora.

"Hey, Zora." I gave her a quick one-armed hug since I still had BJ in my arms. Coconut and jasmine...my favorite combination. I wanted to hold on to her possessively since Squarepants was all in her grill, but I didn't.

"Hey Zeke, I'm glad you made it. This is Doctor Theo Sylvester. He is coming on as the prosthodontist at our practice. Doctor Sylvester, this is Ezekiel Bluette, drummer extraordinaire."

I smiled at her introduction. I'm glad she didn't introduce me as her friend. I was planning on being way more than a friend. Doctor Squarepants extended his hand. We shook. Weak ass handshake.

"It's just Theo. Nice to meet you," he lamely said.

"Zeke," I responded unenthused.

I turned my attention to BJ. I didn't have time to play like I was interested in anything Squarepants had to say.

"Well, I guess I will go and get my sneakers on. The game is about to start. I will see you later, Zora."

"See ya, Theo," Zora responded.

I didn't acknowledge him.

"I have to go and check BJ in with the child care workers. They pay people to keep an eye on the kids while we play the game."

I followed her to the little play area that was gated off. There were several kids in there running around.

"Are any of these kids your friends, BJ?" I asked.

"Yeah, I play with them while Mommy plays kickball."

I put him down so he could be escorted into the enclosure by one of the workers.

"I will see you after the game, BJ okay?"

"Okay."

We turned back in the direction of the fields.

"So, what's up with Doctor Squarepants all up in your grill when I walked up?"

I was lowkey jealous.

"Doctor Squarepants," she laughed. "You are stupid but what's even more stupid is that when I first met him, I named him SpongeBob because his head is square." We both laughed. "He is harmless. He's new to the practice and is trying to get to know everyone."

"I don't know about getting to know everyone, but I see he is trying to get to know you. I may have to trip him when he comes around the bases, or maybe I will turn this into dodgeball and light his ass up with the ball."

She stopped walking to laugh.

"Ezekiel, don't!"

"I'm not making any promises," I threw my hands up in mock surrender. "He's trying to be my competition. He has to go."

"Competition for what?"

"You."

She smiled, "Whatever Zeke. You don't have competition," she winked and walked away.

"Word?" I said while jogging to catch up to her.

I hadn't taken care of her backup problem yet. Not because I didn't want to but because I was scared that once I did get a taste, that would be the thing that will solidify the fact that I am falling for her. The entire time I was away, I thought about her and BJ. I wondered what she was doing. I wondered if BJ was saying his prayers. I wanted to call. I wanted to Facetime. I was ready to get back home. Usually, when I travel, I make the most of each trip. I see the city and find some legs to crawl between, but this time, I was just ready to get back to Houston...to my Lil Dude and his Momma.

Jealousy is not something that I thought I could experience but when I walked up on Zora and Doctor Squarepants, I felt a certain way. I didn't like how close he was. I didn't like that BJ was around to witness him flirting with Zora. I didn't like that he felt comfortable enough to be that close to my wom...Whoa, Zeke. Slow your roll.

The team huddled up to pick positions and the order we would kick. I was hoping that Squarepants would be on the opposite team so that I could get one good lick in with the ball but we were on the same team so I won't be able to get him...this time.

The game began, and I had so much fun. Zora is very athletic and competitive. She tried to kick a homerun every time she got up to the plate. She played center field while I played third base. It came down to the last play of the fifth and last inning of the game. We were tied with the other team. We had two people on base; one on first and the other on third. Zora was up to kick. We all cheered her on.

The first ball rolled under her leg. Strike one. We all cheered and encouraged her. The second ball came, and she kicked the air out of that ball. It went sailing over everyone's heads. She kicked a home-run! Our team went crazy. We rushed to field to celebrate. She was all smiles as she rounded the bases. The team met her at home plate to celebrate her home run. I watched, making sure Doctor Squarepants kept his hands to himself. He did.

"So, MVP what would you like for dinner? My treat."

Zora was still smiling as we walked to her car after picking up BJ.

"Let's eat something, good Mommy," BJ encouraged.

"Okay, something good," She looked at BJ and winked. "What about Italian? Would you like some spaghetti BJ?"

"Yes!" He sang his answer.

"I know a great Italian place," I commented.

"Can we go dressed like this?" Zora asked.

I looked her up and down appreciating how nice she looked in her leggings.

"Yeah, it's a small place, low key. We will be fine."

"Mommy, can I ride with my Zeke?" BJ was holding both of our hands.

"Baby, you have to ride in your car seat. Zeke doesn't have a car seat in his car."

BJ pouted.

"Your mom will follow right behind me in the car. When we get to the restaurant, we will sit together, okay?" I was trying to figure out what to say so he wouldn't be so sad.

"Okay," he smiled.

Zora followed me to a small Italian restaurant. Paxton knew the owner and told me that the food was fresh and good. After we parked, I walked to her car and opened her door then went to get BJ out of the back seat.

BJ grabbed my hand and used his other hand to hold Zora's hand.

We walked into the restaurant. The hostess smiled and directed us to our table. BJ didn't let go of either of our hands until I had to pick him up to put him in the booster seat.

The hostess gave BJ a coloring page and some crayons. BJ busied himself with the coloring paper while Zora and I looked over the menu.

"BJ, would you like spaghetti and meatballs?" He nodded without looking up from his coloring page. "I think I am going to have that also. What about you, Zora?"

"I want the eggplant parmigiana."

The waitress came and took our order.

"The kickball game was fun," I started the conversation once the waitress left with our orders.

"I try to find fun things to do to stay active. I can't get to the gym like I want to because of my schedule."

"You are always welcome to come to my house and use my gym. That way BJ can hang out with me while you work out."

She pulled out her phone and started typing. I felt my phone vibrate. I looked down and saw a text from her.

You're just trying to see me in my workout clothes. - Zora

I smiled and typed out my response. She smiled when her phone chirped indicating she received my response.

Only if you want me to see. I'm more interested in what's underneath.

She typed out her response and looked at me with squinted eyes.

Underneath? – Zora

I responded and smiled.

Yeah. Your heart. Wait...what did you think I was talking about? You nasty.

She busted out laughing after she read it.

"What's funny mommy?" BJ looked at Zora confused.

"Nothing baby. I was just thinking about something funny that happened," she chuckled and looked at me. I smirked and gave BJ my attention.

Our food was delivered to our table. I showed BJ how to use the spoon and fork to collect the spaghetti noodles. He picked up on the concept quickly but decided it was too much work.

The food was delicious.

The waitress came out with the dessert tray.

"What do you want for desert BJ?'

He looked at his mom. She nodded her approval.

"Banana pudding please."

"He's so polite," the waitress commented.

"Thank you," BJ replied.

Our desserts came. It tasted almost as good as my mother's banana pudding.

I had so much fun hanging out with BJ and Zora. I've been on a lot of dates, once they were over, I was glad they were over. I didn't want this one to end.

The waitress brought the bill.

"Thank you for dinner, Zeke. Can I pay the tip?"

Zora reached for the bill. I grabbed it before she could take it.

"No! I asked you to dinner. Why would you need to pay anything?"

I have never been out with a woman that offered to pay anything.

"I don't mind. It's my way of saying thank you."

"I understand English. I heard you say it. You're welcome."

She smiled.

I paid the check, and we left the restaurant.

I carried BJ and followed Zora to her car. I opened the back door, and BJ climbed into his seat. Zora adjusted his straps. I leaned back in to speak to him.

"Thanks for having dinner with me, BJ. I enjoyed you and your mom's company."

His little arms reached up to pull me in for a hug. I kissed his cheek.

"You're welcome, Zeke. I will call you tomorrow, okay?"

"Okay, man. I will talk to you tomorrow."

I got out of the car and closed the door. I smiled at Zora.

"Thank you again for dinner, Zeke."

Zora opened her arms for a hug. I pulled her into me.

I wrapped my arms tightly around her as she melted into my frame. I inhaled her scent and moaned inwardly. I placed a light kiss on her neck before I released her. I smiled. She returned my smile. I moved to open her car door.

"Get home safe, Zora."

"You too, Zeke."

I closed her door after she got in the car. I stood with my hands in my pockets as she and BJ drove away.

ARE YOU HOME?

I hit the send button on the text I had just typed out. I sat eagerly waiting for the response to come. I had never done anything like this before. I found myself headed this direction before I could stop or talk myself out of it. I don't fully understand what led me here, but it was harder to fight it, so I just went with what felt right. This feels right.

What if you get rejected? What if the return text never comes? I had all sorts of thoughts running through my head. I would have to deal with that when it comes because all I know is that right now, there is no other place that I want to be. I tried going home. I tried calling someone that would open wide for me. I don't want any of that I want this, now.

Yes, we made it home. – Zora

Is BJ sleep?

He's out like a light. Lol – Zora

I forgot something. Can you come to the door?

My door? You're here? – Zora

Yes.

I got out of my car and walked to her front door. I saw her look out the window before she opened the door.

"What did you forget?" She whispered when she opened the door.

"This..."

I pulled her into my arms and claimed her lips. I was not prepared for the raw, intense feelings that flooded my system as soon as my lips touched hers. I pulled her in closer using her body to hold myself up under the weight of the electricity that was coursing through my veins. My tongue demanded entry into her mouth immediately, and she obliged. I moved her into her house and closed the door behind me.

"I'm here to relieve you of your backup problem. Are you ready?"

Zora

I nodded my head as I took his hand and led him to my bedroom. I was more than ready. I'd been anticipating this moment since we talked about it at his house. I pulled him into my room and closed and locked the door. I pushed him up against my bedroom door and started to pull his shirt over his head. He pulled me into him by my waist. He used his other hand to stop me from removing his shirt.

"Slow down, Z."

He reached up and undid my bun allowing my hair to fall to my shoulders. He had already released his hair from the bun he had it in earlier. I'd never seen him in person with it down. He is sexy as hell.

He yanked my head back using my hair and peppered my neck with licks and kisses. He lingered in the areas that caused me to moan. He kissed his way up my neck and forcefully pressed his lips to mine in a passionate kiss. He pulled away.

He walked around me and sat on the bench at the foot of my bed.

"Undress."

The masculine rumble of his voice sent a chill through my body and made my sex clench.

He took off his t-shirt exposing his beautiful bare chest.

I put my thumbs in the waistband of my leggings to pull them down.

"Slower," he grunted as his golden eyes penetrated me.

I moved slower and shimmied out of my pants. I stood in front of him in my sports bra and my black thongs.

He toed off his shoes and then pulled down his pants and underwear at the same time. He sat back down. My mouth watered as he used his massive hand to stroke the entire length of his engorged member. It is the prettiest thing I have ever seen. It's long with thick veins running the length of it and a perfect mushroom head. I licked my lips as I watched him stroke it. It seemed to grow longer with each stroke of his hand. I couldn't wait to feel him inside me.

I pulled my sports bra over my head and discarded it beside me. I put my finger in my mouth and used that finger to massage my already hard nipples. He licked his lips while watching me. I moved my hand slowly down my stomach until my fingers disappeared into my underwear.

I threw my head back enjoying the feeling of my finger finding all the moisture that had pooled in my center.

When I opened my eyes, he was standing in front of me. He took my hand and put my fingers into his mouth. He licked each one clean while looking into my eyes.

He led me to my bed directing me onto my back while climbing on top of me. He softly kissed my lips before he started a journey of kisses down my body.

I moaned my pleasure with every lick and kiss as he made his way to my center. I opened my legs wider to accommodate him. He parted my folds and lightly flicked his tongue over my bud. He looked up at me, smiled and then did it again. I like to watch when I am being pleasured. I arched my back to offer myself to him completely. He grabbed my behind in both hands and lifted me slightly off the bed. I watched him feast on me like I was a meal prepared by a five-star chef. He licked and sucked like a skilled lover. I don't know if it's because it's been so long or because of his skill level, but it didn't take very long for me to yell out some gibberish as an orgasm blasted through my body.

He kissed my inner thighs until my body stopped shaking. He lightly blew on my bud before he went back in, licking, kissing and sucking. I wanted to tell him that I am a one orgasm girl. There is no way that I can have another one. I figured after he saw that I wasn't going to come anymore he would stop. However, as soon as he flattened his tongue and licked, I thought I was going to lose my mind! I looked down at him preparing to ask, "What are you doing to me?" My words stalled in my mind because the only thing that was coming out of my mouth was every expletive I've ever known. I was about to come again! I wanted to yell out at the top of my lungs, but I had to remember that my son was down the hall.

"Zeke," I said breathlessly as I ascended into the stratosphere. I think the only things on my bed were the top of my head and the heels of my feet. The second one was more intense than the first one. This has never happened to me.

I came down trying to calm down by breathing in through my nose and out through my mouth.

He was back to kissing the insides of my thighs. I looked down at him and locked eyes with him.

He smiled while he peppered kisses back up my body. He stopped when we were face to face.

"You taste so sweet, Z."

"Let me taste," I responded by closing the space between us and capturing his mouth. He opened for my tongue while I kissed him. I pulled away and sucked each of his lips individually. He moaned as I sucked his lips. "You're right, I do taste sweet."

He growled as he pulled back onto his haunches. He reached behind him to retrieve the condom packages he left on the bench at the foot of my bed.

I watched him as he ripped the package open and sheathed his beautiful member. He crawled towards me on his hands and knees. The movements of his long arms and toned shoulders reminded me of a cheetah that was appraising its prey. I was nervous, anxious and excited all at the same time. I could smell his cologne mixed with my natural scent. I was so turned on. He positioned himself at my opening and slowly pushed himself inside of me inch by inch. I opened to accommodate him as I much as could. He knew it had been a while for me, so he took his time. Each inch felt better than the last. He filled me completely then he paused. He didn't move. Instead, he kissed me. He kissed me like he was making love to my mouth. I moaned my pleasure, then he started to slowly stroke while making eye contact with me. I matched his rhythm while caressing his back.

"Damn, Z. Your pussy is so tight and wet." His strokes became faster and harder.

"No, you're not getting me." He pulled out. "Turn over."

I quickly turned and got on my hands and knees. He forcefully entered me again. He grabbed my hips and pounded into me. I always thought that achieving an orgasm through penetration was impossible. I thought that those women that said that they'd had an orgasm during intercourse were either lying or didn't know what an orgasm was. I felt like that because it had never happened to me. However, with each forceful stroke, I feel my body being worked into another orgasm. I don't know what to do or how to react. I'm so used to getting mine in the beginning and then helping him get his. I gripped the flat sheet on my bed because I knew I needed to stabilize myself for what was about to happen.

He used both of his hands to push my back down right at the top of my butt and created an arch in my back that caused him to hit places that have never been touched.

That's it! I'm coming, and I'm coming hard. I started to convulse. I wanted to breathe, I wanted to scream. I wanted to cry. I wanted to pump my fist in the air, but I couldn't do any of those things. Instead, I held onto my sheets for dear life as another orgasm blasted through my body.

I felt Ezekiel's fingers dig into my hips as his grip tightened on them.

"It's like a vice grip in here when you bust...," were all the words he got out before he stroked a couple more times then, growled and collapsed on my back which caused me to collapse onto my stomach. We laid there spent for minutes before he moved off me so that I could breathe. Honestly, if I had stopped breathing, I would die a very happy and satisfied woman.

After taking a few moments to gain his composure, he rolled on his side and pulled my back into his chest.

8

Ezekiel

I WAS HOLDING Zora trying to play it cool, but this was the most intense experience I've ever had. As soon as I was inside of her, I thought to myself, "This was a bad idea. Now it's official, I've fallen." As soon as I started moving, I felt like I was about to come. A slight panic set in which caused me to switch positions. The second position wasn't much better as far as controlling what I was feeling but at least I wasn't staring into her beautiful, intoxicating blue eyes. She likes to watch which turns me on. It shows a level of confidence that most women I have been with don't have.

I should be getting up to take off this condom, but I don't want to let her go. It feels like she is grounding me. Like, if I let her go, I'm going to float away. That's just how intense this experience was. I would like to say that it's because my last few experiences have not been good ones, but I would be lying. It was spectacular because of Zora. Our connection, our chemistry, and our friendship are what made this spectacular. I want to take her again. I want to experience everything with her all over again.

I need to get up and take care of this condom, but I swear I can't let her go. I don't want to let go.

She moved to get out of the bed.

"Don't move," she whispered as she slowly got up. I watched her as she went into her bathroom. She came back out with two towels and climbed back onto the bed. She skillfully removed the condom and tied it into a knot. She carried it to the bathroom. I heard the toilet flush. She came back to the bed. Using the warm towel, she wiped me clean and then dried me off with another towel. She took both towels back to the bathroom and then climbed back in bed with me. I pulled her close again and dosed off.

I DIDN'T INTEND to stay sleep so long. I was trying to get my strength back so that I could drive home. I knew that I had been asleep for a while because the sun was starting to come up. I have never been comfortable enough with a woman to spend the night with her. Usually, after we do our thing, either she has to go, or I leave. Not with Zora, though. I couldn't leave. I didn't want to leave. I needed to stay. I needed to keep her close to me.

"Hey," I softly said as I ran my finger across her cheek.

"Hey," she softly replied.

"I probably should go before BJ wakes up, right?"

I wish I didn't have to leave, but I can't have him find me naked in his mom's bed.

"Yeah, I guess so, but I don't want you to."

"I don't want to leave either." I can't believe those words came out of my mouth. They did, and I meant it.

She climbed on top of me into a straddled position.

"Look what I found," she showed me the other condom that I had taken out last night. I had every intention of using it, but I couldn't keep my eyes open. "We have to use it before you leave. It's a rule."

"Oh yeah?"

"Yes, if you take it out, you have to use it."

"Is that right?" I asked while rubbing my hands across her thighs.

She looked so sexy with her hair all messy and no makeup.

She ripped the package open. She looked down at my erection and said, "See, he thinks we should use it too."

She moved down my body and situated herself so that she could sheath me with the condom. She spat on my cock and then used her small hand to spread the moisture down the length before she covered it with the condom. She positioned herself over my erection and slid down slowly until I was buried deep inside her. I closed my eyes enjoying the sensation of her warmth and moisture.

She started to move her hips slow at first then she picked up the pace. I assisted her by holding on to her hips and applying more pressure. She pumped up and down with wild abandonment until I couldn't hold on. I could feel her walls pulsating around me and then the constrictions became longer and tighter. I knew she was coming. I flipped her onto her back. I put her legs on my shoulders and pounded into her.

"Zeke," hearing my name come from her caused my own explosion to occur.

"Damn, Z," I panted as I avoided falling on top of her this time.

I held on to her again until I felt enough strength to get up from the bed and go to the restroom.

I discarded the condom and cleaned myself up. I found some mouthwash in her cabinet. I rinsed my mouth and came out. She was sitting up in her bed with her robe on. I walked over to her. She met me at the edge of the bed. We shared a kiss before I started dressing.

"What time does my Lil dude usually wake up?"

"I will wake him up in about another hour to get him ready for school."

I finished dressing. I felt sad that I had to leave. I wanted to throw her back onto the bed and keep her there the entire day.

"I have to fly out for a few days this afternoon. When I get back, I have a gig. I would like for you to be there."

"I would like that a lot."

"Cool, I will call you, okay?"

"Okay."

"Then I would like to see you again, naked."

She laughed.

"I told you that you wouldn't be able to stop yourself. One taste is not enough."

"You are absolutely correct." I pecked her lips before I said, "Walk me to the door?"

She climbed off the bed. I took her hand and walked to the front door.

I pulled her into me and kissed her. I wanted her to remember me for these next few days because I was coming back.

"Have a safe trip, Zeke."

"I will call you."

"If you don't, I will understand. I know how busy you are. No pressure."

I gave her another peck.

"I will talk to you shortly. Have a great day."

"I will." She winked.

I got in my car and reluctantly pulled away.

Zora

I watched Zeke pull away from my house wishing he didn't have to leave. I'm so very sore, but I enjoyed every minute of sex with him. He touched my body like it wasn't our first time. Every time I think about the way he looked into my eyes while he was between my legs makes my stomach drop.

I smiled while I got BJ dressed and dropped him off at school. I was feeling so good that I stopped and picked up coffee and breakfast for my assistants. I blasted that Vivian Green song, "*Get Right Back to My Baby.*" I mean BLASTED! I yelled and screamed singing along. As soon as it would go off, I'd play it from the beginning. I'm sure people in the other cars were looking at me like I'd lost my mind. I didn't care! I even made up some dance moves. I was feeling good!

I had the song on repeat while I was in my office preparing for my day.

There was a knock on my office door.

"Come in."

Susan walked in carrying a bouquet of roses. Each petal of each rose was a different color. They were unique and beautiful.

"These came for you," she smiled. "Does this have anything to do with our impromptu breakfast?"

I smiled while I turned my music off. I stood from my desk to take the vase from her.

"You didn't like the breakfast?"

"I did! It was delicious."

"Well if you ever want it again, I wouldn't ask too many questions."

"Dang...you told me!"

We both laughed.

"These are beautiful. Are they real?"

"Yes, they're real. It's called a kaleidoscope rose. I only know because I saw some on TV and Googled their name. There are more vases up front."

"Really?" I was surprised. I'd never received flowers before.

"Yeah, let me go and get them for you." She walked out to get the other vases.

I saw a card sticking out from the vase. I opened it and read:

One vase for each time...

Zeke

I chuckled and shook my head. I waited until Susan dropped off the other three vases before I called him.

"Thank you for the flowers," I said as soon as I heard his voice on the other end.

"You're welcome."

"They are beautiful."

"So was watching you come last night and this morning."

My stomach flipped. I smiled.

Susan knocked and then opened the door.

"Doctor Chambers your patient is here."

"Thank you, Susan, give me a minute." She stepped back out. "I know you are preparing to leave. I just wanted to say thank you. Have a safe trip."

"I will see you when I get back, right?"

"Yep, you definitely will. Be safe, Zeke."

I disconnected the call and stood from my chair. I felt a shot of pain reminding me of all of the things I'd done last night that I hadn't done in a long time.

I can't wait until he gets back into town.

I turned Vivian back on while I prepared to go and see my patient.

Ezekiel

As soon as I arrived home, I went straight to my computer to order Zora flowers. That's when I realized I don't know how to order flowers.

I called Paxton.

"What's up?"

"Pax, how do I order flowers?"

"Did somebody die?"

"What? No, not that I know of, why?"

"Why are you ordering flowers?"

"Oh," I laughed. "I want to send flowers to a woman, but I don't know how. I've never ordered flowers before."

"I will text you the information of one of the florists that we use for events. They should have something nice. Just tell them what you want, and they will put it together for you."

"Cool, what kind should I send?"

"Women like roses."

"Roses are typical. I don't want to be predictable."

"Dude, you do realize you, Ezekiel Bluette, is sending flowers to a woman. There is nothing predictable about that."

"True. Alright, I will call them and see what they recommend."

"You must have been quite an ass or she is very special for you to be sending flowers."

"It's the latter, Bro."

"That's what's up."

We disconnected the call. I contacted the florist, and he sent me pictures of some kaleidoscope roses. I thought they were unique and special, just like Zora. So, I sent her four dozen.

I thought sex with Zora would be good. I was wrong. Sex with Zora is phenomenal. I can't wait to get back to Houston.

While I was away, I was working with a new soul group, The Brothers. They were working on their first album. Most of it is acapella, but the song I was producing for them had a jazz feel to it.

We were in the studio listening to some old music by male groups so that I could demonstrate what I was looking for on the track.

"It's a love song, so you have to sing the song like you've been in love."

"I have the perfect example," Tony the group's bass singer said. "I found this on YouTube. It's a little before our time, but the name of it is *Last Night* by a group named Az Yet.

"It came out before your time. I think I was either a freshman or about to start high school when this came out."

Tony plugged his phone into the system so that we could hear it through the speakers. As soon as the song began, I got lost in it. It took me right back to the night I spent with Zora. I thought back to the way she undressed in front of me. How sweet she tasted and how amazing it was to watch her climax. There is one line of the song that says: *You felt my body slip into your soul. I almost cried cause it was so beautiful.* That's exactly how I felt when I was with Zora. I made a mental note to add that song to my playlist for the plane ride back home.

"Fellas, let's get to work."

The quicker I get done here, the quicker I can get back to Houston.

Zora

Dr. Gee, one of the partners, has a teenaged daughter who started a babysitting business. I hired her for the evening so that I could go hear Zeke play at a local venue. He had invited me out before he left three days ago. He'd just returned this morning, so I was looking forward to seeing him.

I had chosen to wear my distressed light denim jeans. I wore fishnet stockings underneath so the fishnet could be seen through the holes. I paired those with a sheer black bodysuit. Underneath the bodysuit, I wore a black bra. I wore my black caplet over the bodysuit and red strappy heels. I carried a red clutch. I wore my hair in large loose curls that framed my face and rested on my shoulders. I finished my face off with the reddest matte lipstick that I own. I was feeling myself! It had been so long since I'd gone out. My evenings are usually spent hanging out with BJ. I looked forward to some adult interaction.

I pulled up to the front of the venue. There was a line of people waiting to get in. Zeke told me to text him when I arrived.

Here

I sent my text and sat in my car waiting for a response.

I heard a tap on my window.

"Hey, Percy!" I said as I rolled down my window.

"What's up, Doctor Z. Zeke wants me to escort you in. The valet will take your car."

I was just thinking about how bad my feet were going to be hurting if I had to wait in that long line to get in. I grabbed my clutch and got out the car. Percy motioned for someone to come and park my car.

He bent his arm towards me so that I could grab his forearm.

"Don't start catching feelings cause you feeling my muscles," he chuckled.

"I will try not to," I laughed.

He walked me past the long line and up to security. The security guy moved the rope and let us into the venue. I felt important. We walked down a short hallway and entered a dimly lit room. In the back of the room, there were no tables, only chairs. There were small round tables in the front near the stage. There was soft music playing in the background while people mingled and found their seats. There were several waiters taking orders at the tables.

"This is your table." Percy pulled out the only chair at the table.

"You're not going to sit with me?" I asked as I sat down.

"Doctor Z, I like my job, and I love my life. If Ezekiel comes out on that stage and finds me at this table, I'm going to lose both! That's why it's only one chair here."

I laughed at the funny face he made to get his point across.

"Okay," I chuckled.

"You look amazing, tonight. I wish you had a sister or a cousin or something!"

We laughed again.

"I will send the waiter over, and you can order whatever you like."

"Thanks, Percy."

"My pleasure Doctor Z."

The waiter came to take my drink order. The waiter recommended a Port wine, and I went with her suggestion.

I had butterflies in my stomach waiting for the band to start.

The lights in the venue dimmed. The crowd got quiet as the music started playing from behind the curtain that was covering the stage. The curtains opened revealing the band. My table was situated to have a perfect view of Ezekiel. He looked over and winked as the band started performing their first song of the evening. I winked back. The lead female singer was phenomenal. Her voice was silky and sultry. She captivated the room with her laid-back sex appeal. She was ultra-feminine without trying. She moved like she was alone with the music and the music was her lover. I can see why the place was packed.

The band played a mix of R&B and jazz. The audience stayed engaged the entire time. When Zeke played a drum solo, the women in the room went wild. I whistled too. He was oozing sex appeal with his hair up in his signature bun. He had on a black V-neck t-shirt that hugged his arms deliciously.

During the set break, Ezekiel came out and sat with me. He kissed me on my cheek before he sat down.

"You look fly as hell, Z."

"Thank you, Zeke. I'm enjoying myself at my table for one."

He smiled, "I couldn't have some clown thinking he could come and sit with you while I'm on stage."

"Percy wouldn't even sit with me."

"I know. I threatened him," he winked.

I laughed, "It's really crowded in here," I looked around the room.

"We do this every so often. We post the location on social media the day before."

"It's packed for one day's notice."

"Yeah, and it's always packed. Everyone in the band is successful in their own right, so they bring their own fans."

"You guys sound amazing."

"Thank you. I love playing with these guys. You sticking around until the end?"

"I have a babysitter with BJ, so I will have to go and relieve her. You are more than welcome to come by after you're done, though."

"Word?"

"Word."

"I will text when I get there."

"Can't wait."

9

"HELLO?"

"Z...Eze...Ezekiel?"

"Zora, what's wrong?"

"I called Nette first, but I think she is in a meeting and has her phone off. I'm sorry for calling, but I didn't know who else to call..."

I could hear the panic in her voice.

"Slow down and tell me what's wrong."

"Braeden's school called. He was playing outside and fell and hit his head. They said that he lost consciousness, so they called the ambulance. They said he only lost consciousness briefly but..."

"Where is he?" Panic started to set in, but I knew I had to stay calm for her. I grabbed my keys and went out to my truck.

I had just made it to EZ Blue Sounds. I wasn't far from Braeden's school.

"He's on his way to Children's Hospital, and I am trying to get there, but I feel like I am about to pass out. I am afraid to drive."

"I'm on my way. Where are you?"

"I'm in the garage of my building in my car."

Good. I'm even closer to her job. I pulled out the parking lot of my studio headed her direction.

"I'm coming. Don't hang up."

"Okay. Zeke, I'm so scared. I don't know what I will do if something bad happens to my baby. He's all that I have."

"I know. Listen, we are going to believe together that everything is going to be fine, okay?"

"Okay." She sounded unsure.

"Zora, we know God has him, right? He can heal him. His angels are with him in that ambulance, and they are going to be with him once he gets to the hospital." I started praying out loud, "Fear not for I am with you. Be not afraid because I am your God. By His stripes, we are healed. We thank you, Father God that Braeden is fine. We know that you have everything under control. We trust you because you can do anything but fail. Thank you for giving us peace until we can get to him. Amen."

"Amen."

"I'm here."

I pulled up behind her car. I made it to her in record time. I got out to help her out of her car and into my truck. She was shaking. I wanted to hug her and tell her everything would be fine, but I know that nothing that I would say right now would make her feel better. I have to get her to the hospital.

I got her in and ran around to get back in. I pulled out on my way to the hospital.

"Thank you, Zeke. I just didn't know what to do..."

"You did the right thing." I grabbed her hand as I navigated through traffic to the hospital.

I found a parking space close to the emergency room door. Zora was out of the truck before I put it in park. I trailed close behind her as we followed the signs to the nurse's station.

"Hi, ummm...they brought my son in. His name is BJ..."

I spoke for her, "His name is Braeden Chambers. He came in from school."

I pulled Zora close to me while the nurse typed in his information.

"Yes, he is back with the doctors now. I will let them know you are here. I'm sure he is anxious to see you. Please have a seat. I will be back in a minute." She smiled warmly.

I directed Zora to the chairs, and we both sat down. I didn't feel like sitting. I would have felt better if I could pace back and forth but I knew I had to stay strong for Zora, so I sat. I sent Percy a quick text. I kept my arm around her shoulder until the nurse came back followed closely by another woman I assumed was the doctor. We both stood.

"Mom, Dad?" I was about to correct her, but Zora spoke before I could.

"Yes? Doctor, how is Braeden? Is he okay?"

"I'm Doctor Goldberg. Are you a doctor also, Mom?"

"Yes, I am."

"Well, that explains it. Braeden won't let us look at him. He said his mother is a Doctor and you would check him out when you got here," she chuckled. "He seems to be okay, but Braeden fell and hit his head while he was playing on the playground at his school. The school said that he lost consciousness temporarily. He will probably need a couple of stitches, but we want to run some tests to make sure that there aren't any internal fractures or bleeding. We also want to check for a concussion."

"Okay, can we see him?" Zora asked.

"Sure, follow me."

We followed behind the Doctor. Everything in this children's hospital is so small and colorful. I've never been in a children's hospital. It's so vibrant you would almost forget you were in a hospital until you see a small, frail figure laying on the bed. Then it hits you that all these little people are here for a reason. It's a sobering thought. I silently prayed as we walked into the room and saw BJ laying in the bed. There was a large white bandage on the side of his head. A young lady was sitting in a chair next to his bed. She stood when we walked into the room.

"Doctor Chambers," she moved to hug Zora.

The ladies embraced.

"Hi, Lucy. Thank you for coming here with him."

Zora moved to BJ's bed.

"Hi, Mommy. I felled."

"I know baby that's why you are here at the hospital. Are you in any pain?"

"My head hurts, Mommy."

"I know baby, but the Doctors and nurses are going to make sure you are okay."

I moved to stand behind Zora.

"My Zeke!" BJ held up his arms for me.

I looked at the Doctor to make sure it was okay to move him. She nodded.

I picked him up and sat down on the bed with him. He rested his head on my chest. I felt like I wanted to pull him into my chest and protect him from everything and everyone around him.

"What's up, man. I heard you had a little accident."

He nodded and started crying.

Zora sat next to me to comfort him.

"It's okay baby. You have to let the doctor look at you."

"You can look at me mommy," BJ responded without lifting his head from my chest.

"Remember we talked about the different types of doctors? I told you that I'm not a kid doctor because kid doctors are special?"

He nodded.

"God creates special people to be kid doctors, remember?"

"Yes," he nodded and quickly glanced at the Doctor.

"Doctor Goldberg is special because she knows all about kids. She can help you feel better."

I love watching Zora interact with BJ. She has a way of explaining things to him without dumbing it down.

"Can the special Doctor look at you, Big Man?" I asked.

BJ agreed to allow the doctors check him out.

"If it makes it any easier, you can carry him, Dad," the doctor spoke soothingly. I felt very comfortable with the title the doctor had given me.

I stood from the bed, holding Braeden, ready to follow the Doctor. He rested his head on my shoulder as we followed the Doctor down the hall. Zora and Lucy followed behind us.

The doctor instructed me to put BJ onto a bed on his back.

"Dad, you will have to stand on the other side of the glass, but you will be able to see everything that's happening."

"I will be right there," I pointed to the glass. "You can do this okay Big Man?"

BJ slowly nodded, breaking my heart with each nod. I wanted to keep him in my arms and make sure he was good, but I know that the test was necessary.

I walked out the room and stood next to Zora and Lucy. We watched while the doctor and the nurse did their job.

Zora whispered, "Lucy this is Ezekiel."

"As in *the* Zeke that BJ talks about nonstop?"

Zora chuckled, "In the flesh."

"Zeke, Lucy is BJ's teacher."

"Nice to meet you," I smiled then turned my attention back to my little dude.

I watched as they laid him flat on his back and brought the machine above his head to take the x-ray.

He followed the instructions of the x-ray tech and laid perfectly still. After a few minutes, they beckoned for me to come back into the room. I moved quickly to pick him up from the bed and followed the Doctor back to the room he was in.

"We are going to wait for the Radiologist to read the x-rays. I will be back to let you know the results."

"Thank you, Doctor Goldberg," Zora responded as she left the room.

"Doctor Chambers, my ride is here. I'm going to leave. Will you let me know what they say?" Lucy spoke to Zora.

"Yes, I will. Thank you for everything."

They hugged, and Lucy left the room.

Zora came and sat next to me on the bed while I held BJ. She held his little hand while we quietly waited for the Doctor to return with the results from the x-ray.

Braeden fell asleep in my arms while we were waiting.

"This has to be the scariest thing I have experienced in a long time. He's my little baby, you know? It's just so much sometimes. I try to be everything he needs, but I don't always know what he needs. I don't know if I am a good mother. I don't know if I am raising a strong man or a momma's boy that won't ever want to leave my house. It's just hard."

"I think you are an amazing mother. Your relationship with Braeden reminds me of my relationship with my mother." She looked at me. "I'm serious. You have been given a son to raise, and you are doing it. He's smart, respectful, intelligent and an all around cool kid."

"Zeke, that means so much."

"It's the truth. I admire you, Doctor Chambers."

She rested her head on my shoulder while I held BJ. We sat quietly immersed in our own thoughts.

About thirty minutes later Doctor Goldberg returned with great news. Everything looked fine. No fractures, no bleeding and no concussion. He didn't need stitches. They used skin glue to close the gash and put a bandage on top of it. They gave Zora wound care instructions and released him from the hospital.

"Oh, my God Zeke. We don't have a car seat for him. He's still too small to just strap in the seat belt."

"I have one in my truck."

"You do?"

"Yeah, I sent Percy a text and told him to bring one. He installed it in my truck."

"You did?"

I smiled and nodded. I sent Percy the text as soon as we got to the hospital. It was my step of faith believing that I would be leaving with BJ in my truck.

I carried BJ out to the truck. Zora had to show me how to use the car seat.

"Are you hungry, Braeden?"

"Yes," he murmured as I pulled out into traffic.

"We can go and get your car then I can follow you back to your house. We can order a pizza for him to eat."

"Zeke, you don't have to that. You have already done so much. We will be okay."

I looked at her and then asked, "What kind of pizza do you want BJ?"

"I want cheese pizza," BJ responded.

"Cheese Pizza it is," I turned from Zora and continued down the street.

She exhaled, resting her head on the headrest and closed her eyes. I wasn't planning on leaving BJ until he had a full stomach and was resting comfortably in his bed.

We arrived at her car. I walked around to open her door and help her out of the truck.

"Zeke you don't..."

"Is it that you don't want me to come over?"

"No, no not at all I just don't want to inconvenience you. You've already spent your whole evening with us at the hospital."

"Did you hear me complain?"

"No, I didn't but..."

"Did I look like I didn't want to be there?"

"No," she responded again.

"Then if it's all the same to you, I would like to order my little dude a cheese pizza and make sure he gets in the bed. Is that okay?"

"That's fine Zeke. Thank you," she smiled.

I opened her car door and helped her in. I got back in the truck and followed Zora to her house.

I followed her into her house carrying BJ.

"Baby, let's go and get cleaned up while Zeke orders the pizza."

I put him down. He held on to my leg and didn't move to go with Zora to the back.

"I'm not going anywhere. I will be right here when you come back."

He nodded, let go of my leg and followed his mother to his room. I ordered the pizza and waited for BJ and Zora.

BJ came back down the hall wearing his superhero pajama pants and matching shirt. He had on superhero slippers also. He came and climbed on my lap. I felt so bad because I had never been around him when he wasn't talking a mile a minute.

The pizza arrived. BJ ate a slice while fighting to stay awake. He couldn't take it anymore and feel asleep at the table. I picked him up and followed Zora back to his room.

Zora pulled back his comforter, and I placed him on his bed. She covered him up and kissed him on the cheek. I kissed his other cheek and left out of his room.

"Zeke." I turned and saw tears running down Zora's face. "I need you."

Zora

I didn't mean to sound so clingy, but if he hadn't picked me up so quickly and carried me to my bedroom, I would have begged. I needed the connection to him. I needed to feel him on me and in me.

He put me down on the bed then turned around and locked my bedroom door. He pulled his shirt over his head and toed off his shoes before walking back towards me. I stood and met him in the middle. He roughly grabbed the back of my neck with his calloused hand pulling me close to him while he hungrily kissed me. Our tongues swirled around each other fueling the fire that was already ignited in me. He moved from my mouth placing wet kisses down my neck. I released his hair from his bun while he kissed me.

I worked on getting his pants off while he continued to kiss and suck my neck. I got them unbuckled and down around his ankles. I went down on my knees to help him take them off. He stepped out, and I threw them to the side. I was now facing his large erection. I licked it from the base to the head. His moan prompted me to continue. I placed as much as I could in my mouth and used my hands to cover the rest. I pleasured him until I felt him pulling back.

"Move Z, I'm about to..."

I pushed against him and wouldn't stop. I watched him as I continued. He watched me until his eyes rolled into the back of his head and I felt warm liquid shoot down my throat.

He pulled me up into a standing position and had me naked in record time.

"Bend over."

I turned and rested my hands on the bed. He forcefully entered me.

"Zeke," I called out as I felt every inch of him inside of me. It felt different this time. Bigger, harder, better. He ferociously pumped and I threw it back at him to the rhythm he set. I felt myself about to come. I didn't want it to happen yet. It felt so good. I wanted to switch positions, but I couldn't stop. I didn't want him to stop. I gave in to the feeling of euphoria that was washing over my body. As my legs were giving out, he said something incoherent and came right after I did.

I felt him slowly pull out.

"What the...damn, Z!"

I turned to see what had him so alarmed.

"I didn't put on a condom! I'm trippin'. I'm sorry."

"Zeke," I put my arms around his waist. "It's okay. I'm on birth control, and I haven't been with anyone else, but I was tested when I moved here. I'm okay. It's okay."

He exhaled and placed my face between his massive hands.

"I was just tested too. I'm clean. I am sorry. This has never happened to me before. I never forget."

He kissed me.

"I got that good-good. I told you..."

"Yeah, yeah. Countries have gone to war..."

"Exactly!"

"You sure you're okay?" He asked with concern etched on his face.

"Zeke, I'm fine. Just worry about getting your second wind because I'm not finished with you."

"I got you! Give me a few minutes."

Ezekiel

Zora is quietly sleeping in my arms. I should be sleep, but I keep replaying the day's events in my head: from BJ's accident to my accident.

I've never been as afraid as I was when Zora called and said that BJ had been hurt. I put on a brave face, but I almost lost it when I walked into that hospital room and saw my little dude all bandaged up. I'm so glad he is okay.

When Zora wrapped those full beautiful lips around my erection, I lost my mind. I've had plenty of top but nothing like tonight. She almost had me calling her name like a girl! I mean I wanted to, but she sucked that out of me along with everything else. Then she swallowed...all of it and then licked her lips. All I could think was that I needed to be inside of her immediately. The feeling was overwhelming. That must be what Zora meant when she said, 'heat of the moment.' Now I understand.

I forgot to put on a condom. More accurately, the thought of a condom never crossed my mind. My only thought was burying myself deep inside of her in the shortest amount of time possible. When I did, it was the absolute best thing I'd ever felt; soft, warm and snug. She is the first woman that I've had sex with without using a condom.

"Why aren't you asleep?"

I looked down and saw her looking up at me.

"I was thinking."

"About what?"

"Waking you up."

She climbed on top of me in a straddle position.

"I'm up now."

"So am I."

AFTER THAT LAST ROUND, I was out. Zora is insatiable!

I held her close when I dosed off and woke up with her still in my arms.

"Z," I ran my finger along her cheek.

She opened her eyes and smiled.

"Good morning."

"Good morning. I need to leave before B wakes up."

"Do you want to leave?"

"No, I don't."

"Then stay."

"How will we explain my presence in your bed when BJ wakes up?"

She looked at the clock on her nightstand.

"He won't be awake for another couple of hours. I'm going to stay home today and keep him with me. I'm figuring his head is still going to be a little sore."

"I'm going to go to my house and change clothes. I will come back and make breakfast. Would you like that?"

"I would love that."

"Cool." I pulled her back into my chest. "I'm going to get up in a little while."

Zora

Zeke left to go home and change his clothes. BJ woke up about an hour after Zeke left.

"How are you feeling, Baby?"

"I feel better. My head hurts a little."

My doorbell rang. BJ walked with me to the door.

"My Zeke!" BJ screamed as soon as I opened the door.

He had a bag of groceries in his arms.

"Hey, big man!" Zeke picked BJ up with his free arm and walked to the kitchen.

I followed and watched him deposit the bag and BJ on the counter.

"I heard you and your mom were staying in today, so I brought over breakfast. Is that cool?"

"Yes!" BJ sang.

He placed BJ on the ground and said, "Go and wash up then we can make breakfast for your mom."

BJ started to run down the hall to the bathroom.

"Aye, BJ," Zeke called after him.

"Huh?" BJ stopped.

"No running in the house, man. Running is for outside, okay?"

"Yes, sir."

BJ turned and power-walked to the bathroom.

Zeke walked over and quickly kissed me.

"Good morning."

"Good morning," I smiled.

BJ walked back into the kitchen.

"Alright big man. We have turkey sausage, eggs, pancakes, and hash browns. I also picked up some chocolate chips for your pancakes."

"Yay!" BJ cheered.

"I think we should let your mom go and relax while the men prepare breakfast. What do you think?"

"Yeah, go and relax Mommy. Me and Zeke is gone cook you breakfast."

I smiled, "Okay baby. I will be right out here if you need me."

I smiled at Zeke, and he winked.

I went and sat in my living room. I thought back to when I first met Bahir. He was so attentive and sweet. It felt good being around him. He treated me like I meant something to him. He made me feel important, protected and loved. When BJ was born, he was all in with taking care of him, then something changed. I guess he lost interest in me. Maybe I became too needy. I don't know. What I do know is that I can't go through that heartache again. I can't give Zeke access to my heart. I'm too afraid he will hurt me the same way Bahir did. I watched him laugh and talk with BJ while they were preparing breakfast. After last night and this morning, I know I am falling for him, and I can't afford to fall for someone else who could walk away without warning. I know that a chick with a kid is not what Zeke is looking for. He has a life and a brand. He will get bored with this whole ready-made family thing fairly quickly, I'm sure.

I got sad thinking about what I had to do, but it's about self-preservation. I can't lose what I have built. I can't go backwards I have to move forward. Distance is the key.

10

I FEEL like a stalker right now, but I have to get to the bottom of this. I left town the day after I spent the day with Zora and BJ. BJ and I prepared breakfast. We sat around all day and watched movies, played games and we had dinner together. I thought everything was great. Zora and I put BJ down and enjoyed each other one more time before I left for my flight.

Something happened between then and now. It's three days later and Zora hasn't responded to any of my text messages. All my calls have gone unanswered. I tried to Facetime her to speak to BJ, she wouldn't pick up. I know she is around because she was at dinner with the family on Sunday.

I'm not sure if she is upset about my slip-up with not using the condom. She said she was okay. We used one every time after that. I don't know. I've been racking my brain trying to figure out what I did for her to ignore me. Usually, I wouldn't care if a woman didn't return my text messages or calls. With Zora, I care. I care about her. I want her in my life.

I parked next to her car in the garage of her office building waiting for her to come out. I got off the plane and came straight here.

If she doesn't want to be bothered with me, then I am going to win her over. I need both her and Braeden in my life, so we are going to have to figure this out. I've never chased a woman, but I'm putting my running shoes on because she is not going to get away.

I saw her emerge from the hidden door in the garage and start walking to her car. I got out of my car so that I could speak with her. I leaned on the side of my car and waited for her to notice me.

"Zeke!" she jumped a little when she finally looked up and saw me.

"What's up Zora. You ignoring me?"

I've seen movies where a dude pulls up on his girl at her job, and I always laugh. I knew that I would never be that dude, but here I am, stalking Zora.

"No," she nodded her head. Then she said, "...yes, yes I am."

She leaned against her car facing me.

"Why Z, did I do something to you?"

"Yes, Zeke. Yes, you did! You taught BJ how to pray. You discipline him when he is in the wrong, and he accepts it. You care for him like he is yours. You cook for me. You touch me and make me feel things like you created my body. You send me flowers. You tell me how beautiful I am. I'm falling, Zeke. Hard and fast. I'm falling for you, and I don't want to. I don't want to fall because I'm scared of getting hurt. I'm scared of you getting tired and walking away."

"Z," I ran my hand down my face. "I'm scared too. I've never chased a woman. Ever! I had to ask Paxton how to send flowers. I'd never done that before. I'm terrified of you. I'm terrified of being around the only woman that can make me forget all about being protected because I had to be inside of you. I'm afraid of the way I feel when I am around BJ. How much I want to teach him and protect him. I'm scared, but I'm more afraid of being without both of you. I decided that I would rather be afraid and happy with you than be unafraid and miserable without you."

"Zeke, I..."

"What time does BJ have to picked up?"

"He's going over one of his classmate's house for a play date. I will have to pick him up later."

"Come and take a ride with me."

I had a feeling that she was trying to distance herself from me. I get it. I thought about doing the exact same thing. I wanted to lose her number. I wanted to forget about her and BJ. These feelings scare me but I know I can't go back to how I was before I met them. So, it's balls out for me. I'm all in.

I reached for her hand. She put her hand in mine. I opened the passenger side of my truck and helped her in. I got in and pulled out of the garage. I held her hand while I navigated out of the city. I turned on some music while we rode to our destination.

"Who is this we are listening to?"

"Mali Music."

"Is that a group?"

"No, it's one person. He's cold. He used to be a Gospel singer, but he left the traditional gospel genre to go mainstream. A lot of people were mad that he made that decision, but I understand. I know what it feels like to have all these ideas but nowhere to put them because you are locked into this one genre or box. This is my favorite cut on the album it's called *No Fun Alone.*"

I turned the volume up and let Mali serenade us until we arrived at our destination.

I rode down a secluded road that opened to a large field. I parked the car and got out. I opened her door and helped her out.

"Where are we?"

"This is my land. I purchased it when I first moved to Houston. It's fifteen acres. There is a stream that runs along the property line and separates my property from my neighbor's property. My neighbor is Roman. He purchased the other fifteen acres on the other side of the stream. Paxton has about twenty acres on the other side of Roman.

When I purchased this land, I got it because I figured if I held on to it, at some point someone would want to buy it from me and build on it. I would sell it for probably double what I purchased it for."

"It's so beautiful and serene out here. I can hear the water running in the stream."

I went to my truck and pulled out a blanket. I took her hand and led to an area where I spread the blanket on the ground. I helped her down onto the blanket and sat next to her.

"After I met you and BJ, I started thinking maybe I will keep this land for Braeden. Maybe he will want to build a house on it for his family. Maybe it will be a graduation present, and he can sell it and invest the money."

"Really?"

"Yeah, this is the way my thoughts have gone since I have gotten to know him. I said that I want to help you with him and I mean it. If I can be with you too, that would be great, but I understand your wall. I can't promise that I won't hurt you, but I won't hurt you on purpose. I'm loyal, Z. If I'm in, then I'm in. I just need to know what you are going to do. We are both falling. We might as well fall together."

"Zeke, I'm scared. After Bahir left, I went through a lot. I almost dropped out of grad school and moved back to Saint Louis. I had to readjust my life, and I promised myself I wouldn't let that happen to me again, but I have been miserable without you."

I leaned in and kissed her.

"I've been miserable without you too. Can we figure this out together?"

She nodded, wrapped her arms around my neck and pulled me closer. I kissed her while I massaged her breast through her shirt. I pulled her shirt over her head. I kissed her lightly then created a trail of kisses from her lips to her cheek then to her neck.

I pulled down her left bra strap then kissed her shoulder where her strap rested. I kissed her along her collarbone until I reached her right bra strap. I pulled it down and kissed her right shoulder the same way I kissed the left one. I reached behind her and unlatched her bra. As soon as her breasts were exposed, I sucked one into my mouth while I continued to massage the other one with my hand.

"Did you miss me Z?"

"Yes," she replied softly. "Show me why I should be with you."

She placed her soft hands on my ribs under my shirt and slowly moved them up my sides to remove my shirt.

"I'm not only going to show you why you should be with me but I'm going to spoil you, so no man can come after me."

I went to her breast again kissing and sucking as I worked on taking off her pants. I pushed her onto her back and took a second to look at her body. She lifted her hips so I could remove her black lace panties.

I studied the contrast of her midnight colored areolas against her coffee colored breast. I watched the rise and fall of her chest. Her almost flat stomach with just the right number of stretch marks to prove her womanhood. The little strip of hair on her mound that seemed to be directing me to the area I planned on tasting first. My eyes went back to her. She was watching me. I love it when she watches me. As if reading my mind, she spread her legs giving me access to her center. I could see the moisture seeping from her as I licked her. I was rewarded with an "Oh my goodness!" as I continued to devour her. She is a lot more vocal than when we are at her house. I guess because she knows BJ is in the house. I'm going to make sure we have more alone time. I love hearing her scream out.

I used my finger to penetrate her while I continued to feast on her. In no time her legs were shaking, and she was calling my name. I love when she says my name.

I stood to remove my pants and put on a condom.

"Don't," she looked from the condom to me. "I want to feel you, all of you. Spoil me, Zeke."

I damn near lost my balance getting back down on the blanket and entering her. I couldn't move fast enough. As soon as I was snuggly inside of her, I couldn't think of anything else except making sure she was satisfied.

I stroked slowly while looking at her biting down on her bottom lip. I moved in to kiss her.

"You feel so good, Z. I'm going to do my best to be the man you need. I'm going to mess up, but I won't stop trying. I don't want anyone else but you."

"Be you. I only need you, Zeke. I'm giving you my heart. Take care of it."

"I will, I promise."

I felt her tighten up around me. I felt my ascension building up also.

I was preparing to pull out.

"Don't Zeke. Don't stop," She screamed as she tightened around me.

I didn't stop. We ascended together.

I laid beside her trying to regulate my breathing. I pulled her in close to me.

"Zeke,"

"Yeah?"

"You know we are outside butt-ass naked, right? We can't just lay here!"

"Oh damn! I forgot where we were!"

We busted out laughing. I got up and helped her to her feet. I wrapped my arms around her and hugged her.

"No more ignoring or disappearing, right? Since we are both falling, we might as well fall together."

"Okay," she smiled. "Let's figure it out together."

We found our clothes, got dressed and headed back into the city.

We pulled up to her car in the garage.

"Z, I would like to meet your son."

She looked at me confused.

"Zeke, you already know my son."

"I know. I mean I want to meet your son as the man you are dating or whatever you call it. All I know is that I don't want to see anyone else and I hope you feel the same way."

"So, you want me to be your girlfriend?"

"If that means that I won't have to share you with anyone then that's exactly what I want you to be."

She smiled and leaned over and kissed me.

"Then yes, I would like it to introduce you to my son. Would you like to meet him tonight?"

"Tonight would be nice."

Zora

Zeke and I were laying in his bed after putting BJ down in "his room" at Zeke's house. Since our declaration, a couple weeks ago that we were dating, Zeke, BJ and I have fallen into a routine of spending our evenings together. BJ has claimed a room at Zeke's house as his and has brought over a couple of toys to leave here. Zeke has added to BJ's toy collection.

I tried hard to create some distance between Ezekiel and me. It was torture ignoring his calls and texts. I got scared. I mean for real scared. I had flashbacks to Bahir, and I just couldn't go down that road again. I always hear people say that you can't make the next man pay for the sins of the previous man. That's true but then how do you protect yourself? How do you make sure that you don't become someone else's prey? I don't have the answer because as soon as I saw Zeke resting on his truck in the parking garage, I knew that I couldn't ignore him. I knew that I wanted him. Then he told me about the plans that he'd already begun to make for BJ's future. It was over for me. I thought that I was falling, but after that conversation, I was down. No more falling. I'd reached my destination. That destination was in love with Ezekiel. It's early, and I don't want to scare him away but the feelings I have are true and genuine.

I eavesdropped on the conversation Zeke had with BJ when he told him that we were dating. I thought that Zeke wanted us to have the conversation with BJ, but he said that there were some things that men needed to discuss one on one. So, I stood outside BJ's door and listened.

"Hey man, there is something that I need to talk to you about. Can you sit down with me for a second?"

I couldn't see, but I figure BJ sat in the chair next to Zeke.

"Braeden, you know how we talk about always being honest and telling the truth?"

"Yes, you said we should always tell the truth because it's hard to remember a story."

"Right, when you get a little older you are going to start to like girls."

"I like girls. They are my friends! Candy and Ariel and Heather. That's their names."

"Cool, I like your mom. I like your mom in a way that men like women."

"Oh, are you her boyfriend?"

I covered my mouth to stifle my giggle.

"Yeah...um...B, how do you know about boyfriends?"

"My friend Candy has a boyfriend in class his name is Randy. They sit by each other on the playground, and he gives her his extra Go-Gurt that his mom packs for lunch. Do you give my mommy extra Go-Gurts?"

"Candy and Randy, huh?" Zeke chuckled.

"Um hum," BJ confirmed.

"Yes, I like to share things with your mommy. If I had an extra Go-Gurt, I would share it with her. I wanted to tell you because I wanted to make sure you were okay with me being your mommy's boyfriend."

"I'm okay with it, Zeke."

I tiptoed away so I wouldn't get caught.

"I THINK something is going on with Blue and Nette. She seemed a little weird at dinner tonight. I wanted to ask her, but I figured she would tell me later."

"What do you think could be going on? They went to New York and spent some time with our parents. I thought it went well. My mother is over the moon about them being together."

"I don't know. I just know her. Something is not right. I need to call her."

I heard my phone vibrating on my nightstand.

"I must have talked her up. Hey, Sissy! What wrong?"

She told me about the big blow up she and Roman had. Apparently some random is claiming that Roman is her baby's daddy. Nette is not upset about the baby, she is mad because Roman didn't tell her about it. She had to ask him. I understood why she was upset, but I also understood why Roman hadn't told her yet.

"Sissy, he was just trying to protect you."

I hope it didn't sound like I was taking his side because I wasn't. Apparently, it did sound like I was taking his side because she let me have it.

"Protect me from what Zora?"

"I don't know. He had his reasons."

I didn't know, but I thought this was the best answer to give. I didn't want to see them break-up over a misunderstanding.

"He had his reasons... humph...Is that what you do too, Zora... protect me?"

"Huh?"

"Why haven't you told me that you have been kicking it with Ezekiel?"

"Sissy, I..."

She cut me off.

"If it were me that was having sleepovers at my house with a man and I didn't tell you, all hell would break loose. I would never hear the end of it."

She was right. I hadn't told her yet. I was scared to tell her, but I don't know why. Maybe because what Zeke and I have is nothing like what she and Roman have. Maybe because I put up such a stink about Zeke being a church boy, but here I am trying to build a relationship with him. I don't know why I hadn't told her yet, but I did plan on telling her.

"Sissy, I..."

She cut me off again.

"What is it about me that makes everyone think that I am weak, that I need protection? What is it? Please let me know so that I can change. I'm sick of everyone making decisions for me claiming they are doing things in my best interest. I've lived through some pretty horrible situations. I've experienced hurt, disappointment, frustrations and guess what? I survived. So, you know what? Until you are ready to treat me like I am a grown ass woman and not some little frail, fragile girl that needs everyone's protection, then you can lose my number also."

"Sissy!"

"Bye Zora."

"Sissy!"

I pulled the phone away from my ear and looked at it. She hung up on me. She has never hung up on me.

"What's wrong?"

"Nette hung up on me."

"Lil Sis hung up on you?"

"Yes...I mean she is really upset."

I dialed her number. It went straight to voicemail. I tried again... same thing.

"Maybe I should go over and talk to her."

I got up from the bed looking for something to throw on. Zeke got out of the bed. Took my hand and sat me down next to him on the bed.

"What is she upset about?"

He started rubbing circles on my back with his hand. I love his hands.

"Something that went down between her and Roman but she is

mad at me because I haven't told her about us; me and you. She figured it out and was waiting for me to talk to her about it."

"She and Roman have been busy. I haven't talked to my brothers about it yet either. I plan on it. You did plan on it too, right? Or did you just want me to stay your dirty little secret?"

I giggled even though I didn't want to.

"I did tell her that I liked you. I told her that the day you took BJ with you and met me at her house."

"Oh, that day we fell asleep over there?"

"Yeah, but I hadn't told her how we've progressed since then."

"She doesn't know I be all up in those guts?"

"Shut up Zeke." I laughed, "I planned on telling her about us dating not necessarily about you being all up in my guts." We laughed. "I still want you to be dirty just not secretly."

He laughed again and pulled me closer to him.

"Give Lil Sis some space. If she is mad enough to hang up on you, then it's serious. She will need you in a couple of days but let her cool off. Leave her a message and tell her whatever you need to say then let her breathe. Hopefully she and Blue will figure it out."

"Alright."

I called her number again after the beep I said, "Hey Sissy. I'm sorry that I offended you by taking Roman's side. That was not my intention. I love you both, but I will always have your back no matter what. As far as Zeke and I are concerned. Yes, we are dating. I like him a lot. I would love to talk to you about it. Can you call me when you are ready to talk? I love you, Sissy."

Ezekiel

I called Paxton the next morning and told him to meet me at Blue's house so we could workout. I had been working out almost every morning with Zora either at my house or at the gym in her office building. She's been making us these protein shakes in the morning that I thoroughly enjoy.

I pulled up to Blue's house and used my key to get in. I went to the gym and started my workout. Paxton came in shortly after I did. We talked a little before Blue came in and joined us. We worked out silently. Once we were all finished, we sat down and talked.

Roman told us his side of the story. There is a chick claiming he has a six-year-old son. I know Tasha from around the way. She has slept with several dudes that I know. No telling who her son's father is. I'm positive the baby is not Roman's, but he's getting a DNA test to be sure. Paxton gave him some good advice that I'm sure Blue will follow.

Then the conversation turned to me.

"So, Zeke, what up with you and Zora?"

I finished my protein drink that Zora prepared.

"Man look, I'm not gone even front. I'm sprung for real."

"Not the eternal bachelor!" Paxton laughed.

"She got you, huh?" Blue added.

"Yep, she has me following her around like a little puppy," I chuckled. "Nose wide open."

We all laughed.

"Don't you leave soon for the tour with Lyrica? How is that going to work out?" Blue asked. "How long will you be gone? Isn't it six months?"

"Yes, it's six months. I thought about only doing the first half of the tour and letting someone else do the second half. I don't want to be away from Zora and BJ that long."

I looked up, and both of my brothers were staring at me.

"What?"

"You are considering not touring, the thing that you live for because you want to be around for Zora and BJ?" Paxton questioned.

"Yeah, but since I am the MD, it's not possible, not to mention professional, for me to leave the tour early."

"Whoa, this is serious," Blue added.

"I tried to fight these feelings. I mean I tried! The harder I fought the more intense the feelings became. Zora tried to put some distance between us because she had the same fear as me, and I almost lost it. She had me at her job waiting for her to come out. I was in stalker mode, straight up." We all laughed. "I'm happy when I'm with them. I can't say I'm ready for marriage, but I know that I don't want to be without her or Braeden."

"This is the first time you've ever discussed a woman outside of how fire her body is," Paxton commented. "I'm guessing she is who you sent the flowers to?"

"You sent flowers?" Blue questioned.

"Yeah, I sent her the flowers. She's the first one worth talking about. I also wanted to talk to you both because while I am away, I would like for you to help Zora with BJ. You know, picking him up from school or spending some time with him on the weekends to give her a break. I'm asking you because she won't ask. She will just shoulder all the responsibility like she was doing before. I wasn't around then to help her, but as long as I am around, she won't have to take care of him alone."

"You've fallen for both of them," Blue smiled.

"I have. I've been thinking long term like starting a college fund for Braeden and some even scarier things that I don't care to share."

They both laughed.

"I understand. You have to reconcile those thoughts in your head before you can speak them," Blue assessed.

"Right."

"We got you, Bro. We will make sure both Zora and BJ are taken care of while you are away." Paxton said.

I looked down at my vibrating phone and saw my mother was Facetiming me.

"It's mom," I said as the call connected.

"Hey baby!" she smiled brightly. I moved to sit between my brothers.

"Hi, Mom we are all here."

"All my babies! I'm making one phone call instead of three! How is everyone?"

"Good!" Paxton answered.

"I'm cool," I responded.

"I'm okay," Roman finished.

"I had a very interesting phone call with Sister Simmons."

"That's Tasha's momma, right?" I asked.

"Yeah. She was trying to tell me that Tasha's son is your son, Roman. She talking about we share a grandchild. I already told you about the way Tasha used that baby to marry that nice young man. Now she is trying to use him against you?"

"Yes ma'am," Roman solemnly replied.

"Is it a possibility that he is your son?" my mother questioned.

"It's a very slim possibility but, yes."

"So, you smashed?"

"Momma!" Both Roman and Paxton said at the same time.

I laughed because I'd already heard her use that word.

She waved her hand like it was not big deal and continued, "Well, I told her I don't discuss my children's business so whenever we find out the truth, then we can talk. What did Zanetta say? I'm sure she will love him and you, right?"

"Yes, ma'am. That's what she said."

"Then why are you looking like somebody scraped all the crème filling from in between your Oreo cookies and replaced it with toothpaste?"

"Nette and I had a little disagreement about this."

"He didn't tell her mom," I interjected. Roman looked at me and rolled his eyes. I smiled back. I enjoyed watching him squirm under mom's scrutiny. I was always the one in trouble when we were younger. It's nice to see Blue and Pax in the hot seat. I continued, "She found out from Tasha. Rome didn't mention it to her. She had to bring it up." Both Paxton and Roman elbowed me at the same time. That was my queue to be quiet.

"What in the ever-loving world is your problem? So now my daughter is somewhere sad because you are on some foolishness? I need to call her. You better fix this Roman. I'm serious."

"I am mom. I love her."

"When do you get the DNA test?"

"I did it today."

"Either way, I got your back Baby. We're going to be happy either way, okay? I just need for you to fix things with Nette. She is good for you."

"Yes, ma'am."

"So, what else is happening?"

"Zeke has a girlfriend," Roman was trying to get the heat off him. I didn't care because I was going to tell mom about Zora and BJ soon.

"Oh, I know," she said matter-of-factly.

"How do you know?" I questioned.

"I knew when you called me asking me for a recipe to impress the baby and his mother. You have never even mentioned a female that you were interested in to me, so I knew it was serious. Tell me about her."

"She has a great sense of humor. Well, she's funny to me because most of the things that come out her mouth are sarcastic. She's an amazing mother to my Lil Dude, BJ. She's mad cool Mom. She is finishing up her residency so she can be an oral surgeon but she already has her DDS. She's confident, but sometimes she's unsure. She's independent because she has raised BJ all by herself, but she's not so independent that she won't accept help. She's smart, but she doesn't make everyone else around her feel dumb, though. She just mad cool."

"And the baby? How old is he?"

"My Lil Dude? His name is Braeden James. He's three. His birthday is coming soon. We call him BJ. He's extremely smart. He's learning the basics on the drums. He's a cool kid. I love being around him."

"I'm coming to town, and I would love to meet them."

"I would like for you to meet them."

Again, the room went silent.

"What?" I looked from my brothers to my mother.

"I was just kidding. You actually want me to meet Zora?" My mother questioned.

"Yeah, I do. Why? You don't want to meet her?"

I was confused.

"Ezekiel, you've never introduced me to anyone. This is serious."

"It is, Mom. I mean I'm not buying any rings like Blue, but I'm serious."

"I'm happy for you Baby. Paxton, it's your turn."

"Mom, you know I don't have anything to report. I'm content right now. If I meet someone, I will be okay with that, but right now, I haven't."

"Your heart is a muscle..."

She went into her speech about the same way we exercise the other muscles in our body we should exercise our heart by loving someone and letting them love you back. I would always hear her say that and I would zone out, but today, it makes a lot of sense.

"Your dad and I will be in town in two days to begin the first round of interviews for the Abundant Blessings Academy. Now explain how this works?"

"Zanetta hired a company to vet the applications. They sent us the top ten applicants. All of them will be interviewed by Dad and his team. They will choose the top five. My team will interview the top five and make the final selection." Roman explained.

"That's a process!"

"It is but we are trusting these people with our children, so we have to make sure we are choosing the best candidate. With your education background, your input will be invaluable." Roman said.

"Oh, I thought you were going to say my ability to call *bull manure* would be invaluable."

We laughed.

"That too, Mom!"

11

IT HAD BEEN a few days since I had spoken to Zanetta. I took Zeke's advice and didn't force her to talk to me. I gave her some space, but now that's over. She can't ignore me anymore.

I used my code to open the door to her apartment. I knew she was home because I parked next to her Shelby in the garage.

"Hey, Sissy." She whispered and smiled.

"Hey, Sissy."

We apologized to each other even though she really didn't have anything to be sorry about. I should have told her about Zeke and me. At first, I told her I didn't know why I didn't tell her but then I had to tell her the real reason.

"Sissy, I didn't tell you about Zeke and me because," I paused and took a deep breath and exhaled, "I didn't want you to think that he was too good for me."

She looked offended.

"Zora, what in THE hell are you talking about?"

"He's a good person. A church boy. I'm not good. We are the exact opposite."

"I don't know if you tripped up the steps and bumped your head or if you've inhaled too much laughing gas but either way you must have lost your damn mind! Yes, I said a curse word because it's the only one that fits. Well, another one would have fit, but I'm not saying it. It starts with an F and rhymes with trucking."

I laughed at her. I would have just said the word.

"Zora, why would you think something like that? It is so not true! If anything, you are too good for him! He is the lucky one, not you. I mean he's an amazing guy, and I love you two together. You guys balance each other. However, I would never think like that about you. Have I ever given you a reason to think that I feel that way about you? If I have, I didn't mean to do it because it's not true."

"No, Nette. You've never judged me or ever made me feel judged. It's just that he's so different than any other man I have been with and I did all of that big talk about church boys, and now I've fallen for one. I didn't want to like him. I certainly didn't want to fall for him, but I have. So has BJ."

"Zeke is not your typical church boy, but based on the way your skin is glowing and the permanent smile that is on your face, I'm sure you have figured that out."

My stomach did flips thinking about being with him.

"Yeah," I cheesed, "I know."

"Seriously, Sissy. I don't ever want to hear you say anything like that about yourself again. You are amazing! I admire your strength, courage, and wisdom."

"It's been inside of me all along," I laughed as I sang the words to the old India Arie song.

"Shut-up! I'm serious. I love the woman that you are."

"Thank you, sissy. I love you too."

"Tell me about him. What is he like to date? First, let's acknowledge that you are dating!"

"Right! I am, and I am scared shi...crapless. He's so attentive, and he loves BJ. More importantly, BJ loves him. Oh, and look at this."

I pulled out my phone to show her the picture of the flowers he sent.

"Oh, my Goodness, Sissy. Are these real?"

"I know right! Yes, they are real. They are called kaleidoscope roses. He sent four dozen!"

"Four dozen? Why four?"

I cleared my throat and adjusted my legs beneath me.

"Oh, nevamind! Y'all are so nasty, but after that night I had with Roman, I totally understand now!"

We giggled. We laughed and talked for a couple of hours before it was time for me to leave.

"Well, I'm going to go. Zeke and BJ were hanging out tonight, but I'm sure they are headed back to my house. I love you, Sissy. Thank you for understanding me."

"I love you too."

"I MEAN, what does she like to do? What does she like to eat? Should I cook something for them or are we going out to eat?"

"Z, you nervous?"

"Hell yeah, I'm nervous!"

Ezekiel had just finished telling me that his parents were in town and he wanted to introduce me and BJ to them. Nervous is the understatement of the century! I want to call Nette and get some information from her, but I couldn't call Nette. After I left her apartment, she decided to go and meet Roman in Atlanta. I didn't want to disturb her because they are probably doing a lot of making up.

"It's not like it's an inquisition or something it's just Roland and Grace Bluette."

"Who are also your parents!"

"Z, come here," He pulled me next to him on the couch in my living room. "Why are you acting like this? It's cool. They are cool people."

"I lived in a house with a woman for my whole childhood that hated me. She never said it, but I knew she did. Her actions showed it. Because of her, I have a hard time developing relationships with women. It always feels like they don't like me but there really isn't a reason why, you know? I don't even try anymore. When I was in school girls didn't really come for me. I had three older brothers, and they knew that I could scrap like a dude, but that didn't stop them from saying things about me. They were jealous of me for no reason. So, when you say I have to meet another woman who is the mother of the man that I am completely infatuated with, it scares me. What if she falls into the same category as my mother and sees something in me that she hates? Not to mention that I have a baby out of wedlock. That's like the number one sin, right?"

He pulled me in closer to him and kissed my forehead.

"So, you're infatuated with me?"

"Really Zeke?" I smiled.

He chuckled.

"I just wanted to make you smile. I know things were hard for you and I'm sorry you had to live through that but you did. You are a fighter. They are not the type to judge you. You're an amazing woman Doctor Chambers. You are an amazing mother with an amazing son. I'm sure my parents, especially my mother, will see that in you."

Ezekiel

Zora, BJ and I were meeting my parents at their condo in the city. They visit Houston a lot, so my brothers and I purchased them a condo in the Galleria area of Houston. I held Zora's hand the entire car ride. She was trying to put on a brave face, but she was nervous. When I picked her and BJ up, I told her how beautiful she looked in her long African print skirt and yellow tank top. She wore yellow sandals with it and wore her hair up in a bun. She dressed BJ in some khakis and a denim shirt. He had on a red bowtie. I had purchased him several since he has shown such an interest in wearing them. I pulled up to their building and parked. I got out and helped BJ out of his car seat then we opened Zora's door. I kissed her hand as we all walked hand in hand into the building.

I knocked and then used my key to enter their condo. My parents were standing in the living room.

"Hello Beautiful Lady," I walked over to my mother and embraced her.

"Hi, Baby!" She smiled brightly.

"Hi, Dad!" We hugged, and he kissed me on the cheek.

"Mom, Dad, this is Doctor Zora Chambers, my girlfriend and this my Lil Dude, Braeden. My mom Grace Bluette and my dad Bishop Roland Bluette."

"Hi Sweetheart, it's a pleasure to meet you," my dad gave Zora a hug.

"Bishop, the pleasure it mine. Zanetta used to share the CDs of your sermons with me while we were in school. They were amazing."

"Thank you," my dad smiled.

"No, thank you, Bishop. Those words came during some really challenging times in my life. They helped me tremendously. First Lady Bluette, it's a pleasure to meet you, too. Zanetta always speaks so highly of you."

I love the way Zora carries herself. She can be young and free like when she came to hear me play, or she can be subdued like she is with my parents. That's my lady.

"I can say the same for you. Congratulations on the new practice." My mother responded.

"Thank you, First Lady."

They hugged.

"And now who is this small person?" My dad was speaking to BJ.

BJ smiled and said, "My name is Braeden James Chambers. I'm three years old, but I'm going to be four soon."

My dad extended his hand, "It's a pleasure it meet you, Mr. Chambers."

BJ laughed and said, "Noooooo, not Mr. Chambers my name is B-J."

We all laughed.

"Excuse me, pardon my mistake. It's a pleasure to meet you BJ."

BJ shook his hand.

"BJ, my name is Grace. I'm happy to finally meet you. Your Tee Tee talks about you all the time." My mother bent down to speak with BJ eye to eye. Braeden smiled and extended his hand to touch her cheek.

"You are pretty like my mommy," he hugged her. My mother looked from me to Zora to my dad while she embraced BJ. She was a goner. He got her just like he got me. She may have had some tears in her eyes behind that one. That's my Lil Dude.

My parents followed me to the Mexican restaurant where we had reservations. BJ sat between my parents during dinner.

"Zora, what made you want to become a Dentist?" My father asked while we were waiting for our meals to be delivered.

"I had a dentist growing up that was like the dentist to the black community. All the black people went to Doctor Bixby. My family saw him religiously, every six months. My older brothers kept cavities. Every time we went to our appointment, they would need to get a filling. I never did, but Doctor Bixby would let me stay in the operatory while he did the fillings on my brothers. I thought it was amazing how he could fix a tooth with this silver metal. It would be a liquid first and then become solid. He saw how much I liked dentistry and told me that I should be a dentist. He said the dental field needs more African-American women in it. He was the first person to ever talk to me about my future, so I listened. Now I'm here."

"Is there still a shortage of African-American women in that industry?" My mother asked.

"Absolutely, I don't know the numbers, but I was the only black female enrolled in the dental program while I was at Columbia. The problem is that black dentists treat black patients. So, when there isn't a black dentist around, a lot of people in our community go untreated. Not to sound preachy but we have health fairs all the time and always omit the dental screenings. Gum disease can lead to heart problems. I hope I'm not being too preachy. I'm just passionate about dental care."

"Zora wants to start a free clinic, Dad. She wants it to be non-profit. I told her that I could introduce her to Sister Jones since that is her area of expertise."

"Of course, Sister Jones is the church administrator, and she is also a lawyer. She knows all the ins and outs of the not for profit. I'm sure she would be happy to help." My dad smiled.

"That's a wonderful idea, Zora." My mom complimented.

"Thank you, First Lady. I just want to help people. I don't believe that just because you don't have insurance that your treatment should be sub par."

"I agree, Sweetheart," my dad smiled.

Between Zora and BJ, my parents were entertained the whole dinner. Zora relaxed, and BJ commanded the conversation for most of dinner.

"Ezekiel, don't let me forget to give you a box of Roman's things that we found in the house."

"Yes ma'am, I will remind you."

"EZEKIEL, I LIKE HER A LOT!" my mother confessed.

The day after my parents met Zora and BJ, I went to my parent's condo to have lunch with them. My mother had prepared a fresh salad topped with grilled chicken. She made me a pitcher of cherry Kool-Aid.

"And that BJ. He is such a little charmer. And boy is he smart! You almost forget you're talking to a three-year-old." She continued.

"I know," I smiled. "He's getting smarter every day. I love having both of them around."

"What are your plans for her, son?"

"I don't have it all figured out Dad, but I want them in my life. I want Zora and BJ to share my life and my world. Like I told Mom, I don't know if I'm ready to be married, but I want them in my life permanently."

"She's a great choice. I didn't think you would ever make one," my Dad chuckled.

"Me either," my Mom cosigned.

"Bluette men know when we've found the one. Make sure you make her number one. No one or nothing should come before her. She is successful and strong. Let her be those things but still treat her like the most precious thing in your life because she is. Guard her heart and always consider her feelings. Pray for her and for Braeden. When the time is right, make her your wife."

"Yes, sir. Thank you for the advice."

"Ezekiel, do you think that Zora would like to come over for dinner before we leave for New York? I would love to spend some time with her again and BJ."

"I will ask her and let you know."

Zora

"Tell me about your family, Zora."

I was in the kitchen of First Lady Bluette's condo helping her with dinner. She had invited us over before she and Bishop go back to New York.

I wish she would have asked me about anything else other than my family. I hate this subject.

"Well, First Lady, can I be honest with you?"

"That's the best way to be."

"Okay, I haven't spoken to my family since I was seventeen years old. So almost ten years."

"Why?"

"I left home and moved to New York by myself. My home life was a disaster and I felt like leaving was the best solution. My mother hated me. My dad disappeared behind the pulpit, and my three brothers got old enough, left home and never looked back."

I don't know why I just bared my soul to her. I don't want to have to pretend. Either she is going to like me, or she isn't.

"I didn't have the best relationship with my mother either. She never really understood me. I didn't understand her either. It was not until I was older and she was sick that we had a conversation about our feelings for each other. She was jealous of me because of the attention that my father gave me. I was the only girl. She asked for my forgiveness for competing with me instead of being my mother. I forgave her. We had a couple of good years together before she went home to be with the Lord."

I don't know why her story made me cry, but it did.

"I tried to reach out to my family, but it didn't work out."

She pulled me into a hug. I cried on her shoulder.

"You are going to be just fine. I believe that God will restore those severed relationships. In the meantime, I would love to get to know you."

"You would?"

"Yes, I would. My son is an excellent judge of character. Zanetta believes you walk on water. If they think you're amazing, then I do too." She winked.

"SISSY! HE PROPOSED!"

"WHAT! WHEN?"

I was awakened by my phone vibrating on the nightstand. I reached for it hoping it was not some emergency at the hospital. It was Zanetta.

"Last night, at my auntie's birthday party!"

"WHAT!"

"What!" Ezekiel sat up in the bed. My screaming startled him.

"Blue proposed to Sissy," I said to him while holding the phone away from my ear.

"Oh, yeah. He said he was. Tell her I said congrats." He laid back down, pulled the covers over his head and mumbled, "I thought something was wrong."

"So, tell me what happened," I lowered my voice.

She told me all the details of his proposal from picking out her dress to wear to the guys singing to her while he got down on one knee. She sent me a picture of the ring. It is huge. He did a great job picking it out. We talked a little longer before we hung up.

"It looks like we are going to a wedding, Zeke."

No answer.

"Zeke...you sleep?"

Is he ignoring me? I know he's not sleeping that hard. I know what will make him respond.

"I wore that ass out last night. You should be tired."

I turned to lay down, but before I could, Zeke had me pinned on my back.

"You talking a lot of stuff for someone that tapped out."

"Tapped out? The last thing I saw you doing last night was sucking your thumb all balled up in a fetal position."

He laughed as he moved down my body.

"Let's see how many jokes you are cracking in a few minutes."

"Oh, I'm sure I will still be cra...."

My words were lost when I felt the first swipe of his tongue on my bud.

"You still talking? I can't hear you?"

I wanted to respond and say something smart, but he knew exactly how to shut me up. I sat up a little and rested on my elbows, giving me the perfect view. I massaged my breasts while I watched him pleasure me.

"Damn, Z, you taste so good."

I moved my hips in concert with his tongue.

"Oh, Zeke, you are so good at this. Yes, baby. Just like that."

He wasn't down there very long before I felt my release coming. With every lick and flick of his tongue, I felt myself getting closer to my ascension.

"Zeke!" I called out his name as my body started to convulse. It took me a minute to calm myself down enough to open my eyes.

He smiled and said, "Now go back to sleep."

AFTER ROMAN PROPOSED, we all went into planning mode because they decided they wanted to have the wedding a few weeks later. Nette arranged to have the wedding in Saint Louis and only invited close family and friends.

I felt some kinda way about going back to Saint Louis. I hadn't been since the night of my high school graduation almost ten years ago. I wouldn't have to worry about seeing my parents because they weren't on the guest list but I still have a little anxiety about going back.

I was sitting in Nette's apartment while she finalized the last details of the trip back to Saint Louis.

"I am going to fly in a few days early. Roman and the rest of the family will be there the day before the ceremony. When are you coming?"

She looked at me waiting for my response.

"Um..."

"Oh my goodness, Sissy! I didn't even think about how this will impact you. I know you haven't been back to Saint Louis in so long. How are you feeling? Why didn't you say something? We could have done something here."

She stopped what she was doing and sat down next to me.

"I would never ask you to compromise your dream or happiness for me. I'm a big girl. I will be fine. I'm just so excited for you that I hadn't thought about it until Zeke and I were discussing our travel plans. BJ and I are coming in with the men unless you need me earlier."

"No, I understand your schedule is tight. Your dress will be ready when you get there. If any adjustments need to be made Philip will do them on the spot. I love you so much for being uncomfortable for me."

We embraced.

"I will do it a hundred times more for you. I'm so hyped that we are living in the same city again, but do you want to know what I'm most excited about?"

"What?"

"You 'bout to get some. You 'bout to get some."

I stood up and started dancing to the made-up song I was singing. She stood and danced with me.

Ezekiel

We sent Roman and Nette off on their honeymoon the morning after their wedding. Paxton flew out with the rest of our family, but Zora, BJ and I spent the day after the wedding driving around Saint Louis. Zora hadn't been back since she left. She wanted to see how things had changed. I thought that she would have wanted to get back to Houston but she requested that we stay an extra day, so we did.

"Where are we headed to first?" I asked after pulling off the hotel parking lot.

"I want to go to Forest Park first."

She put the destination in the GPS, and I followed the prompts to the park. We arrived at the huge city park and found a parking space.

We walked down the sidewalk while Zora pointed out things to me and BJ.

"Over there is the Muny Amphitheatre."

"What's an pampatheter, mommy?"

"It's an AMPhitheatre baby. It's a place where you watch plays outside. Remember when we went to see Sesame Street Live?"

He nodded.

"It's like that but outside not inside a building."

"Oh! I like-did Sesame Street."

"I saw the Little Mermaid at the Muny when I was a little girl."

We continued walking as she pointed out other sights.

"Oh, Zeke look, boats! Can we get on the boats, Zeke?"

BJ could barely contain his excitement in seeing the paddle boats. He and I had gone on a paddle boat during one of our outings.

"If your mom says it's okay."

"Can we Mommy?"

"Sure baby."

We went to the small boat dock. I paid for one of the boats that Zora and I would have to paddle with our feet. We put BJ's life vest on him and sat him in the seat between Zora and me.

Paddling those boats will give you a serious workout! We paddled out and back. It took us about an hour. BJ clapped and screamed the entire time. He really enjoyed himself. That's because he wasn't paddling.

After we docked back at the Boathouse, I went to turn in BJ's life vest.

"You have a beautiful family," the lady behind the counter commented.

I turned around to see my Lady and my Lil Dude waiting on me. I smiled.

"I do. Thank you."

"Now I'm hungry. I want to go and get pizza." Zora said.

I followed her directions to a pizzeria named Imo's.

"Just so you know, this pizza is not like the pizza in New York, but it's delicious."

"New York has the best pizza, but I will try it."

"This was one of my most favorite things to eat."

She ordered a pie (pizza) for all of us to share. The pie came to our table straight out of the oven. It looked different.

"Why is it so flat and cut into squares?"

"That's how they make it. Just try it, Zeke. You will like it."

I watched the elation on Zora's face when she bit into her first piece. I was happy to see her enjoying herself. I followed her lead and tried a piece of the square pizza. It was delicious. She also ordered some toasted ravioli which is also a Saint Louis staple. Those were good too.

We finished our pizza and toasted ravioli.

"Where to now?" I asked while we walked back to the rental car.

"I want to show you where I grew up."

That surprised and concerned me. It surprised me because she'd mentioned not wanting to run into her family. Seeing where she grew up could possibly mean that we would run into her family. It concerned me because I didn't want to see her sad. Anytime we talk about her family she gets so melancholy. I don't like to see her sad.

She put the address to her childhood home in the GPS. I followed the prompts until we were driving into a neighborhood of old stately homes.

"That's it, right there."

She pointed to our left.

Her childhood home was a Tudor style brick house. The architecture of the house put you in the mind of a small castle.

"It hasn't changed a whole lot," she said while examining the house.

"This doesn't look like the neighborhood were Nette grew up. I thought you lived close to each other?"

"No, we didn't live close to each other. We went to the same private school. This is the Shaw neighborhood. Nette and her family lived in the Central West End. It's about a fifteen-minute drive from here. That's why I really didn't go anywhere when I lived here, because I didn't have friends in the neighborhood."

I could see the sadness in her eyes.

"Okay, I'm ready."

I pulled away.

She gave me directions to her father's church. We rode for about ten minutes before we pulled in front of a large white-washed brick church. *Pool of Siloam* was illuminated on the sign attached to the front of the building.

There was a flash of sadness in her eyes when I asked, "Do you want to go in?"

"No, I'm good. This short trip down memory lane was enough. I don't want to end this trip on a sad note."

I pulled away from the curb and headed down the street.

She perked up when she said, "Look, that's the basketball court where I schooled many dudes that thought I couldn't play because I was a girl."

"You're lucky I didn't bring any recreational clothes because I would see you on the court."

"Zeke, I wouldn't do that to you. I know how fragile your ego is. I wouldn't want to shatter it out there."

"Whatever, Z. We will play when we get back home."

"Okay, don't say I didn't warn you!"

"I want to play on the playground mommy," BJ said from the backseat.

"Okay baby, you can run around for a little while."

We stopped at the small playground that was next to the basketball court. Zora and I found a bench under a tree while BJ ran to the slide.

"So, how are you feeling?"

I straddled the bench and pulled her between my legs. I wrap my arms around her waist while she rested her back on my chest.

In the not so distant past, I would have never asked a woman how she was feeling. I didn't want to know what she was thinking. I could care less if something was adversely affecting her. With Zora, I need to know what she is feeling. It's like her feelings are connected to mine. As strange as that may sound. When she is happy, I'm happy. When she is not, I'm not.

"I feel okay. Actually, I feel good. The air is different here. I don't know if you can tell, but I feel like I can breathe. Not that I wasn't breathing before, but I don't know. Being here is refreshing. I thought that I would be sad and depressed, but I'm not. I mean, I would love to clear the air with my family but right now, sitting here in your arms, watching my son play...I'm happy."

I bent down and kissed her cheek.

"I'm happy too, with you and BJ."

She turned her body to face me.

"You are?"

"I am," I smiled. "Preparing for this tour with Lyrica has been difficult for me. I've never had anyone else to consider when leaving for months at a time. Now I have you, and I have BJ. I don't want to leave you."

I touched her face with my hand. She moved into my touch.

"I'm so glad I'm not alone in feeling the same way. I know its work for you but the thought of being away from you for six months makes me sad. Not because I don't think that we can handle the separation but because I'm going to miss you."

That's exactly how I was feeling. I leaned in and kissed her. When we separated, BJ was standing next to us smiling. He walked over to Zora and gave her a kiss on the cheek.

"Thank you, baby," she smiled.

"Are you ready to go Big Man?"

"No, I want to be pushed on the swings."

"I got you." I took his hand as he led me to the swing set.

I've never been that dude that wanted this: family, responsibility, and love. Now I realize I might not have wanted it, but I needed it. BJ has become an essential part of my life. I anticipate our daily conversations and interactions. His hugs make me feel invincible. When he says, 'My Zeke,' I feel important. I crave Zora. I adore the feeling of her next to me in the bed. I prefer the smell of her body wash in my bathroom. I love the scented trail of coconuts and jasmine she leaves behind when she moves. My life is better with them in it.

ONCE WE ARRIVED BACK to Houston from Saint Louis, my

schedule was jammed packed with meetings, rehearsals and studio time. I was preparing for the release party of my signature drum kit. The drum company is going all out for the party. They are live streaming it on their social media sites as well as mine. The guest list is packed with all the coldest musicians in the game right now. I began rehearsals with the band for Lyrica's tour, and I am working on some new music. My schedule is hectic.

I have figured out ways to incorporate BJ and Zora into my schedule no matter how hectic it gets. They have become my number one and number two priority. Some nights while I am working in the studio, she and BJ will come to the studio and have dinner with me. If they can't make it to me, BJ and I will Facetime so that we can say our prayers together. I spend some nights with Zora at her house, and then other nights she and BJ will stay at my house.

I've never been in love before. Since I've never been in love, I didn't think I would recognize it if it ever happened to me but I'm certain that I am in love with Zora. Who would have ever thought that it would happen to me? But it has. She gets me. She hasn't tried to change me into what she wants me to be, she rolls with me just the way that I am. She doesn't ask for anything. Which makes me want to give her the world. She gives me space to create, but when I need her close, she curls up right next to me. I have to force her to let me pay when we go out. There have been a couple times where she's paid the bill without me knowing. After each occurrence, I hid money in her purse or in her car. She told me to stop giving her money. I told her to stop paying when we go out. She hasn't stopped trying to pay, so I haven't stopped hiding money for her.

She encourages all my ideas and ventures. I haven't told her that I love her, but I hope that my actions show it.

12

TONIGHT IS Ezekiel's signature kit release party. I am so nervous like I am going to be the one on the stage. He doesn't seem fazed. Zanetta's style team came to Houston for the occasion.

She and Roman just got back from their honeymoon. I think Zanetta has a permanent smile on her face. Before the glam team started on my hair and make-up, I pulled Nette into a private area so that we could talk.

"So, how was it?"

"How was what?"

"Zanetta, don't get cussed out. How was everything on the honeymoon but specifically the D?"

She chuckled.

"Everything was great, but the D was phenomenal!"

We slapped a high five and laughed.

"No, for real. He has been very patient but passionate at the same time. He shows me how to touch him and pleasure him. He talks to me about our experiences to find out what I like and don't like. I like sex, Sissy."

"Sex is amazing when it's with someone you love and who loves you."

"Love? Are we talking about me or you?"

"Both," I smiled.

"Wow, does he feel the same way?"

"I don't..."

"Z," I heard Ezekiel call from the other side of the door.

"I'm in here with Nette," I called out.

He came into the room.

"Oh, what are you two in here talking about?"

"None of your business, Creep! You are so nosey." Zanetta smiled.

"You think you grown now 'cause you married little girl?"

"Shut up Zeke," Zanetta rolled her eyes.

"Z, what were you talking about?" Ezekiel turned his attention to me.

"Zeke, she said none of your business."

"You're not going to tell me?" He moved closer and ran his finger from my neck to the end of the V of my tee-shirt. I knew that look of mischief in his eyes.

"Zeke, stop playing."

"What?" He leaned down to kiss my neck. My head moved involuntarily to give him access to my neck. "I'm just asking a question. You know I could get it out of you if I wanted to, right?" He kissed my neck again. I moved my hands to his chest with the intention of pushing him away, but they rested there instead. He pulled me closer so I could feel his erection through his shorts.

"Zeke, you play too much." I finally found the strength to push him away. He knows I can't deny him when he touches me a certain way.

"I'll find out later," he laughed and walked out of the room.

I felt like I need to adjust my clothes even though nothing was out of place. After I finished pulling on my shirt, I looked at Nette.

"Dang, now I'm turned on."

We laughed.

"He plays too much!"

We laughed again.

"So, you haven't told him how you feel about him?"

"No, I haven't."

"I'm sure he feels the same way. Look at the way he fusses over you and always wants to be around you."

I don't know when I realized I'd fallen in love with Ezekiel but I have. At some point, my strong *like* for him evolved into love. I thought that I knew what love was, but he's shown me something totally different. His main goal is to make sure I'm satisfied. He takes care of me mentally and physically. I can talk to him about everything. He hasn't tried to get me to go to church, but he shares Roman's message topics with me. He takes BJ with him every Sunday, never making me feel guilty about staying home. He gets me and it's a wonderful feeling.

"Yeah, I hope so. Anyway, enough about me. What did Roman think of the tattoo?"

"He loved it!" she beamed. "Sissy, I think I fell more in love with him during our honeymoon. The way he touches me and is always concerned about how I feel and what I need...I can't ask for anything better."

I swooned.

"Aww, Sissy. I am so happy for you. How long were you sore after the first time?"

"Girl, I'm still sore! It ain't stopping nothing though!"

"And orgasms?"

"Every time."

"That's what I'm talking about!" We slapped hands again.

After our conversation, Zanetta's team and Marlan; Zeke's locti-cian went to work. Marlan worked on twisting Ezekiel's locs while Nette's hair stylist flat ironed my hair. As soon as Marlan lowered the lid of the dryer, Zeke fell asleep. He's been going non-stop between getting ready for this release party and practicing for Lyrica's tour, he's been busy. Everyone in the room was speaking in hushed tones so we wouldn't wake him up. My poor baby is exhausted.

Zanetta dressed me in a blush colored cigarette pant jumpsuit. The top of the jumpsuit had a sweetheart neckline. She handed me a pair of crisscrossed strappy sandals that buckled around my ankle. The straps were a sparkly material while the back of the shoe was painted cork.

"These are amazing."

"I know, right? These Bluette men and their taste in shoes."

"Huh? Who picked these out?"

"Zeke did. He asked me to match your outfit to them for tonight."

I smiled, "He did?"

"Yep."

My outfit was completed with a gold teardrop necklace that rested between by breast, gold hoops, and a painted cork clutch purse.

Zanetta was killing it in a black catsuit that she wore under a long red duster. She wore strappy black heels and carried a black clutch.

"Did Roman see what you were wearing tonight?"

"No," she laughed. "He's going to like it. Don't you think?"

"I don't think you will be at the event very long once he sees you."

"Good, that's my plan." she winked.

Yes! I am loving this sexually active Sissy!

The men went to the venue early. They sent a car for Zanetta and me.

The venue was buzzing with photographers, reporters and musicians. People were snapping pictures, posing for pictures and doing interviews.

"Mrs. Bluette, Doctor Zora." Percy met us at our car.

"Hey Percy, don't you look handsome." I complimented him on his black slim fit suit that he paired with a black shirt and skinny black tie.

"Both of you look stunning."

"Thank you," we both said as we linked arms with him while he led us through the crowd.

He directed us to a table right in front of the stage.

"This is your table. The fellas will join you later."

"Thanks, Percy."

"No problem."

I turned to Zanetta, "This is so exciting. I'm nervous like I'm about to do something."

"I know," she smiled. "I'm so proud of Zeke."

"Me too."

The event began with two men on the small stage that was in the center of the room. They talked about the process of creating a unique product for Ezekiel and how much fun he was to work with.

"Without further ado, we present Ezekiel Golden Drummer Bluette on his signature drum kit."

Someone yelled from the back of the room, "One, two, three!"

All of a sudden, a marching band dressed in blue and gold uniforms filled the room. The drum majors wore their signature hats as they led the band down the aisles of the room playing one of Ezekiel's songs. This was the band that won the competition. Ezekiel donated drums and cymbals for the entire drumline. The band's music slowed as the spotlight landed on Roman and he began playing a melody on the keyboard.

"Yes!" Zanetta screamed when he started playing.

Then you heard the rumblings of a bass drum and what sounded like a million cymbals as all the lights in the venue rested on Ezekiel. The marching band accompanied him for a portion of the song then he performed a solo.

My heart pounded with excitement, anticipation of what he would do next, pride and love. He looked delicious in his black sleeveless t-shirt showing off his toned and tattooed arms.

He played a couple of songs accompanied by Roman and a small band that consisted of a lead guitar, bass guitar, and saxophone.

When he finished the lights in the room came up. He stood from his stool smiling and out of breath. The room erupted in applause followed by a standing ovation.

"They were amazing!" I smiled at Zanetta.

"Yes, they are." She smiled without taking her eyes off Roman.

The look on Roman's face was priceless when he took in Zanetta's full ensemble. I don't know if he was supposed to leave the stage, but he did and headed straight towards her.

They are so cute.

Ezekiel's eyes scanned the room until they locked with mine. He smiled and winked.

I smiled and winked back.

Someone handed Ezekiel a microphone, "I would like to say thank you to..."

As he was talking, Percy came and tapped me on the shoulder.

"Doctor Chambers, Zeke wants you to meet him in the back in his dressing room."

I leaned over and told Nette I would be back, but she and Roman were too busy staring each other down to notice my departure. I stood and followed Percy to the back of the venue.

He opened the door to the small dressing room. I stood inside waiting for Ezekiel to join me. About ten minutes later he burst through the door all smiles.

"Babe! You had an amazing performance!"

He kissed me quickly and removed his shirt. I hiked up one eyebrow.

"We about to get down like that?"

He laughed, "You're silly. No, I need to take a quick shower and change into my suit."

"I was about to say..."

I laughed as he moved past me and disappeared through a door that I didn't realize was a bathroom. He reemerged a few minutes later with a towel around his waist.

He walked toward me smiling.

"Now."

He grabbed me by my waist and pulled me into his chest. We kissed like we hadn't just seen each other a couple minutes ago. Instead, we kissed like we were long lost lovers who had just encountered each other again.

"Stop playing, woman. We have to get back out here to this party."

"You started it," I replied with my arms around his waist. "What I want to do is snatch this towel from around your waist and take in a mouthful, but like you said, we have a party to get to."

"Why would you say something like that knowing I have to get back out there? You're getting it tonight. For this little stunt and for not telling me what you and Lil Sis were talking about earlier."

I laughed as he turned from me to put on his suit.

Nette chose his suit. She put him in a gray suit with a gold plaid detail. He wore a vest with the same print under the jacket. His white shirt was left open instead of wearing a tie. She chose gray loafers to finish off the ensemble. He looked good enough to eat.

"This look okay?" He asked turning to me from the mirror.

"You look delicious," I said as I adjusted the white handkerchief that was sticking out of his jacket pocket.

"Thank you, Z. So, do you." He leaned in and kissed me again before taking my hand and leading us out of the dressing room.

We walked out into the party that was in full swing. There was food and a DJ. People were eating, dancing and drinking. I left Ezekiel to mingle with the guests, while I went to find Nette. I didn't want to cramp his style.

I found Zanetta sitting with Roman and Paxton.

I sat next to her and whispered, "What did he think of your outfit?"

She smiled and said, "We're leaving soon."

A few minutes later Roman said something to her in her ear that made her giggle. He announced they were leaving. I hugged them both, and they left.

I scooted next to Paxton.

"Pax, why didn't you bring a date tonight?"

"I don't have time to date, Zora."

"Can I ask you something without you getting offended?"

"I don't offend easily."

"Do you like women or..."

"Are you asking me if I'm gay?"

I nodded my head.

"I'm not gay, Zora. I just don't have time for the games. I'm at a point in my life where I want to find my wife. I want to be with someone that wants me for me. I'm a lot to take on."

"I understand. I wasn't trying to be in a relationship either. It just sort of snuck up on me."

"I hear you. I think that's how it works. You find that one person when you are not looking for them. Women are constantly telling me what they can do for me or to me. Sometimes I want to take them up on their offers, but I know that anyone that is bold enough to come at me like that is not the one I want to introduce to Grace and Roland. Then there's Nigel and Giselle, my biological parents...she has to be built for me."

I had never heard him mention his biological parents.

"I respect that."

"I can't just bring anyone around my family. There is no way I am going to expose my nephew to the likes of these women that I have come across."

"Thank you for accepting BJ as your family."

"Please! Thank you for letting me. When I introduce you to a woman, she will be my wife."

"Got it."

We talked for a little while longer before he decided it was time to leave.

"Excuse me," I felt someone tap my shoulder. I turned around and was eye to eye with a woman looking like she was concerned about something. "You're Ezekiel's date correct?"

"Yes, I am."

"I need to share something with you about Ezekiel."

"Okay..."

At first, I was going to say no thank you, but I wasn't sure who she was so I listened. I stood from my table to talk to her.

"My name is Lindsay. Ezekiel and I dated on again off again for several years."

My bullshit meter went off when she used the word "dated." I know she is about to say some stupid crap because Ezekiel doesn't date...well didn't date.

"He started out being a sweetheart as I am sure he is with you right now. Eventually because of the way he is, his nature, he will cheat on you. Just like he cheated on me. I know for a fact that he is not only with you. There are at least two other women who he's dating or at least kicking it with. That's how he operates."

I processed what she said before I lightly grabbed her elbow and moved her to a more secluded area.

"You're having dick withdrawals, huh? No, no I get it. If he ever decided to stop giving it to me, I would be out at public events making a fool of myself just like you, trying to get it back. It's superb, right? What's your favorite position? Mine is the one where he is behind me, and he uses his hands to put that arch in my back...whew, it gets me every time."

I fanned myself with my hand.

"You say there are at least two other women he is currently dating? Wow, the dick downs I get are superb, and that's only like half the dick if I'm sharing it with two other women. Wait, not even half more like thirty-three percent. I've had some whole dick that doesn't compare to the percent I'm getting from him. As a matter of fact, it's so good that I would be willing to call those other two broads sister wives just so he won't take it from me. Shit, let's all live together in harmony!"

The look of disdain on her face was hilarious. I held back my laugh, but it was hard.

"He will get tired of you just like he does everyone else. You're not special. As a matter of fact, you're basic. Who still wears blue contacts?" she spat angrily.

"Maybe I'm not special. Probably could be called basic. Blue contacts...okay," I shrugged my shoulders. "What's for sure is that after this event is over, I'm going back to his house, which I'm positive you've never been inside of. I'm going to get onto his California king bed, which I'm sure you've never seen. Then I am going to let him do some extremely nasty things to me. I'm talking about triple X-rated things. Without a condom.

For the record, I was decorous this time, but if you ever come at me again about my man or what he is doing, it's going to be catastrophic for you. Enjoy the rest of the party." I smiled and walked away from her.

I knew it was just a matter of time before some thirsty, slut bucket tried me over Ezekiel. I don't know what she thought was going to happen, but I rides for mine!

I found Ezekiel standing with a group of people.

"There you are! I was looking for you," he smiled and pulled me close to him.

"I just met someone who thought she was your ex-girlfriend."

He threw his head back and laughed. He noticed I wasn't laughing then said, "Are you serious?"

"Yes," I shook my head.

"Who?" He looked at me with concern on his face.

"Lindsay."

"Lindsay? She was never my girlfriend. What the hell? She was here?"

"Yes, I know, and yes she was here."

He looked around the room angrily before I used my hand to direct his face back to me.

"I handled it."

"What do you mean, you handled it. What did she say to you?"

"She said you had some other broads you are having sex with at the same time as me."

"Zora, you know that's not..."

"I know, Zeke. I responded and told her that she was probably having dick withdrawals because I know that I would, if you ever took it away from me."

"You said that?"

I nodded.

He threw his head back and laughed.

"You are stoopid! That's why I fools with you!"

I laughed too.

"I told you I handled it."

"Come on are you ready to go? I want you to back up all of that big talk you were doing earlier."

"Oh, I am more than capable."

"Show and prove, Doctor Chambers. Show and prove."

Ezekiel

I was sitting in my music house with my headphones on listening to some playback on a song that Lyrica recorded for the concert. I felt a small hand touch my arm. I turned to see BJ dressed in his superhero pajamas. Zora was standing next to him holding his other hand.

I stopped the playback and removed my headset.

"Hey man, you all ready for bed?"

"Yes, I took a shower so now imma go to sleep."

"I'm going to come and tuck you in, okay?"

I cut my eyes at Zora as I stood from my chair and picked him up. We walked back into my house and to his bedroom. I purchased him a new bed for his room at my house. Zanetta is going to decorate his room for me while I am away on tour.

We said our prayers together, and I tucked him in. I kissed his cheek and turned to leave his room.

"I love you, Zeke," BJ called out as I was walking out. I stopped in my tracks and turned around.

"What did you say Big Man?"

"I said I love you. I love my new bed too."

I walked back over to his bed and sat down.

"Man, you know that I'm leaving because I have to, right? It's my job. If I didn't have to leave you, I wouldn't."

"I know. You have to go and direct the music for Ms. Lyrica so she can sing."

"Right but if I didn't have to do that, I wouldn't, okay?"

"Okay."

"I love you so much, man. Do you know that?"

"Yes, I know."

"Alright, go to sleep, so you won't be tired for school in the morning."

I kissed him again and walked out his room.

Zora was sitting in a chair in my bedroom reading something on her laptop. I closed the door behind me.

"I thought I told you I was going to get him ready for bed?"

She looked up at me with a confused look on her face and then looked back at her computer.

"Zora!"

"It's obvious that you are trying to start another petty ass argument with me and I'm not falling for it. You were out there working on something and had lost track of time apparently. I was not going to interrupt you to get him ready for bed, so I did it."

"You know I'm leaving and I want to spend as much time with him as I can before I leave!" I couldn't understand why she was acting so nonchalant. It was only pissing me off more.

"I'm not doing it, Zeke. Either go back outside or shut up cause you're going to piss me off again and I don't feel like it today. You have been Petty Peter..."

"Petty Peter?"

"Yes! First name: Petty, middle name: Ass, Last name: Peter for a couple days now and I'm sick of playing nice. You complained because my gas tank in my car was three-quarters full instead of full."

"You were talking about driving to the other side of town, and you know how traffic is!"

"You complained when they put pickles on your burger, but you didn't tell them not to."

"Pickles don't always come on those burgers. I shouldn't have to say it."

"You had that little boy that worked there about to pee his pants! You got all irate over pickles!"

"Whatever, people need to do their jobs."

"You got mad when they changed BJ's zoo field trip date."

"They can't be messing with people's calendars like that! Now I won't be able to chaperone because I won't be here!"

"So, like I said, either carry your petty ass back out to the music house or shut up cause you're pissing me off!"

"I'm not being petty, Z."

"Yes, you are, and I don't understand why."

She was right. I had not been the nicest person lately. I wasn't trying to be petty, but everything was annoying me.

"Maybe it's because I'm stressed about leaving."

I sat down on the ottoman in front of the chair she was sitting in.

"Stressed? Because of your level of responsibility on the tour?"

"No, because I don't want to leave you and Braeden behind. I've never been on tour and in a relationship at the same time. I don't know if I'm built for it." She closed her laptop and scooted closer to me.

"What do you mean by built for it?"

"I mean tour life is totally different than everyday life. It's fast-paced, exciting and full of..."

"Women?"

"Yeah, women. I mean, I know that you're the only woman that I want to kick it with. I don't even see other women the same way I see you, but I've seen the road destroy relationships which is another reason why I didn't do them. Before you and BJ all I had to worry about was myself. Now I have both of you. I'm not complaining because it's an honor to have you in my life. I just don't want to mess it up."

It felt good to be able to say exactly what I had been feeling.

"Ezekiel, when we first said that we were going to do this, you told me that you were loyal. You have been loyal. I love what we have. The ease of conversation and the ability to be myself. I hope you feel like you can be yourself with me."

"I do."

"Then be yourself. I'm not asking for you to be anyone other than Ezekiel Levi Bluette. You make the best decisions you can when the time calls for it, and I will respect your decision. I trust you. I'm not saying go and smash every broad that comes your way. What I'm saying is that I trust you to make good choices. The same way I shut Lindsay down is the same way I will shut anyone else down that tries to tell me something about you. BJ and I are going to hold you down on the back end while you go and be great. Have fun. Live your life. We will be waiting on you."

"What if Doctor Squarepants steps up his game? I won't be around to shut him down. Or one of those other doctors at the hospital that's always trying to get with you."

"I'm spoiled. You spoiled me, Zeke. I don't want anything from any other man. All I want is you. You should know that by the way I've put up with your pettiness!"

"You're spoiled, Z?" I asked as I pulled her onto my lap.

"Rotten," she nestled her face into my neck.

"I'm sorry for being petty."

"Prove it."

I planned on proving it every day until I left.

"YOU HAVE the keys and all of the codes, right?"

She nodded her head.

"You have the bank cards, right?"

She nodded again.

I was trying to make sure I didn't forget anything before I got on the plane for the first leg of the tour. I had given Zora the keys to my houses and my cars. I put her name on one of my bank accounts just in case she needed something and couldn't reach me. I wanted to make sure she and BJ were taken care of. I knew she was capable... more than capable of taking care of herself but it gave me peace of mind knowing she had backup. I'd had several conversations with my brothers and Nette about helping her with BJ. I knew it would happen without me saying it, but I just wanted to make sure.

I didn't want her to drive me to the airport, but she insisted. I thought it would have been easier to say goodbye at the house, but she wasn't going for it.

I SPENT the day before I left with BJ making sure to prep him for my time away. Zora let me keep him out of school so that we could have our men time. He seemed to be in better spirits than I was. I was still battling a level of guilt about leaving him for so long. I know he's not my son...biologically but the bond that I have formed with this kid feels paternal. It feels like he came from me.

We spent time at the arcade center then we went to a few stores to pick him up some clothes, shoes, and underclothes. Then we went to the toy store, and I let him pick out a few things.

"Aye Big Man, you know I'm leaving in the morning, right?"

"Yes, sir."

"You remember what we talked about as far as keeping up with your responsibilities while I'm away?"

"Yes, I have to be good in school. Help my mommy and keep my rooms clean."

"Right. Do you think any of that will be a problem for you?"

"No, 'cause I do it now. Imma hold it down for you while you away, Zeke."

Where did he get that from?

"Okay, I appreciate it."

We had his favorite meal before we went back to my house to meet Zora. BJ and I put all of his new things away before he took his shower and went to bed.

I spent the rest of the night making love to my Lady.

NOW WE ARE at the airport meeting some of the other band members to board the plane

I got down on one knee to talk to Braeden.

"I'm going to miss you Man, but I will call as often as I can okay?"

He nodded as tears began to silently fall down his cheeks. I blinked hard to keep mine at bay.

"I love you, Braeden, okay?"

"I love you too, Zeke. This much," He opened both his arms wide. That almost got me. I cleared my throat to help relieve some of the pressure that was building from the tears I was fighting.

I gave him a long hug. I released him and wiped his cheeks.

"I will call you soon, okay?"

"Okay."

I stood up to look at Zora. Maybe I should have asked her to marry me. Maybe I should tell her I love her before I leave. I decided not to do either. I don't think it would be fair to put a ring on her finger now. She would think that I was doing it because I wanted to tie her down while I was away which would be partially true. I'm not going to declare my undying love for her and then fart around and mess up while I'm away. I would never hurt her like that.

"I'm going to miss you, Z."

I pulled her into me and hugged her. I was having a hard time letting her go.

"I'm going to miss you too, Zeke."

I wanted to just say it. I wanted to say, "I love you, Zora." I couldn't...I mean I can, but I'm not.

I kissed her gently, knowing that two little eyes were watching me.

"I will call you when I get settled, okay?"

"Okay."

I hated the sadness that I saw in her eyes. It was enough to just call off the whole thing, but I knew I had a responsibility, a career, and reputation.

She teared up a little, but she didn't let any tears fall. Her strength was giving me strength.

I turned to walk through the TSA line. Once they checked my boarding pass and ID, I turned and waved goodbye to them...my family.

Man, this crap is hard.

Zora

Ezekiel had been gone for four weeks. The first couple of weeks were hell, but now things are better. I missed him so much those first few days, I didn't know what to do with myself.

Zeke calls as much as he can. He will Facetime at night to pray with Braeden, and then he and I will have a conversation. He sends me text messages all day long, and he is continually posting on his social media pages. I miss having him here but thanks to technology, I feel like I am there sometimes.

Obasi and Lyrica have called to check on me and BJ. Lyrica asked if I wanted to come and spend a week with them on tour. I told her if my schedule would allow me to, I would love to come. She said, "my brother is happier when you are around." That made me smile. I am happier when he is around too.

I thought that was so sweet. If I can get some time off, it will be towards the end of the tour. She even said BJ could come. He is going to be so siked.

Roman and Paxton have definitely stepped in to help with BJ. They have scheduled days to pick BJ up from school. Roman takes him to the studio where he is teaching BJ the piano. He also helps him with the drums. Paxton and BJ are working on forming a company called BJ's Bow ties. Since BJ likes bowties so much Paxton came up with the idea to turn it into a company. Nette is helping them with fabrics, and she found the company that will produce them. Of course, Nette helps a lot also. She's been working hard to get her boutique open. The building Roman purchased for her is in the perfect location. She is still working with the church, but she stopped taking a salary once she and Roman got married.

I arrived at Roman and Nette's house to pick up BJ.

"Hey Sissy," I said as I entered the house after she opened the door.

"Hey, Sissy."

"Where are the men?"

"They are on their way home. Paxton said the meeting with the fabric distributor ran a little long."

"Girl, I can't believe my son really has his own company."

"I know, right? It's so cool though. It could really grow into something if we handle it correctly."

"I know. That's so amazing."

"So how is Zeke? How is life on the road treating him?"

"He's good. I just saw where he posted a picture in Detroit. He knows I like snow globes so he's sent me a snow globes from every place they have gone so far."

"That's so cute and thoughtful."

"I know, right. Listen to this radio interview he did the other day."

I took out my phone and went to the website for WPAB. They have an afternoon radio show that is number one in the country.

I found the link and turned up the volume so we both could hear.

"Good afternoon everybody, it's ya boy DJ Ratio. I'm here with my crew Cashmere and Thor. We are joined in studio by the beautiful and talented Lyrica and her musical director and one of the coldest drummers around, the golden drummer, Ezekiel Bluette. Welcome to the both of you."

"Thank you," both Zeke and Lyrica said at the same time.

"Lyrica, you are on tour right now. I hear that every venue has been sold out."

"That is correct," Lyrica confirmed. "Let me say a huge thank you to all of my family for buying those tickets to come and spend an evening with me."

Cashmere spoke next, "It really is like spending the evening with you. You not only perform, but you give us a glimpse into your life which you never do. You are so fiercely private."

"I do. I want to connect with my family in a way that I've never done before. I share some videos and some new songs that Zeke and I wrote right before the tour started."

"Ezekiel, you have been with Lyrica basically from the start, right?" Ratio asked.

"Yeah, we worked on her first project together but before that, I worked with her mom, so we've been family for a long time."

"Now by family does that mean you two are romantic? Or have been romantic?" Thor asked.

"Naw, man. Never that. She has been like a sister to me for a lot of years."

"Right, right, right cause Lyrica you are dating Obasi, the model, right? You guys have been together for a long time," Cashmere stated.

"Yes, Obasi is my man. Hey, baby! I know he's listening."

"I know that's right, girl. He is fine as hell! Kudos to you."

Both women laughed.

"Since we are talking about relationships, Ezekiel, what about you?" Cashmere asked.

"I have a lady holding things down for me back in Houston."

"Wud?" Thor replied, "Zeke I have known you for years. I've never heard you say that you were in a relationship."

"Yeah, they had you listed in *Black Majic* Magazine as one of their most eligible bachelors," Cashmere added.

"Well, Thor, I guess I grew up. Cashmere, that publication is old."

"So, is she the one?" DJ Ratio asked.

"She's the only."

I looked at Zanetta and smiled. The interview continued with more questions about the tour and what people could expect. They asked Ezekiel one last question.

"Ezekiel, I know you play the drums, but I heard that you know how to play a couple other instruments, is that true?" DJ Ratio asked.

"Yeah, I started out on the piano, but it didn't make enough noise for me, so I moved to the drums. I can play any stringed instrument, just about, but my brother Blue is the virtuoso on the keys."

"Out of all those sounds which one is your favorite?" DJ Ratio questioned.

"My lady's voice."

Everyone on the broadcast said something like, "That was smooth," or "That's what's up."

I clicked off the web page and locked my phone.

Zanetta was smiling, and so was I.

"That was so sweet!"

"I know! I just keep listening to the whole thing just to hear him say that at the end. I miss him so much!"

"I miss him, so I know you do."

I felt my phone vibrating. I looked down and saw Ezekiel was Facetiming me. I accepted the call.

"Hey, Babe!"

"Hey, Z. I miss you!"

"I miss you too!"

"Hey, Clown!" Nette called out.

"What's up, Lil Sis. What are you up to? Playing like you grown?"

"Shut up Zeke," she laughed. "Actually, I'm trying to finalize the hiring of the new ABA director and getting my boutique opened."

"That's what's up. I'm proud of you Lil Sis."

"Thank you. I love you, brother. I will let y'all talk."

"Alright, love you too, sis."

Nette left the room while I continued my conversation.

"How has your day been?"

"It's been busy. We are about to hit the stage as soon as Lyrica gets herself together. She's been sick for the past couple of days."

"Really? What's going on with her?"

"She's been throwing up. She's been getting dizzy too, like almost fainting. The doctor thinks it's exhaustion, but they are going to run some test tomorrow. We couldn't get her to postpone tonight, so she's in her dressing room with an I.V."

"Awe man! But the performances have been great according to the reviews."

"They have been amazing. Once she hits that stage, we forget that she is battling something, but as soon as she stops performing, we have to be there to catch her, literally."

"It's probably just a bug because I've been sick too. I have a hard time keeping anything down. I think it's a virus going around."

"Oh yeah? You didn't tell me that the last time we talked."

"That's because I'm fine. I have everyone here looking out for me. It's gotten a little better, but I'm still cautiously eating soup and crackers."

"Z, why didn't you let me know? I could have sent chef over to cook."

"Zeke, I'm good. I'm a doctor, remember? Surrounded by doctors all day. If it gets bad, I will get looked at. You know a virus has to run its course."

"Yeah..."

"Ezekiel, I'm fine!"

He turned around to address someone that entered his room.

"Is she ready? How is she acting? Alright, here I come."

He turned back to me.

"Where is my Lil dude?"

"He's on his way back from a meeting."

"With Pax and the distributors, right?"

"Yes."

"I will try to call back tonight. If I can't, I will catch him in the next couple days, okay?"

"Sounds good."

"Z, take care of yourself. Don't make me leave this tour to come and force feed you because you know that I will."

"Babe, I'm good. I shouldn't have said anything. I don't want you to be concerned."

"I won't worry as long as you promise you are taking care of yourself."

"I promise."

"Alright, I have to go. I will talk to you later."

"Dream about me."

"Always..."

13

Ezekiel

ONE OF THE hardest things about being on tour this time is the fact that I am missing BJ's birthday. He's turned four, and I was not there to celebrate with him. I wanted to try to catch a flight back home to celebrate with him, but I couldn't make it work. I hounded my brothers and Nette trying to make sure his birthday is a special one even though I couldn't be there.

I paid for his class to take a field trip to the Children's Theater. After the production at the theater, they had cake and ice cream.

Everyone on tour got tired of me talking about missing his birthday, so every single person on tour from the stage hands to the sound engineer sent BJ a gift for his birthday. He would open those at the party at my house.

"Hey, Z," I smiled when I saw her face fill my phone's screen.

"Hey, Zeke."

I heard kids screaming in the background.

"I guess the party is in full swing?"

"Yes, all of his classmates showed up plus all of the partner's kids. There are a few kids from the church here too."

"That's what's up!"

I ordered three giant bouncy houses for the party. Chef was preparing hot dogs for the kids and barbecue for the adults. My mom and dad were in town for the party as well.

"Is he having fun, Z?"

She turned the camera on the phone to face the other direction so that I could see him jumping into the deep end of my swimming pool.

"Doesn't he look like he's having fun?"

I smiled. I was happy he was having fun, but I hated that I was not there.

"He does look like he's having fun. Are the lifeguards doing their jobs?"

I had hired two lifeguards since the kids would be in the pool, I didn't want any accidents.

"Yes, they are working. Blowing those darn whistles at the kids."

"Z, do you think he's disappointed I'm not there?"

"Zeke, stop beating yourself up about not being here. You couldn't do it. Did he seem disappointed when you talked to him last night?"

"No, he was too busy telling me about the production at the Children's Theater."

"Right. Did he seem disappointed this morning when you spoke to him?"

"No, but I don't feel like I've done enough. My dad never missed our birthdays. He always figured out a way to be with us. I just don't want him to feel like he's not important to me."

She walked away from the crowd and closed a door behind her. It looked like she was in the bathroom.

"Ezekiel, you have done so much. You paid for the field trip. You planned this party by yourself basically. He has at least a million gifts to open. Baby, you've done more than enough. He understands you have to work. He's fine."

"Are you sure?"

"Positive."

Her words made me feel a little better about not being there.

"Did he give you your gift?"

"He did! Zeke that was so sweet."

I'd asked Paxton and Roman to take BJ out to pick out a gift for Zora for his birthday. My father taught my brothers and me to celebrate our mother on our birthday. We give her a small gift on our birthday every year to thank her for giving birth to us. I wanted BJ to continue that tradition with Zora. My brothers took him out and let him pick out her gift.

"Paxton sent me a picture of the necklace he found. Is it edible?"

"Yes, it's a candy necklace." She moved the phone so that I could see her wearing it.

"He has great taste."

"He does," she laughed.

"It was important for him to choose the gift himself."

"Well, I love it. Thank you, Zeke."

She smiled. I love her smiles.

"Alright, enjoy the party. I will call you tonight if it's not too late."

"Zeke?"

"What's up?"

"Thank you. This means so much to me and to BJ. I don't know what we would do without you."

That made me smile.

"I'm the lucky one."

"Dream about me."

"Always."

Zora

I was startled awake by my phone singing Zeke's ring tone. I looked at my clock. It was two in the morning. He never calls this late. I sat straight up in the bed to answer it.

It had been two weeks since BJ's party.

"Zeke?"

"Z, is BJ asleep?"

"Huh? Um..." I was trying to clear the fog from my brain after being jarred from my sleep. "He's with Doctor Mill..."

He interrupted, "Come open the door."

I jumped up from my bed, grabbed my robe and put it on as I ran down the steps to the front door. I disengaged the alarm and snatched the door open.

Zeke was standing on the other side smiling. I didn't give him a chance to say anything before I jumped into his arms and wrapped my legs around his waist. He caught me and moved into the house. Our lips violently crashed into each other like ocean waves crashing into rocks. He held me up while he kicked the door shut and re-engaged the alarm.

He pushed my back into the wall of the foyer while I worked frantically at getting his shirt pulled over his head and out of my way. He opened my robe and saw that I was naked underneath. He growled his approval. I held on while he shoved his jogging pants and underwear down to his knees, freeing Clyde (I had given *him* a nickname). I could feel Bonnie (Zeke's nickname for *her*) weeping in anticipation of being reacquainted with him.

With no preamble, I sank down onto him while he thrust into me. We both yelled out in pleasure. God! This felt like being in a desert for weeks and finally finding a fresh source of water. He felt so good. He filled me completely. He held on to my rear cheeks as he aggressively pumped in and out. Hearing his grunts and feeling his strong muscles holding me up turned me on. We locked eyes and didn't break eye contact until I felt my release coming.

"Zeke," I cried.

I wanted to hold out. I wanted to make this last longer, but I had lost all control.

"I know. Make it wetter for me baby."

He changed his angle slightly, and that was it for me. I came so hard! I tightened my legs around his waist as I soaked Clyde with my juices.

"Damn, Z," he thundered as he came right behind me. He held

me in place several minutes before he slowly slid out of me and lowered me to the ground. I rested my head on his chest while we both fought to regulate our breathing.

He kicked off his shoes and pants that were still resting at his ankles. He grabbed my hand and led me to my bedroom. He went into the bathroom and turned on the water to fill the tub.

He came back out smiling.

"What are you doing here?" I smiled back.

He put his arms around my waist and said, "Lyrica's doctor told her she needed to take a few days off. She is canceling the shows for the next couple of cities. I missed you, so I got on the next thing smoking to see you."

"I missed you too."

"Come on and take a bath with me."

He helped me into the tub, and then he got in behind me. I rested my back against his chest as he began to tell me about all the things he'd been experiencing on tour.

"I think this is the last touring gig I am going to take for a while."

"Really? Why? I thought you loved being on the road."

"I used to love being on the road. I guess you get older and your priorities change. I would much rather be on a field trip with B or spending quality time with my Lady."

"You're still sad that you missed Braeden's zoo field trip?" I chuckled.

"Yeah! I love the zoo. I wanted him to experience that with me for the first time. Not some random soccer mom."

"You sad for real!" I laughed.

He laughed too.

We washed each other and got out. He put on a pair of his pajamas that were left at my house while I put on my nightgown.

We laid in the bed together quietly for several minutes before I said, "How is Lyrica doing?"

"She's better now that we know what was wrong with her."

"Was it a virus?"

He hadn't told me if my diagnosis of a virus was accurate for Lyrica, but I was totally off with the diagnosis for myself.

"No, she's pregnant."

My stomach dropped.

"Really? Is she happy about it?"

"I think she is. She seems to be happy. She just found out which is why the doctor told her to chill for a few days. We may even postpone the rest of the tour indefinitely. Obasi wants her to postpone, but of course, Lyrica thinks she will be able to be violently sick every day and still put on a great performance."

I sat quietly for a few minutes thinking about how I should continue this conversation.

"What's on your mind, Z? You got quiet on me."

"I was just thinking about kids. Do you want kids?"

"If you would have asked me this question before I met BJ then I would have told you absolutely not. Now that I have Braeden, I want fifteen more just like him," he chuckled.

I love the way he calls BJ his. I know that he genuinely loves him. Hopefully what I say next will go over well.

"What if the next one would be here in about seven and a half months?"

"Seven and a half months," he chuckled. "You would have to be preg..."

He sat straight up in the bed. I sat up and faced him. He reached over and turned on the light on my nightstand.

"Z, you're pregnant?"

I nodded my head.

"With my baby?"

I nodded my head again. I was searching his face trying to figure out if he was happy or mad. Right now, he looked...confused.

"So, what you're saying is in seven or so months, I'm going to be somebody's father? There is a human being growing in your stomach that we created?" He looked at my stomach and then at me.

I nodded my head.

"Wow," he whispered.

I started feeling nervous not knowing what he was going to say next.

"Ezekiel, I'm sorry. Remember I was adding the flax seed to our shakes? I had no idea that it could interfere with birth control. I mean it's rare but that the only thing I can think of that could have happened. If I had known, I wouldn't have let us go with a con..."

"Z, what are you talking about? Why would you apologize? You don't want to have my baby?"

"What? Yes, I want to have your baby. I thought you were upset and I was trying to explain..."

He interrupted my sentence by leaning in and kissing me.

"I'm very excited. I'm the first one to give Momma a grandbaby. Now she's about to have two! My brothers are going to be so jealous!" he laughed. "Did the virus that you were sick with affect the baby at all? I mean is she okay?"

"I didn't have a virus. It was the baby."

"So, you're good? Our baby is good?"

He said, 'our baby.' That made me smile. I nodded my head.

He leaned into me forcing me onto my back. I opened my legs so that he could lay between them.

"That's why *Bonnie* felt different. Softer, wetter, more responsive; if that's possible. I thought it was just because you missed me."

He kissed my neck knowing he would get a response from me.

"Yeah," I moaned as he kissed the most sensitive area on my neck.

"Let's see if she will respond that way again."

"Let's."

Ezekiel

I'm laying here with Zora in my arms. She fell asleep after our third round. I'm tired, but I'm so wired with the news of my impending fatherhood. I haven't moved my hand from her stomach since I pulled her close to me while she was falling asleep. I'm going to be a Dad.

That is so crazy. I love Peanut already. Yeah, I started calling our baby Peanut in my head as soon as it registered that Zora was pregnant. I didn't think I wanted a Lady or a family, but right now, I couldn't be happier.

I rubbed her flat stomach as I spoke out loud," Hey Peanut. It's your daddy. I just found out about you a couple hours ago, but I love you so much already. Your mommy is going to make sure that you grow big and strong while you are in there. When you come out, your big brother Braeden and I will make sure you are taken care of. I plan on making sure that you have everything that you need for the rest of your life. I want you to know that you were created in love. You have the best mommy. I love your mommy so much and you will too. I can't wait to see you, Peanut. I love you."

I love Zora. I haven't said it out loud until now. I realized I loved her when it became easier to sleep with her in my arms. I knew it when she began to dominate my thoughts. Not because of our amazing sexual chemistry but because of the way she gets this squint in her eyes when she is about to do something mischievous or the way we silently judge people without saying a word to each other. Like one time, we were together at a store in the mall. A woman came out of the dressing room to ask her husband how she looked in a dress. She wasn't a bad looking woman but her breasts were very small, almost non-existent. Her husband told her she filled the dress out nicely. Zora and I locked eyes and both of us knew what the other one was thinking. She was going to need a padded bra with that dress. Another time we were at dinner together and the waitress kept saying 'pacific' or 'pacifically' instead of *specific* or *specifically*. Every time the waitress used the word incorrectly, I would look at Zora. We never said a word but I knew exactly what she was thinking.

I've never told a woman that I love her because honestly, I never have. With Zora, it's different. I want a future with her and my kids. I could not have chosen any better than Zora to be the mother of my children. I guess since she is pregnant now I can say that I wanted the condom to break a long time ago. When we stopped using them, I wanted to hide her birth control. I wanted her to have my baby.

I WALKED into the kitchen the next morning to find Zora making breakfast. She had on my shirt that I wore last night. I walked up behind her putting my arms around her waist. I kissed her neck.

"Good morning, sleepy head."

"Good morning. It smells good in here."

"This is my second go at these eggs. I had to stop cooking the last batch to go and throw up. This morning sickness is wearing me out. When I was pregnant with BJ, I had it for the first three months."

"Awe man. I'm sorry. Here, let me finish cooking this," I moved to take the spatula from her.

"No, I'm okay. Usually, after I throw up a few times in the morning, I'm good."

"So, what else do I have to look forward to during this pregnancy?" I grabbed a cup out of the pantry to pour a cup of coffee.

"Let me think." She moved the eggs from the skillet onto our plates. She walked over to the island and put my plate in front of me. I pulled her between my legs as I sat on the stool. "They say all pregnancies are different, but with BJ, I started out sick in the mornings for the first few months. Then I was horny and hungry all the time."

"So, no different than before the pregnancy then?"

She laughed and hit my arm. "Basically." We laughed.

I pulled her closer to me and rested my hands on her behind.

"How do you feel about this? I know that it was not in your plan to finish your residency pregnant."

"I freaked a little when my doctor told me that I was pregnant, but after I thought about it, I was fine with it. We're together. You are a fantastic role model for BJ, and I know you will be the same for this one. I think the thing that scared me the most was how you would react to the news. I know that you didn't plan on having children."

"It's not that I didn't plan on having kids, I had never thought about it. I'm excited. Mostly because you're her mother." Her eyes filled with tears. "Don't cry."

She smiled, and a couple tears fell.

"You are amazing, and my hormones are all over the place."

She leaned in and kissed me. I grabbed the hem of my shirt that she was wearing and pulled it over her head.

"Your food is going to get cold."

"I'm about to eat."

I led her back to her bedroom.

I FOLLOWED Zora back into the kitchen to help her prepare breakfast, again. I didn't want to leave the bedroom, but I'd worked up an appetite.

"Watch this."

I pulled out my phone to Facetime, my mother.

"Hey, beautiful girl!" I said once her face came into view.

"Hi, baby!" She smiled brightly.

"Zora's here." I moved the phone so both of our faces could be seen.

"Hi, Baby! How are you?"

"I'm good, Momma Grace. How are you?"

Zora had started calling my mother Momma Grace instead of First Lady. My mother requested the change. They are forming a close relationship.

"I'm fine. Thank you for asking. Did you go out on the road to meet Ezekiel?"

"No ma'am."

"No Momma, I'm home for a couple of days. Lyrica had to take a break. Doctor's orders. I flew in last night to spend some time with Zora and Braeden."

"BJ called me last night. He said he was with Doctor Miller."

"He did?" I questioned.

"Yes, he calls at least once every other day. He tells me all of the places he is going to take me when I come for a visit next time."

We all laughed.

"Momma, is Dad around? I want to speak to you both."

"Yes, he's here."

She moved a short distance in the house, and my dad's face could be seen next to hers on the screen.

"Hey, dad! It's good to see you."

"Hi, Son. Hi, Sweetheart."

"Hi Bishop," Zora smiled into the phone.

"Zora and I are having a baby."

"What! Ezekiel! Are you playing with me?" My mother screamed and covered her mouth.

"No," I chuckled, "I'm serious!"

My mother's smile warmed my heart. I didn't really know how they would respond since Zora and I aren't doing things the traditional way.

"I'm going to have two grandbabies! I just don't know what to do with myself!"

We all laughed.

"Congratulations son."

"Thanks, Dad."

"Zora, how are you feeling? How far along are you?" My mother was wiping tears from her eyes.

"I feel okay after I get past the morning sickness. I'm going into my seventh week."

"I was sick with both Roman and Ezekiel. I know what you are going through. Bishop, I have to be there for our grandbaby's birth."

"I know, baby, you will be there, don't worry," my dad assured her.

"I'm so excited! I went from zero grandkids to two in no time flat! You know there's a possibility that this baby could be born with blonde hair like her grandmother and blue eyes like her mother?"

"How do you know it's a girl, Grace?" My dad questioned my mother.

"I just know, Roland. I just know," she smiled. "Call it grandma intuition."

"We are calling her Peanut until she gets an official name."

"See, *her*. Even Ezekiel already knows," my mother winked.

"Alright, son. We will talk soon. I love you. Take care and be safe on the road."

"I love you, baby. I love you, Zora. I will check in on you this week, okay?"

"I love you too, Momma Grace. I will keep you informed."

"I love you both," I said as I disconnected the call. "Have you told BJ?"

"No, I haven't. I haven't told anyone yet."

"Cool, I would like to sit down with him and tell him. After we finish breakfast, I have a run I need to make and then we can go and get BJ."

Zora

Momma Grace and Bishop both seem to be excited about Peanut. I was excited when I first found out, but that was quickly replaced with nervousness. I didn't know what Ezekiel was going to think when I told him. He's excited too.

I hadn't thought about having any more children. I though BJ was it for me. I didn't plan on opening myself up to anyone like I did with Bahir but I've opened myself up for Zeke. I'm so glad I took a chance on him. He has taken care of me and my heart. I know he is going to be an amazing dad because he already is to BJ.

"You have so many people that love you Peanut."

I said out loud as I rubbed my stomach.

I'm going to eat, wear my stomach out, take pictures and enjoy this pregnancy. I'm experiencing it with someone that wants to be with me. I'm so excited.

"Z, I'm back." I heard Ezekiel call from downstairs.

I came down the steps with my purse all ready to go and pick up BJ. He is going to be thrilled to see Zeke. I got to the bottom of the steps and saw Zeke standing there with a bouquet of red roses. I walked up to him to get the roses when he dropped down on one knee. He produced a box from his pocket and held it out as he spoke.

"Zora, will you marry me?"

It felt like someone had sucked all the air out of the room and I couldn't breathe. I looked at the ring and back to Zeke. He was still on his knee waiting for my answer.

"Zeke...um..." I shook my head and backed away.

"Zora, I'm pretty sure that's not how this is supposed to go," he stood and walked towards me.

"I...I...I don't think I want to do this. I like things the way that they are."

"What do mean the way they are?"

"I mean I like how we are. We are good together. Just like this."

"Zora, you are carrying my child. In every way that counts, BJ is my son. Don't you think that this is the next logical step?"

"Yes, but we are not a logical couple. We make our own rules. I don't think marriage should be something that we do just because it's logical."

He looked at me for a minute. I watched him go from confused to angry.

"So how would this work then? I would get to come over and see my kids as long as it suits you?"

"No, Zeke. That's not how it is now. You will always have access to them." He turned and walked away from me. I followed behind him and said, "you could move in, or we could move to your place."

He turned to me and said, "No, I'm not playing house with you. You're either in, or you're out. This thing that we have is changing. There are kids involved, and I don't want them confused as to my role in their lives."

"I don't want them confused either. I'm just saying..."

He interrupted me, "Is there someone else?"

I looked at him confused, "Huh?"

He moved in closer to me, "I said are you fucking someone else?"

"EZEKIEL!" I was shocked that he would mold his mouth to ask me that question but then to use the mother of all curse words. The only expletive I've ever heard him use is damn. I backed out of his space a little. I knew that he was pissed off. I know that he won't put his hands on me, but if looks could kill, I would be six feet under.

"Answer the question, Zora."

"Ezekiel, we..."

He interrupted me again, "ANSWER THE GOTDAMN QUESTION!"

Did he just yell at me like I'm a child? Now I'm pissed.

"First of all, who in the hell do you think you are talking to? Second, as long as you are black and breathing don't you ever raise your voice at me like I'm your child. I am not your child! Third, I'm not going to justify that question with an answer. You know me well enough to know what I will and will not do. If you think that I am going for this old raggedy ass proposal on the strength that your careless ass knocked me up, then you got another thing coming. I don't need you or any other man. I have made it all this time on my own. You can't decide something for my life and think that I won't have a say in it. You can get on with all of that bullshit."

"Get on? Get on, Zora?"

"Yes, I mean with all these demands. Zeke come on this is stupid."

The way he was looking at me was making my heart break. There was anger and fear in his eyes. I want to stop the yelling and have a conversation about it. I understood where he was coming from, and I appreciated the gesture, but I'm not ready for marriage.

"No. Let's go with your original thought. I'm out."

He walked to the door.

"Zeke, come on. We can talk about this without yelling at each other."

"I will call BJ later to talk to him about Peanut."

He slammed the front door.

I looked down and realized I was still holding the flowers that he'd given me. What in the hell just happened? Did we just do that? Did he just walk out? I tried calling his phone, and it went straight to voicemail. I left him a text asking him to call me, but he didn't respond.

I ARRIVED back home after picking up BJ from Doctor Miller's house. My phone rang, and I saw it was Ezekiel Facetiming me. Cool, we can finally talk and hash all of this out.

"Hey," I connected the call.

"Is BJ home?"

He's still pissed.

"Um...yeah...hold on." I passed the phone to BJ.

"My Zeke! Hi." BJ smiled at the phone.

"What's up Lil Man! I miss you!"

"I miss you too! When will you be home?"

"Soon man. It may be sooner than we expected."

"Yay!"

"I'm excited too. I need to talk to you about something very important."

"Okay." BJ sat down on the couch. I sat next to BJ but stayed out of the frame.

"Do you remember when your teacher had a baby in her stomach?"

BJ nodded his head. "Yes, she said that the baby had to linkubate in her stomach. That means her baby had to live in her stomach until he was big enough to come out."

I held in my chuckle and nodded my head as BJ looked pridefully at me.

"Yes, it's incubate, but that's true. Your mommy has a baby in her stomach just like your teacher did. That means you are going to be a big brother."

BJ looked at me and said, "You do?" He eyes were wide as saucers.

"Yes," I smiled.

"How did it get in there?"

"I put Peanut in your Mommy's stomach, so she is my baby too."

"She is?" BJ looked at me to confirm again.

"Yes," I smiled again.

"Peanut has to stay in your mommy's stomach for a few more months then she will be able to come out. I need for you to do something that only a big boy can do. Can you help me?"

"Yes, I'm a big boy. I can help."

"Okay, I need for you to help your mommy. She may be a little sick in the mornings, or she may be sleepier than usual. Can you be on your best behavior until I get back?"

"Yes, I am going to help my mommy and baby Peanut."

"I knew you could do it."

BJ smiled brightly and nodded his head.

I heard a female voice say, "Zeke, we are all about to leave. Are you ready?"

I looked at the phone and saw him looking over his shoulder at a dark skin girl with long black weave parted down the middle.

"Yeah, give me a minute. I'm talking to my Lil man."

She peeked over his shoulder and said, "Oh he's handsome. Hi," she waved.

"Hi." BJ politely responded.

She walked out of frame. Ezekiel turned his attention back to BJ.

"Where are you?" I asked trying to rein in my anger. How in the hell did he just leave here and already has some chick all in his face? He's got some nerve.

"I'm with the tour."

"With the tour? You just lef..."

"I'm back with the tour. I just got back." He mugged me like he was waiting for me to say something else. I mugged him back. He is so lucky BJ is sitting right here.

"Hey BJ, remember you are going to help your mom until I get back."

"Yes sir, I am. I love you."

"I love you too."

Can I speak to your mother?"

BJ handed me the phone.

"Put your earphones in."

Usually, when I was instructed to put my earphones in, he was about to say something naughty. This is about to be a different conversation.

"BJ, go and get ready for bed. I will be in after I get off the phone."

"Okay."

"Goodnight, BJ."

"Goodnight, Zeke."

I waited until BJ left the room. I closed the door before I put my earphones in and said, "How are you back on tour. You said you didn't have to be back until tomorrow evening. I thought you would be back after you cooled off."

"I found a flight leaving out right after I left. So, I caught it. Now, I'm back."

"Why would you do that? We needed to talk through everything that happened."

"I think we said everything that needed to be said."

"How can you say that when we just said a bunch of stuff out of anger."

"Were you angry when you turned down my proposal?"

"No, but I..."

"Look, Zora. I don't feel like it. I just need for you to send me the doctor's appointments for Peanut. I want to work my schedule around them. As far as you and me, we don't have anything to talk about outside of BJ and Peanut. Let's at least be cordial for the kids and the family."

I can't believe he is acting so cold. This is not what I want. I want my family, and that includes Zeke. I just wish he could understand where I am coming from.

"Cordial? Zeke what are you..."

"I will call BJ again as soon as I can."

He disconnected the call.

It felt like someone had ripped my heart from my chest. I felt sick, like I was going to throw up. I ran to the bathroom, but nothing came up. I put some water on my face and went into BJ's room to tuck him in.

"Come on Big Boy, it's time for bed."

BJ climbed into his bed and sat next to me holding on to his drumsticks.

"Mommy is baby Peanut going to sleep in my room?"

"No, I think we are going to give Peanut her own room. Will you help me decorate it?"

"Yes, I will help. My Zeke will help too."

"That would be nice."

I felt the tears trying to come, but I forced them back.

"Come on. Say your prayers." He got on his knees like Zeke taught him and began his prayer.

"Dear God, thank you for my mommy and my Zeke. Thank you for my grandma Grace and my grandpa Bluette. Thank you for my Tee Tee and my uncles Blue and Paxton. Oh, and thank you for Baby Peanut. Amen."

"Amen."

I kissed his forehead and helped him under his covers.

I closed his door and went into my room. As soon as I stepped over the threshold, the tears started falling uncontrollably.

I called Zanetta.

"Hey Sissy," Zanetta said as soon as she answered the phone.

"Hey Sissy," I tried to sound upbeat.

"What's wrong?"

I cleared my throat attempting to clear the large lump that had formed, "You're going to be a Tee Tee again."

"Zora! What! I am?"

"What?" I heard Roman ask in the background.

"You can put me on speaker. I might as well tell everyone at the same time."

"Babe, I will tell you in a minute. I'm going to talk to Zora in the other room." Zanetta spoke to Roman.

"Hey, Sis!" Roman said loud enough for me to hear.

"Tell him I said hello."

"Okay, hang up. I'm going to Facetime you so I can see you."

"Okay."

I disconnected the call and waited a few seconds before my phone was ringing with a Facetime call. I knew as soon as I saw her face I was going to start crying. I didn't even try to fight it.

Her face filled the screen. She saw me and immediately looked concerned.

"What did he do?"

I chuckled even though I didn't feel like laughing. Zanetta was ready to fight and didn't even know what was happening.

"He is excited about Peanut."

"Peanut?"

"Yes, he's already declared the baby is a girl and has nicknamed her Peanut."

"Okay, so what did he do?"

"He asked me to marry him, and I said no. Then he got mad and left." I wiped the tears from my face.

"Left? He was here?"

"Yes, he came in because they had a short break and he said he missed us. We were going to get BJ and spend the day together, then he got down on one knee. I thought he would come back once he cooled down but he got on a plane and met back up with the tour!"

I didn't share the ugly things we said to each other when we argued. I know we were both upset and those words didn't mean anything.

"You don't love him, Sissy?"

"I do Nette, I love him but..."

"How can love have a *but*? Doesn't but negate everything that came before it in the sentence?"

"I love him. I love him so much. I'm excited to be carrying someone that he and I created together. I don't want to be married."

"You don't want to be married, or you're afraid to be married?"

"Both?"

"Are you asking me or telling me? Does this have anything to do with the things you experienced in your past?"

I didn't answer.

"I thought so. You're still letting your past dictate your future? You're never going to fully embrace the present if you keep looking back. You've made it! Do you understand? You made it! In spite of everything that life threw at you, you made it! You have to live and enjoy it!"

"I don't know how Zanetta!"

"You're going to lose the first man that you've ever loved because you don't know how? You didn't know how to be a dentist, but you learned. You didn't know how to be a mom, but you are the best around. You didn't know how to be a best friend, but I can't live without you! You have proven that you can do whatever you want to do!"

"Stop yelling at me!"

"I'm not yelling! I just want you to finally hear me!"

"You're saying I was wrong for turning down his proposal?"

"No, I'm not saying that! I'm saying make your decision based on the present. Not on your past. I'm not taking sides. I just want you to be happy. What do you need from me? Do you want me to come over? Do you want me to call him and curse him out? What do you need?"

"No...I just need you to do what you just did. Tell me the truth."

"I'm happy to be an aunt again. I'm happy that you're in love and I'm happy that I will be around to experience every step with you. Zeke will get out of his feelings and y'all will be okay, I know it."

"You think we will be okay?"

"Yes. I know it. You want me to pray with you?"

I nodded my head, "Please."

Ezekiel

I kept replaying the argument Zora and I had three days ago. I know that the way I asked her to marry me was not the most romantic. I know that I probably should have prefaced my request with I love you or I can't live without you, probably both. Both are true.

I never thought she would say no. Not only did she say no, but she backed away from me like I was some stranger and not the father of the child she is carrying. She's carrying my baby...wow. I know I was wrong for cursing at her and accusing her of sleeping with someone else. That was low...gutter low. She hurt my feelings and my pride, so I lashed out. It was stupid and immature. I need to apologize, but right now, I'm sulking.

I was staying with my mom and dad instead of at the hotel with the band. The last show of the tour was at Madison Square Garden. I didn't feel like being bothered with people.

Lyrica's doctor demanded that she stop the tour. She wanted to fight it, but Obasi made the call for her. We will resume after their baby is born.

My mother knocked on the door before she entered my old bedroom.

"Hi, Baby."

"Hi, mom."

"Can I talk to you for a minute?"

I sat up on the bed, "Sure."

When I arrived, I asked for a little space. I knew my Mom

wanted me to talk to her so that she could find out what was going on but I didn't feel like rehashing the whole thing.

"How are you feeling, sweetheart?"

"Pretty stupid. I overreacted."

I ran down the sequence of events to her. I omitted the yelling and cursing part.

"I can agree that you overreacted. Have you spoken to Zora?"

"No."

I hadn't spoken to her since the conversation we had after the argument. I want to call her, but I don't know what to say.

"Zora reminds me so much of you. Did you know that?"

"Why do you say that?"

"She is driven, and goal focused. Those are two things I admire about you. She had this master plan to keep love out of her life, just like you, but look what happened. You both found each other anyway. Now you both are scared but for different reasons. Instead of figuring it out together you both are hiding.

Marriage is important, very important but did you ever think to ask her why she said no? Does it have anything to do with all the important men in her life abandoning her? Does it have anything to do with the strained relationship she has with her mother? Maybe it could have something to do with her residency?"

"I didn't ask."

"You just walked out of her life like every other important man in her life has done?"

That revelation made me sick to my stomach. Did I do exactly what Braeden's father did? Did I turn my back like her father and brothers did?

"Momma, I didn't realize..."

"I know. I know you didn't but now that you do know, what are you going to do about it? Do you love her?"

"Yes, I do."

"How do you know?"

"I know because she is the first thing I think about when I wake up in the morning followed closely by BJ. Even when I don't have time in my schedule, I figure out a way to at least see her. It could be something as simple as asking her to stay over at my house so when I get home she is there. The smell of her hair on my pillows help me to sleep better at night."

"You're not worried about taking on the responsibility of another man's child?"

"BJ is mine. I know I didn't create him, but I'm molding him. He may not carry my DNA biologically, but he is my legacy. When I look at him, I see pure love."

My mother swiped at a tear that had fallen from her eye, "Have you told her? Have you said these things to her?"

"No, but I show her through my actions."

"Not speaking to her for days or not apologizing is showing her you love her?"

I nodded my head.

"No, it doesn't."

"Fix this Ezekiel. It's your responsibility to make sure your family is whole. Do you understand?"

"Yes, ma'am."

14

"DOCTOR CHAMBERS there are two gentlemen here to see you." Liz, my assistant, said after knocking on my office door.

"Two men?"

"Yes, um..." she looked at piece of paper in her hand, "Roman and Paxton Bluette?"

I walked down the hall to the front desk of my practice. I rounded the corner and saw Roman and Paxton standing by the front desk.

"Roman, Paxton. Hi, what are you doing here?"

Both men smiled.

I noticed the little huddle of women behind the desk whispering and staring at them. I don't blame them. Both men are handsome.

"We came to take our sister to lunch. You are hungry, right?" Roman asked.

"Is the sky blue? Of course, I'm hungry. Pregnant women are always hungry! I am going to grab my purse. I will be right back."

I changed out of my scrubs, used the restroom and grabbed my purse. I went back up front and followed Roman and Paxton out of the office to Paxton's truck.

"What would you like to eat?" Paxton asked.

"Anything. Peanut and I are not particular," I rubbed my stomach.

It seems like as soon as I told people that I was pregnant, I developed a little baby bump. It's small, but it's noticeable.

"How about Italian?" Roman asked.

"Sounds good to us."

We chose an Italian restaurant that was close to the office. We entered the restaurant and were seated immediately by the hostess.

"To what do I owe the pleasure of having two Bluette men as my lunch dates?" I figured it had something to do with Ezekiel.

"The pleasure is all mine. You are my sister, my only sister. I plan on spoiling you the same way my brothers spoil Nette. I always wanted a sister. As a matter of fact, I wanted Ezekiel to be a girl, but God decided to play a cruel joke on me and give me Zeke instead." Roman answered.

"Same here. We were together and decided to come by and check on you. We told Ezekiel we would make sure you were okay while he was away. Now you are toting around a little family member in there, you won't be able to get rid of us." Paxton added.

We all laughed.

"I appreciate you both. I can't say it enough."

After we ordered our food, I was certain that one of them would bring up Ezekiel, but they did not. Roman told me about BJ's piano lessons and how well he was picking up the keyboard. Paxton talked about BJ's bowties and what he wanted to do with the company.

"BJ is so very talented. He can do anything that he puts his mind to," Roman said.

"Yes, and he is such a blessing. He is so excited about being a big brother."

"I'm excited about being an uncle, again. Maybe Peanut is a girl then we will have a nephew and a niece," Paxton added.

"I miss him so much," I blurted.

Roman looked at me and smiled, "I can tell you miss him."

Ezekiel and I hadn't spoken since our argument three days ago. I refused to call because I was being stubborn. I guess he was too. I know we need to talk, but I don't know where to start.

"No, I mean, I miss him so much it's hard to breathe. I miss him so much I can't sleep."

"We didn't bring you out to lunch to discuss Zeke. We really just wanted to check on you and feed you but since you brought him up, did you know that you are the only woman he has ever introduced to our parents?"

I knew that Ezekiel didn't make a habit of introducing women to his parents, but I figured they had at least met one before me.

"It's true. Our parents have never even heard about a female he was dealing with. Ezekiel has always marched to the beat of his own drum, literally!" Paxton added.

We all laughed.

"When we were young, after finding out that his light eyes were a chick magnet, he decided that he was never going to settle down and get married. Remember Pax?"

"Yeah, he always talked about being an eternal bachelor," Paxton chuckled.

"After I got married and settled down, I was positive that he would follow suit, but he didn't. He was serious about staying single. He didn't bring women around my mother at all. He never mentioned being serious about anyone, ever. Oh, and if she had a child? He wouldn't date her. Then you and BJ came along. My brother is talking about what college he wants to send BJ to," Roman explained.

"He introduced you to our mother and father. He's talked about reducing his travel schedule." Paxton interjected.

"He told you about missing the zoo trip?" I laughed.

"Yeah, he did."

We chuckled.

"His whole outlook on life has changed since he met you. I understand why you don't want to be with him, though. He's too immature, right?" Roman questioned.

I shook my head. "No, he is very mature. There is no aspect of him that is immature. I mean he's silly and funny, but when it comes down to business, he handles everything promptly and makes great decisions."

"Oh, well then he must be inconsistent."

"No, if he says he is going to do something, then he does it. Everything he has told me he was going to do, from putting a picture up on my wall to getting the oil changed on my car, he has done it."

"He doesn't show you how he feels about you, right? All words no action?" Roman continued to question.

"I know he loves me. He shows me his love through his actions. He cooks for me. He rubs my feet after a long day. He takes BJ for hours at a time so I can rest. He prays with me."

"Then, what is the problem?" Paxton asked.

"I am the problem. There are things about me that would ruin his opinion of me. I am messed up."

Roman passed me a handkerchief so that I could wipe my face. I was crying all over the place.

"I don't believe that there is anything that you could tell my brother that would change the way he feels about you. Except, did you have anything to do with his pet turtle dying when he was in the third grade?" Roman asked.

"What was that turtle's name? Oh, Speedy!" Paxton chuckled.

"Zeke loved that turtle. One day he came home, and the turtle had 'gone on to be with the Lord.' Those were the words my father used when he broke the news to him," he chuckled as he thought back. "Zeke swore up and down that someone did something to that turtle. Was it you?"

I chuckled and nodded my head, "No, I didn't do anything to his turtle."

"Then you are good."

"I wish it were that simple. I was..."

Roman cut me off, "Don't tell us. You need to tell Ezekiel first. If you feel like you need to talk to us about it after you tell him, then we will be here for you. I don't want you to tell me and then think that Ezekiel and I will have the same reaction."

"We have your back Zora, okay? Anything you need. We're here. I know that my brother is crazy about you and you feel the same about him. It's not every day a person finds that one person that gets them, you know? Talk to him for me, please." Paxton finished.

"Okay, I will."

Ezekiel

"I'm sorry," I said as soon Zora answered her phone.

It had been four days since we'd spoken and I was a mess. I didn't know how to apologize, so I just blurted it out as soon as she answered the phone. I wasn't sure she would answer. After talking to my mother and realizing how my leaving probably made Zora feel, I knew I needed to call. Between getting prepared for the last show, packing up and getting to the airport, I didn't have the time to call her until now. I thought about taking the coward way out and sending a text, but I hurt the woman that I love, and I had to man-up and fix it. I was sitting in the airport waiting to board my flight, but I couldn't go another minute without apologizing.

"I'm sorry too," she said softly.

I exhaled a deep breath and moved further into the corner I'd found near the airport gate where I would be boarding my flight.

"Z, I overreacted. I was stupid."

"I miss you."

"I miss you too. How are you feeling? How are my kids?"

"I feel okay. BJ and Peanut are good."

"Aye Zeke! They are boarding the plane." One of the band members called from behind me.

"Alright. I'm coming."

"Z, I'm about to board the plane. I will be back in enough time to get ready for church. Can you have BJ ready for me? I would like to take him with me. After church can we talk?"

"Yes, he's going to be so excited. I would like to talk."

"Cool, I have to go."

I didn't want to hang up. I wanted to tell her that I loved her. I needed her, and I couldn't live without her, but I needed to say it in person.

"Okay. Zeke?"

"Yeah, Z?"

"...dream about me?"

"Even when I'm awake."

I ARRIVED in Houston with enough time to get to my house, shower, change and head to Zora's house to pick up BJ for church. I was nervous and excited to see them both.

"Zeke! You're home!"

BJ came running down the hall as I entered Zora's house.

"Hey, big man." I kissed him on the cheek and gave him a hug. "I missed you so much!"

"I missed you too!"

"Guess what?"

"What?"

"I'm home for good. I'm not on tour anymore."

"You're not?"

"Nope, I'm not leaving again for a while. Were you a big boy for your Mommy like I asked you to be?"

"Yes, I was. My apple stayed on the tree at school."

"Great job Man! I have some things I brought you back, but they are at my house. We will get them later, okay?"

"Okay!"

"You look nice today. Is this one of the new designs from your bowtie collection?" He was wearing a colorful plaid bow tie with his denim shirt and khaki pants.

"Yes, Tee Tee helped me pick out the fabric."

"You did a great job. I'm proud of you. Do you know that?"

"Yes, 'cause you tell me that all the time."

"That's because it's true! I missed you too, so much!" I hugged him again.

As I was finishing my sentence, Zora appeared in the hallway wearing a fitted black dress and hot pink stilettos. She had my undivided attention as she walked towards us.

"Welcome back," she smiled.

"Thank you."

I examined her from head to toe. She was wearing her hair down with a part in the middle. I love it when she wears her hair that way. She had on a little makeup and pink lipstick that made her lips extra kissable. Peanut filled the dress out in her midsection. She's starting to show. It's not a whole lot but because her stomach was flat before it's very noticeable. I wanted to touch her, but I knew that I had some more apologizing to do before I touched her like that.

"You look stunning, Z. Are you headed somewhere?"

"Yes, I'm going to church with you guys if that's okay."

"That's okay Mommy, right Zeke?"

"Of course it is, Big Man."

Zora smiled.

I missed her smile. She grabbed her purse off the table and followed BJ out of the house. I locked the front door and proceeded to open her door to my truck.

I helped her in and closed her door. I walked to my side thinking this is how Sundays are supposed to be. My little man, my Lady and my baby all on the way to church together.

I pulled into the street headed in the direction of the church.

"Does Lil Sis know you are coming?"

"No, I thought I would surprise her. I didn't want her making a big fuss over me being there."

BJ carried the conversation as we made our way down the highway to the church. He seemed to be excited that his mom was joining us for church. I know I was.

I reached for Zora's hand. She laced her fingers in mine. I smiled and kissed the back of her hand. I know we still have a lot to talk about, but this gesture lets me know that things were going to be okay.

I pulled up to the church and parked in my usual spot. I let BJ out of the truck first and then opened Zora's door. I held her left hand to help her out of the truck. I glanced at her finger wishing my ring was there.

We went through the side door of the church that leads to the offices. I knocked on Blue's office door. Nette opened the door and squealed when she saw Zora standing beside me.

"Sissy! You're here!"

BJ and I walked into the office while Nette hugged Zora.

"Come in Sissy! I'm so glad you are here!"

"Hey Lil Sis," Roman also hugged Zora. "It's good to see you."

"What's up Zora. Glad you're here." Paxton hugged her. "How are you feeling?"

"I'm good, Pax," she smiled.

"You can sit next to me just in case you need to go to the restroom or anything during service," Nette said excitedly.

"Where do you sit? Not up there where Roman sits right? I can't be up on no stage. I'm here but don't push it, Sissy."

"Zora," Zanetta laughed, "You know I would not have you sitting up in the pulpit! We all sit on the floor on the front row. We can sit near the door to this area just in case you need to leave for any reason."

"Oh, okay, cool."

We all filed out of the office. I took BJ to children's church and took my position on the drums. Zora walked out of the back with Nette and sat next to her. I watched her the entire time I was on the drums. She seemed to be enjoying the service. After the praise and worship portion of the service, I usually sit with the other musicians in the office and watch the service from there until we are needed on the instruments again. This Sunday, I had the Usher save me a seat next to Zora. I went and sat by her before Roman began his message. She grabbed my hand as soon as I sat down.

"Because your loving kindness is better than life, my lips shall praise you!" Roman exclaimed.

The church responded by clapping, standing and saying amen.

"I'm a movie person. Some people are more television people, but I like movies. Who else likes movies?"

Some people in the congregation raised their hands.

"One of my most favorite movies is The Wiz. It's the African-American adaptation of The Wizard of Oz, just in case you didn't know. My wife enjoys the original version more than she likes the adaptation. I informed her that her black card is in jeopardy for speaking such blasphemy."

People laughed. He smiled and winked at Zanetta.

"The premise of the movie is that there is a young woman who finds herself in a strange place and is trying to get back home. She encounters some obstacles as she follows this path to get her to the person that can ultimately get her back home. She meets people who are willing to walk this path with her and others who are only on the road with her to deter her or hinder her progress.

Did you know that we are all like Dorothy? We are all on a road going somewhere. That somewhere is our destiny. In the Bible, we see this story over and over again. Let's use Joseph as an example. Joseph's ultimate destiny was to be the person that saved his family from the famine. His brothers were on the road with him to his destiny. They were like the accordion people in The Wiz. They were not on the road to help him, they were there to deter him. They threw him into a pit and then sold him into slavery. Guess what? He still made it to his destination.

We can use Jesus as an example. Jesus was on the road to his destiny. He had people on the road that wanted to see Him succeed. He also had people on the road that wanted to see him fail. Guess what? He still made it to his destination. We are so grateful that He did!"

The audience applauded.

"There is a scripture in Ecclesiastics that talks about seasons. We all have seasons in our life. There are some friends that you will see you through to your destination, and there are some that are seasonal. They may be like the munchkins who could only point Dorothy in the direction of the yellow brick road but could not make the trip with her. Then there will be some friends like the Scarecrow, Tin Man and Lion that will make the journey with you.

You have to be aware of those that are ordained to walk with you and those that are ordained to point you in the direction you're supposed to go. People are placed in your life for three purposes: a reason, a season or a lifetime. Don't confuse people's purposes in your life. Understand that on your road to destiny you will have to leave some people behind.

Could you imagine if Dorothy had to make that trip with all of those singing little people? At some point, she would have turned around and said, "Shut up!" Well, that's what I would have done. You know what it's like when you are trying to follow directions and you turn the radio down? Like the volume of the radio somehow helps you navigate better."

The audience laughed again.

"They were ordained to encourage her to begin, but they were not ordained to follow her through to the end. Out of all of the people she met, only three saw her to her destination. Please don't be sad when your level of growth or progression causes you to have to leave some people behind. They were not ordained to go with you in the first place. You cannot take them with you. They will hinder you from getting to where you are going. They will make your trip longer, more strenuous and you will miss the blessings along the way.

If Dorothy had taken all the Munchkins with her, she might not have stopped to slide a little oil to the Tin Man. She probably would have missed his muffled cries for help because of all the singing the Munchkins would have been doing."

The audience laughed.

"Beloved, let me encourage you today. If you find yourself not progressing, not moving forward, not seeing that next destination that you were promised, re-evaluate who you have along for the ride. Do you have a reason with you or are you stuck with a season?"

Zora didn't move during Roman's message. She took notes on her phone and stayed fully engaged. When Roman called a prayer line, she didn't get up to go to the line, but she did ask Zanetta to pray with her.

After they prayed together, I said, "I'm going to get B from children's church."

"I will come with you. I would like to know how it works so I can take him if I need to."

Her response made me pause. Does this mean that she is going to come back? I would love it if my whole family were here with me on Sundays.

I placed my hand on the small of her back to direct her through the crowd to the children's church. I held out my wristlet with a bar code on it. It is used to check the children in and out. That way we aren't passing children out to the wrong adult.

"Hi, Brother Ezekiel. Welcome back."

"Sister Janet," I smiled, "Thank you. This is BJ's mother, Zora."

"Well, aren't you beautiful! Look at those blue eyes!"

Sister Janet is one of the women that oversees the children's ministry. She's worked with children for years. All the children love her.

Zora smiled, "Thank you, Sister Janet."

"Oh, and look at that glow. Do you know what you are having yet?"

"No, ma'am, I don't know yet. We are hoping for a girl but either way I will be happy," Zora smiled.

"What a beautiful baby that is going to be," she winked at me. I smiled back at her.

BJ ran up to the door with a juice packet and a bag of Cheez-its.

"Mommy! I learned about a man that was living in a big fish until God saved him."

"Wow, you will have to tell me all about it."

"I will. Bye Sister Janet. I love you."

"I love you too, BJ."

BJ held my hand and Zora's hand as we walked to my truck.

"We are going to dinner at Blue and Nette's house, right?" I asked Zora as I helped her into the truck.

"Yes, I would like to go and change before we go over there."

"Okay, hey B, what did you learn today?"

We drove back to her house. BJ told us the story he learned in children's church about the man that lived in the fish. Some of his facts were a little distorted so Zora, and I had to correct him, but he had most the story correct.

We arrived at the house.

"BJ, go to your room and change out of your clothes into some play clothes. Bring your swim trucks. You may be able to get in the pool."

He took off running to his room.

"B!" I yelled. "I know you're not running!"

He stopped and started walking, "No sir, I'm walking."

Zora turned with her back facing me and said, "Can you unzip this?"

I reached for the zipper and slowly pulled it down. I watched as her beautiful brown skin was exposed. It looked so soft. God, I missed her so much. I got to the bottom of the zipper track and couldn't stop myself from wrapping my arm around her waist and pulling her into me. I rested my hand on her stomach and buried my face in her neck.

"I'm sorry," I said while still resting my face in her neck.

"I'm sorry too," she whispered.

She turned around to face me. We stared at each other for a few minutes before BJ yelled, "Zeke!"

"What's up man?" I asked without taking my eyes off Zora.

"I pooped!"

We looked at each other and laughed.

"I missed hearing that! Go and get changed. I will take care of him."

I pulled her into me and lightly kissed her on the lips.

"We will talk after dinner, right?"

"Right," she smiled.

She turned and went to her room to change. I went and tended to BJ.

"WELCOME HOME, ZEKE," Zanetta hugged me as we entered the house.

"Thanks, Lil Sis."

We walked into the living room and saw a new face.

"Olivia Callahan, this is my best friend Zora and my brother, Pastor Roman's youngest brother Ezekiel. Olivia is the new director of the Academy."

"I saw you both at church this morning. It's nice to meet you." Olivia extended her hand.

She shook Zora's hand then mine.

"Zora, Olivia you want to help me in the kitchen?" Nette asked.

I know that's girl code for let's talk without the men listening.

"I got B," I smiled.

Zora

I decided after my quick phone call with Zeke last night that I was going to go to church. It was time. I had to face those things that I ran from so many years ago. I was starting with church. I thought that I would feel weird being there, but it was so peaceful. It felt like a part of the puzzle of my life was finally in place. One of the singers on the praise team sang *Center of my Joy*. Richard Smallwood sang it originally. My dad would sing it at church. I loved hearing him sing it. He always said it was his favorite song. Hearing it today brought back so many memories. I still remembered all the words.

I am overjoyed to have Zeke back home. I know we need to talk. I am prepared to be completely honest with him. I need him to understand why I said no.

"What's for dinner? I'm hungry!" I asked after I followed Zanetta into her kitchen.

"Pot roast, roasted potatoes, and green beans," Zanetta replied.

"Is there something to eat now? I'm starved!" I rubbed my stomach.

"It's some fruit in the refrigerator, Drama Queen."

I chose the red grapes that were in the fridge then sat next to Olivia at the island.

Olivia was shorter than me but taller than Nette. Her close-set brown eyes had a sadness to them that she tried to mask. I can see sadness because I am so familiar with the emotion. Above her eyes, she had thick, full eyebrows that looked like they'd never seen a piece of thread, wax or a razor. Her natural brown hair was pulled back into a ponytail. I could tell her hair was long by the way she had it tucked into a knot. She was basic but pretty. She had a beautiful smile and nice teeth. Her dress was too big for her, in my opinion. I could tell when I walked into the kitchen behind her that she was hiding some curves.

"Olivia, are you from Houston?" I asked while popping a grape into my mouth.

"No, I'm from Savannah, Georgia. I moved to Houston after my divorce. Well actually before my divorce...that's a long, complicated story."

"He messed up, huh?" I asked while popping another grape into my mouth.

"Yes, he did, terribly."

She looked a little sad, so I didn't press her for more information about her divorce.

"You will be the director of the academy at the church?"

"Yes, I was fortunate to be selected for the position," Olivia said meekly.

"Please, you are the most qualified plus you did so well during all your interviews. We are fortunate to have you." Zanetta responded.

"Do you have family here?" I asked.

"No, I don't have any family here. That is one of the reasons why I chose Houston. I wanted a fresh start. I needed to go where no one knew my name. I spent a lot of years in my ex-husband's shadow. Now I want the sun to shine on me so that I can cast my own shadow."

"I know that's right!"

"I've survived having lived with one of the most heartless, callous, vile, vituperative, supercilious people on earth; my ex-husband. Now I just want to live."

I saw how much anger was behind each word she said.

"You better use your words! Come through thesaurus!"

We all laughed. We needed something to lighten the mood.

"I'm sorry. It was a hard time in my life."

"You don't have to apologize! We are glad you are here now," Nette said.

"I'm glad too. Everyone has been so nice and helpful."

"Especially Paxton," Nette smiled.

I looked between Nette and Olivia. Nette nodded and smiled.

"Really?" I questioned.

Olivia nodded and blushed.

That's interesting.

"Sissy, do you want BJ to stay with us tonight?"

"I don't know if you will be able to get him away from Zeke, but that would be great if he could stay."

It would be easier for Zeke and me to talk without BJ being there. I don't want him to overhear what I need to say to Ezekiel.

Zanetta cooked a ton of food like she does almost every Sunday dinner. We ate, laughed, debated and enjoyed each other's company. It felt good having everyone together again.

"Zora, you met Olivia?" Paxton asked.

"I did Pax, Nette introduced us."

I thought back to me and Paxton's conversation at the release party and smiled.

Olivia fit right in. Paxton sat next to her. He studies her like these Bluette men have a tendency to do. It was interesting to see this side of him. I'm so used to him being the quiet protector. He was fully engaged in the conversation and trying to get to know Olivia. She seems to be a little shy but the way he is already all in her space, I don't see that shyness lasting too long.

Zeke

I noticed Zora yawning.

"Are you ready to go home?"

She nodded.

I didn't think BJ would go for spending the night with Blue and Nette, but he had fallen asleep, so we were going to leave him with them. I'm sure he will be calling me first thing in the morning to come and pick him up.

Zora and I rode back to her house. I held Zora's hand while I drove. Neither one of us said anything. We both were immersed in our own thoughts. I was going over everything in my head that I needed to say to her. I needed to apologize for cursing at her. I needed to let her know that it was never my intention to make her feel like the men in her past made her feel.

We made it to her house. I turned off the engine and sat for a moment.

"It's time to talk, right?"

"Yes, it is."

I opened my door and came around to open her door. I led her into the house by her hand. We sat on the couch in the living room.

"Let me go first, Zeke."

"No, I need to go first because I need to say..."

"No, Zeke, I really need to say this because..."

"Z, I know but it's not really necessary to..."

We were talking over each other until she yelled, "BJ was not my first pregnancy!"

Zora

Ezekiel stopped talking and looked at me like I had two heads.

I stood from the couch and backed into the wall as I continued to talk.

"BJ was not my first pregnancy because I was pregnant when I was seventeen years old. I was pregnant when I was seventeen years old because..." I took a deep breath and continued. "I was pregnant when I was seventeen years old because I was molested by my uncle and he got me pregnant."

Ezekiel shot up from the couch and came to stand in front of me.

He reached for me, but I waved my hand, "Let me finish please, Zeke." I closed my eyes to hold in the tears that were threatening to fall. I took another deep breath.

"My uncle, my mother's brother, started molesting me when I was fourteen years old. He moved in with us after he and his wife divorced. I told my mother the first time he touched me and she said that she didn't believe me. She said that if it were true, it's because I was fast and probably did something to provoke it. Even though I was a virgin and sex was the furthest thing from my mind. I never told my father because he was so wrapped up in the church. I felt like his response would have been the same as my mother's. Besides, I know she told him. She wouldn't keep something like that a secret."

I glanced at Ezekiel. He was quiet, but I noticed his jaw muscles clenched.

"My brothers were already gone out of the house basically, and they never came back to check on me. I thought about calling my oldest brother, Countee and telling him but my uncle told me if I told them, he would murder them in their sleep. I believed him because he had been locked up before. I didn't know why he was in jail, but I knew he had been in."

I wiped the tears from my face and continued. "I know that it was stupid to believe that he would murder them but I did. I believed him. Since my parents were so into working in the church, he had a lot of opportunities to get to me. They wouldn't let me go anywhere, so I was always home. He took my virginity, my innocence away from me. He stole it, and I knew I could never get it back. I never just laid there and took it. I fought. I fought until I was exhausted. That's when he would rape me.

I found out I was pregnant about two weeks before I graduated from high school. I had already decided that after I graduated, I was leaving home and never looking back. I didn't tell Nette that I was pregnant before I left because I knew that a secret that big would be too hard for her to hold on to. I did tell her that my uncle touched me, but I didn't tell her about the rape until we were in New York. I made her promise not to tell Uncle JD and Auntie because I knew they would force my parents to do something and then they would hate me even more. At least that was my reasoning at the time.

I saved up some money and purchased a one-way bus ticket to New York. I stayed in a homeless shelter for a couple of days before I could go to my school. The lady at the homeless shelter and the woman at my school helped me get a summer job. They also directed me to a clinic where I got an abortion at no cost to me. I had the hardest time going through with the abortion. I was tormented at night feeling like God would hate me because I did it. Then once I did it, I felt nothing. I thought God would curse me for not caring about killing a life.

I wanted to take control of my sexuality. I didn't want to be afraid to have a real relationship with a man. So, I went through my hoe stage. Then I meet Bahir. He treated me so nice. He was attentive and persistent. I adjusted my plans to be with him. I got pregnant with BJ, and he was around for a little...then one day, he was gone. Poof! Into thin air.

I evaluated my track record with men. My daddy was too busy with church to see that he had a pedophile living in his home. My brothers were all too busy with their lives to even come by and check on me. Bahir got me pregnant and left me. Now, there is you."

"Zora, I..."

"Let me finish, please. I love you more than air. Like if I had to choose between breathing and loving you, I would choose loving you. I'm no good for you Zeke. I have a terrible past. You have built a brand with your drumkit, your studio, and your businesses. Being married to me would tarnish all of that. I can't ruin your life and everything you've built. That's why I said no."

Ezekiel stepped in front of me and placed his hands on the wall locking me into place.

"Zora, what are you talking about?" He used his thumb and first finger to move my chin so that I was looking at him. "Tarnish? How could you tarnish anything?"

"You are good Ezekiel. I'm not," I looked down again.

He moved my face again and said, "Z, look at me." I made eye contact with him as he continued. "You are not responsible for what that asshole did to you. You were a baby, and he took advantage of you. There is a special place in hell for him. He better hope that I'm not the one that sends him there."

He took my face in both of his hands.

"Do you understand that none of that was your fault? None of it Zora."

I nodded my head as he pulled me into a hug.

"You are perfect for me. Your past is just that, your past. You are an Ivy League educated, Oral and Maxillofacial surgeon that graduated at the top of her class and is the partner of a highly successful dental practice. Zora, I went to a state college, and I play the drums for a living. If anyone is not good enough, it's me."

"Don't say that Zeke."

"It's true. I knew you were out of my league when I first met you, but I wanted you so bad that I at least had to try. Every day I would wake up with you in my arms, and I would thank God that is was not a dream. I knew at some point you would come to your senses and see me for who I am, but you didn't until I asked you to marry me."

"That's not what it was at all Zeke."

"I realize that now. We were both afraid, but we were afraid of different things. I love you so much, Zora."

"You do?"

"Yes, I do. I didn't think that I would ever want to love a woman, but I live to love you and BJ. I'm sorry."

His lips crashed onto mine with so much passion. He pulled me into a tight hug.

"I'm sorry baby. I'm sorry for what your uncle did to you. I'm sorry that you had to go through the abortion on your own. I'm sorry that your family didn't believe you. I'm sorry Bahir walked away. I'm sorry that I was afraid and didn't understand. I'm sorry that I raised my voice and cursed. I'm sorry that I left instead of listening to you. I'm sorry it took me four days to call you and apologize. I apologize for every man in your life that has wronged you. Please let me make it up to you."

I cried harder and harder with each I'm sorry. It felt like each time he said it a little piece of me was put back together.

"We don't have to get married as long as I know that you are mine, I will take you any way that I can get you."

"I'm your's, Zeke."

"Do you forgive me for walking away. For being selfish, immature and petty?"

I laughed.

"Yes, I forgive you. Do you forgive me for not expressing how I felt sooner? For not giving you the full story a long time ago?"

"Yes, I forgive you."

"Prove it."

He smiled as he lifted me into his arms and started walking to my bedroom.

"I was hoping you would say that."

Zora

After our talk, we made love all night. I missed him so much. His apology meant so much to me. Then he told me that he loves me! He is the first man to ever say that to me. I've never heard it from my father or my brothers. Bahir never said it. Ezekiel did. I wish I could describe the way those words made me feel. The closest description would be like the feeling you get when you are extremely thirsty, and you finally get something to drink. Sometimes you can feel the liquid coat your stomach. That's the way those words made me feel. It was like something coating me from my head down to my feet. I literally felt his words.

"Doctor Chambers."

The OB nurse was calling me back for my appointment. This is Ezekiel's first prenatal appointment with me. We stood together and followed the nurse to the small examination room.

"You don't have to take off anything as long as the doctor has access to your stomach. Please have a seat on the table. The doctor will be in shortly."

I climbed up on the table while Ezekiel roamed around the room touching things. He looked at all the posters. Then he touched the model of the uterus. He was nervous.

"Babe, here is a seat. Come and sit down."

He sat down and reached for my hand.

"What is he going to do today? Will we be able to see Peanut?"

"I'm not sure."

As soon as I finished my sentence, the doctor entered the room.

"Doctor Chambers it's good to see you again," he smiled.

"Doctor Ingram, it's good to see you too. This is my boyfriend, Ezekiel Bluette."

Doctor Ingram extended his hand to Ezekiel. They shook.

"Bluette...you're not related to Roman Bluette are you?"

"Yes, I am. He's my brother."

"Wow, small world. I visited his church for the first time last week. I was very impressed."

"Thank you. You are always welcome."

"I plan on returning. So, Doctor Chambers, how are you feeling?"

"Aside from the morning sickness, I'm good."

"Great, let's have you lay back on the table so we can measure you and get a look at baby Chambers."

"Baby Bluette," I corrected.

"Of course."

I laid back on the table and lifted my shirt above my small bump. I rolled the top of my scrubs pants down to give him total access. He pulled out a small measuring tape and measured my stomach. He wrote the measurement down on my chart. He turned on the Doppler machine and put in on my stomach. He moved it around until Peanut's heartbeat filled the room.

"What is that?" Ezekiel asked.

"That's your son or daughter's heartbeat."

Ezekiel pulled out his phone and tapped a few buttons.

"I'm recording this."

He beamed with pride while Doctor Ingram held the machine in place to let Ezekiel record it. I watched him close his eyes and listen like he was listening to a song. He opened his eyes and smiled at me. A couple of tears fell that he quickly wiped away.

"You know, we may be able to get a peek at baby Bluette."

"An ultrasound?"

"Yeah would like to see her or him?"

"Absolutely!" Ezekiel responded.

I smiled and nodded in agreement.

Doctor Ingram put the jelly on my stomach and turned on the ultrasound machine. It didn't take but a moment for Peanut to show up on the screen.

"There is your baby," Doctor Ingram pointed to the screen.

Ezekiel stood and held my hand.

"This is the arm. Here is the little heart beating. Look, there is a leg."

I watched him point to the monitor, but it was hard to see through the tears that were falling. I was already so in love with this little baby.

"Look at daddy's baby," Ezekiel whispered while Doctor Ingram continued to point out body parts.

He finished the ultrasound. He printed out a couple of pictures and handed them to Ezekiel.

"Well mom and dad, the baby looks healthy. I will see you back here next month."

"Thank you, Doctor," Ezekiel replied.

Doctor Ingram left the room.

Ezekiel helped me sit up after I wiped the jelly off my stomach.

"Did you see my baby?"

"I did," I smiled.

"She's beautiful, isn't she?"

"Zeke, what if she's a he?"

"She's not," he said confidently.

He helped me down off the table then said, "Z, where did you find this Doctor? Soap Opera Doctors-R-Us?"

"Shut- up Zeke," I laughed. "He delivered a couple of the partner's babies."

"You're lucky I'm secure in my manhood!" He said as he held the door open for me to exit.

I laughed again.

"You're stupid!"

It's funny because when I first met Doctor Ingram, I thought he could be an actor or a model. He is fine.

AFTER SHARING the pictures of Peanut with Braeden and letting him hear the heartbeat, we ate dinner and put him down.

Zeke was doing one of my most favorite things, rubbing my feet. I had my eyes closed enjoying the sensation of his huge, coarse hands massaging my feet.

"Z, where is your uncle now?"

He hadn't asked me any questions about my uncle since I shared with him a few days ago.

"I think he is still in Saint Louis. I don't know. Since I haven't talked to anyone in my family, I'm not sure where he is."

"Do you think you should have a conversation with your parents about everything that happened?"

"Yes, I do. I would like to sit down with them and ask why they didn't believe me. I would like for them to know what he did to me."

"If we could organize that meeting, would you do it?"

"Yes, I would."

"Good, then we will be going to Saint Louis in the next couple of days. I'm going to locate that bitch ass child predator as well."

"Zeke, I don't think it will be that easy. My parents don't care..."

"Z, don't say that. We just had a whole huge misunderstanding based on misconceptions and fear. I'm not going to let you continue down this road. If your parents and your brothers don't want anything to do with you, then let them tell you to your face. None of them have said it, outside of that letter you received from your mother. You have assumed, and so have they. You've never told them that you don't want to have anything to do with them, right?"

"Right."

"Then let's stop assuming and get to the bottom of this whole thing."

I had never thought about it like that. What if it is a misunderstanding? What if I can get my family back? BJ can know his uncles and his grandparents. That would be wonderful. I sat quietly thinking about how different things could be this time next week while Zeke massaged my feet. If I could fix my relationship with my family, I will be content, but if I can't, I am so very happy with Zeke, BJ, and Peanut. Either way, at least I will know.

Ezekiel

We walked into The Encounter Worship Center in Saint Louis. Zanetta's uncle, Pastor DeLucas felt it would be the best location for the family meeting. I contacted him after Zora said that she wanted to meet with her family. Roman said it would be important to have a neutral party present to mediate. He knew he couldn't be that neutral party because all he wanted to do was find the uncle and take care of him.

Zora shared her story with my brothers and Zanetta. As hard as it was to hear again, I held her hand as she said the same things to them as she said to me. It took so much control to listen to her tell me the details of what her uncle did to her. I wanted to walk right out of the house, find him and murder him. I hate that she had to experience all those things on her own. She's mine now. I'm going to make sure no one ever hurts her again. Part of the reason why I wanted to have this meeting is that I want her to be able to close the door on her past. I want her to know the reasons why things went the way they did when she was growing up. I need for her to be whole for our family but most importantly for herself.

"Zora, Ezekiel, it's good to see you both."

"Hi Uncle JD." Zora hugged him. I shook his hand.

"Come on in. Your family is already here."

Zanetta refused to let Zora come to this meeting without her. BJ stayed behind at the hotel with my brothers. I didn't know what we would be walking into. They were going to take him to breakfast and to the park to keep him entertained.

Zora, Zanetta and I followed Pastor DeLucas into the office. Zora's mother and father were seated along with her three brothers. No one spoke as we took the seats across from them. Zora looks a lot like her father and her oldest brother Countee. No one else has blue eyes, but they all look related.

"We are going to have a quick word of prayer, and then we are going to get started."

Pastor D said a prayer. He finished it with amen and spoke again. "We are here because Ezekiel called me and asked me to mediate a meeting between your family. If you don't know, Ezekiel is Zanetta's brother in law and him and Zora are expecting a child together. I have prayed a long time for this family's reconciliation, and I believe that God is answering my prayer. The key is getting to the root of the problem and dealing with it. We can agree that one of the things that caused the division is when Zora left after graduation and cut off communication with all of you. I would like for you to start Zora. I would just ask that everyone, please let her say everything she needs to say without interrupting her. Everyone will have a chance to speak. Zora."

I moved in closer to Zora and held her hand as she began to speak.

Zora

I cleared my throat and sat up straight.

I'd been so nervous about having this meeting with my family. I had considered all the worse outcomes. They could all tell me that they hate me. They could still call me a liar. They may listen but still not want anything to do with me. Zeke and Zanetta have kept me from flipping out every time I think about it. I'm glad we could schedule this meeting so quickly.

"Thank you, Uncle JD for being here. I wanted to have this meeting because I need to explain why I left home when I was seventeen. First, I want to apologize for the heartache I caused with my decision to leave." My mother made a tsk noise with her throat like she could care less. I glanced over at her but continued, "I know now as an adult that it could have been handled better. It should have been handled better, but at the time, it felt like the only thing I could do."

I braced myself to speak the next words out loud to my family. I felt Ezekiel scoot a little closer and Zanetta held my other hand.

I took a deep breath and said, "When I was fourteen years old, Uncle Humphrey started molesting me."

My mother went into a whole tirade.

"Here you go with these lies. I thought we were coming here for you to finally say something that is not a lie but you don't know how to tell the truth, do you?"

"First Lady, I'm going to remind you of what I said before. Please don't interrupt Zora. Let her speak," Uncle JD shut her down.

I continued, "Humphrey started molesting me when I was fourteen years old." I looked over at my brothers. All three were watching me, waiting for me to continue. I didn't have enough courage to look at my father. "When y'all would go to church and leave me alone in the house with him, he took full advantage of the time. At first, he would touch me inappropriately then he moved on to full penetration. He stole my virginity from me and made me clean the sheets that I bled on." I fought so hard to keep the tears from falling, but it didn't work. At this point, I had tears and snot running down my face. "He told me that if I told anyone they wouldn't believe me. He told me that the boys didn't care about me because they never come around to check on me. He said that if I did tell them that he would murder them in their sleep." I heard Amiri release a breath and sit back in his chair. "He continued to molest me until it was time for me to graduate from high school. I missed my period, went to planned parenthood and found out that I was pregnant."

Uncle JD shoved a trash can into my father's hands just as he was throwing up. Uncle JD went into the bathroom and brought out a towel for my father to wipe his face. My dad didn't look up from the towel as I continued. "I left after graduation with a one-way ticket to New York. I told one of the women that worked at my school what happened, and she made sure I got the abortion and set me up with a small job so that I could live in the dorms for the summer."

I finished my last sentence, and the room was silent. I looked at my brothers, and each one was deep in thought. Countee pulled out

his phone and tapped away for several seconds before he put it away
and stared off into space.

"Do you have anything else you need to say, Zora?"

I nodded my head at Uncle JD.

"Like I said, this has all been a colossal waste of our time. She
brought us here to tell lies and disgusting lies at that!" My mother
spat while looking at me like I repulsed her.

"Why didn't you say something?" My father finally spoke, but he
said it so low that I almost missed it.

I looked at him, and we finally made eye contact.

"I did say something the first time he touched me," I cried.

"To whom? Who did you say something to?" I could see the
agony in his eyes.

"I told Mom," I whispered.

"She has always been such a liar. I wasn't going to let her tell
those lies on my brother when he..."

Before she could finish her sentence, my father lunged at her. She
fell backward out of her chair trying to get away while my brothers
jumped in front of my father just before he got his hands on her.
Ezekiel jumped in front of Zanetta and me while my mother ran to
the corner of the room. My brothers wrestled with my dad for several
minutes. He was taking on all three of them until he realized he
couldn't get past them.

"James, you tried to put your hands on me!" My mother screamed
at my father.

"No," my dad said in a cool tone while my brothers stood in front
of him, "I was not trying to put my hands on you. I was about to take
your life."

Ezekiel moved to the side of me once my dad calmed down.

"James!" My mother yelled.

"You knew that bastard was touching my daughter..."

"I didn't know..."

"I make a vow right now that if you open your mouth and lie to
me again, today will be your last day on this earth. That lie that you

tell me will be the last breath that you take. Did Zora tell you something was happening to her."

My mother nodded her head then started shaking and crying.

"You knew that bastard was touching my daughter and you didn't do anything to stop him! Let me go, son. She needs to die."

My brothers didn't move.

My mother covered her mouth and moved further into the corner of the room like the walls would magically protect her. I wanted to go to her, but Ezekiel had a grip on me while Uncle JD stood close to Zanetta.

"I have never in my entire life put my hands on a woman, but I promise to God if I get back to that house and you or your stuff are still there I am going to spend the rest of my life in jail because I am going to end your life. GET. OUT!"

My mother didn't move at first. My father charged her so quickly that my brothers had to scramble to catch him. As soon as my dad was about to put his hands on my mother, I yelled, "Daddy, please don't kill my mother."

He stopped mid-stride giving my brothers time to hold him back again. He looked my mother in the eyes and said, "She is not your mother."

"What?"

It felt like someone knocked the wind out of me. I slowly sat back down in my chair.

What did he mean she wasn't my mother? Did he mean because of what she allowed to happen, she wasn't my mother or did he mean that she was never my mother from the beginning? I was confused. If she's not my mother, then who is? Where is my mother? Did my brothers know? Why would my father not tell me? Why did he let me live with a woman that hated me? Is that why she hated me because I'm not her daughter?

"Shelia, there is a car waiting for you outside. Some of my men will help you get your things. Please just leave. Once Dad calms down we will find you," Countee said.

"James, I..."

"Please just leave Sheila. We won't let him hurt you," Langston added.

"You're not worth it," Amiri added.

My moth...Sheila was escorted out of the office by one of Countee's employees. She didn't even look back to apologize.

My father came over to where I was sitting and got down on his knees in front of me. He took my hand and said, "Baby girl, I am so sorry that I was not there to protect you. I trusted you with her, and that was my fault. I lost sight of what was important, and I let you down. I promise I had no idea. If I'd had an inkling of something happening, I would have ended his life. I am so sorry. Please forgive me."

He laid his head in my lap and cried. I never thought that I would hear my father say something like this to me.

"Daddy, I forgive you. I should have come to you and told you myself. I just thought that..."

"No," he cut me off. "You don't have anything to be sorry about." He wiped my tears. "It was my responsibility to keep you safe, and I failed. If you will let me, I will spend the rest of my life making it up to you. I love you Baby Girl. I love you so much, and I am so proud of the woman you are."

He stood and pulled me into a hug. I was back in my daddy's arms again. It felt so good. We hugged for several minutes before he sat me back down in my seat and sat next to me.

"What did you mean when you said that Sheila was not my mother?"

"Baby Girl, your mother's name was Kasima."

He pulled his wallet from his pocket and handed me a picture. It was like looking into a mirror and seeing me in the future.

"Daddy, I've dreamt about this woman since I was a little girl. Yes, she would sing a lullaby to me while she rubbed my hair or let me lay my head on her shoulder."

"What lullaby?" Langston asked.

"Hush a bye. Don't you cry..."

"Go to sleep, my little baby..." Langston finished the song.

"She used to sing that song to all of us when we were small," Amiri smiled.

"Kasima?" I ran my finger along the picture. "She is beautiful."

"She was beautiful, and she was the love of my life. She was so excited when she found out that you were a girl. We had already tried three times and produced these three knuckleheads," he motioned to my brothers.

"You all knew about our mother?"

"Yes, we did," Langston answered. "None of us cared for Sheila, and we definitely did not agree with keeping our mother from you, but pop and Sheila insisted, so when we were old enough, we left. We always talked about telling you about our mother, but we didn't. I'm sorry Baby Girl."

I nodded. I guess I never thought about why she let the boys call her by her first name. I was the only one that called her mom.

My father continued, "Your mother died after you turned one. She loved you so much. She would never let me put you in your crib. You slept with us until she passed," he smiled thinking back.

"What happened to my mother. How did she die?"

"When she was born, she had a heart defect that was corrected with surgery but even with the surgery, she wasn't supposed to live past her sixteenth birthday. She did though. She was amazing. I pursued her from our first day of kindergarten until she finally gave in when we were thirteen. She loved poetry and literature. That's why all of you are named after a poet or author. She was quoting Paul Laurence Dunbar when she was in elementary school. I loved her more than I have ever loved anyone. She loved me too. I wanted to marry her as soon as we graduated from high school but she was afraid that she would die and leave me a widower, so she refused my proposals."

"Sounds like someone I know," Ezekiel mumbled.

I shot him a side eye and continued to listen to my father's story.

"She went to college, so I went too even though the streets were my home. My uncles introduced me to the streets, and I fell in love with them. I loved the streets almost as much as I loved Kasi. Drugs, guns, gangs, I was into everything. She wanted me to leave the streets and get an education. We compromised, I got the education but still stayed in the streets.

After our first year of college, we got pregnant with Countee. I thought that having your brother would make her want to marry me, but she didn't. Then we got pregnant with Amiri right after Countee. Of course, Langston came after Amiri. We finished school and moved in together. We thought we were finished having kids and four years after Langston, you came. You were the prettiest baby girl I had ever seen. Your eyes are just like your mother's. Right after you turned one, she collapsed at home and never regained consciousness."

"You never married her?" I asked.

"No, I had planned on asking her again, but she died before I got the opportunity. I don't regret one single day that I had with her. She wasn't my wife, but that didn't matter because she was my everything. She never judged me for being in the streets. She didn't like it, but she always had my back. She was the best mother to you and your brothers. I never felt like I was in competition with my kids. She managed to give me what I needed and still be a wonderful mother."

"She's where I get my blue eyes from?"

"Yes, you look just like her. When I met Sheila, I was just being introduced to church. I was still hustling when your mom died, but there was a minister that would always come on the block and tell us about Jesus. After I lost Kasi and found myself a single father with four kids, I didn't know what to do. I followed the minister to church, and I have been there ever since. I didn't give up the streets right away, but eventually, I did.

I thought that Sheila was a good church going woman that would help me raise you. I still had so much of the streets in me, and I didn't want that for you. I had already influenced your brothers to some degree so I was determined that I would not influence you too.

I was wrong about Sheila, very wrong. I lost you because I was too stubborn to recognize her manipulative ways."

"Why didn't one of you come and find me?" I looked at my brothers.

"We did find you, Baby Girl," Countee responded.

"We knew you were in New York at Columbia," Amiri added. "That scholarship that you got every year, that was us. We set it up through the university so that you would be taken care of."

I always wondered who the donors were for the scholarship I was awarded every year. The school always said that the donors wanted to remain anonymous.

"Why didn't you say something? I needed you."

I felt myself becoming emotional again. Ezekiel kissed the side of my forehead.

"Sheila..." Langston began.

"I told y'all not to trust that bitch," Countee interrupted. "Sorry Pastor JD but I told my brothers not to believe her!"

"You're good. I understand," Uncle JD responded.

"What did she do?" My father looked at my brothers for an answer.

"She told us you left and didn't want anything to do with the family," Langston finished.

"But you should have asked me!"

"We know, Babygirl. We know," Langston replied. "It was shame, guilt, not knowing what to say or what to do. So, we just stayed in the background and made sure you were okay financially."

"We realized it was wrong for us to do that. When we decided that we were going to come to New York and speak with you, you'd moved," Amiri finished.

I broke down and cried. They all moved in to hug me. Each one of my brothers hugged me and apologized.

"Thank you for taking care of me. I survived off the money I received from that scholarship."

"You deserved it. We are all so proud of you," Langston said while still holding on to me.

"Baby Girl, I know it's been a lot all at once. Why don't you go and get some rest? We can all meet at my house later for dinner."

I nodded my head. It had been a long day already, and it was still early. I needed a little time to process everything, but I did want more time to spend with my family.

My dad helped me stand.

"I will see you later, okay? I love you."

"I love you too, Daddy."

I hugged him again.

Ezekiel

Watching Zora go through such a wide range of emotions was hard. Her father was genuinely repentant for everything that she'd gone through. I'm so happy that she found the answers that she was looking for and some she wasn't. She stared at the picture of her mother the whole ride back to our hotel. She went into the bedroom and closed the door. I wasn't sure if I should just leave her alone or go into the room with her.

"God, please give me some direction on how to handle Zora. Should I give her space or should I go and make sure she's okay? I really need your help."

I sat back on the couch for a minute until I thought back to our conversation about every man in her life walking away. I knew that she needed me.

I shot up from my seat and went into the bedroom. She was sitting on the side of the bed with the picture of her mother still in her hand. I ran a tub of water and undressed before going into the room and standing her on her feet.

She had tears running down her face. I undressed her and carried her into the bathroom. She stepped into the tub, and I followed situating myself behind her.

We sat quietly until she broke the silence.

"Zeke, do you understand how this changes everything?"

I didn't respond, I let her talk.

"My mother is Kasima, not Sheila. My mother loved me, not hated me. My brothers took care of me financially while I attended college. My father loves me and always has. He was trying to protect me. Nothing is what I thought it was.

I used to dream about my mother all the time. I thought she was just someone that I made up, but she wasn't. She existed, and she loved me."

"I know baby," I pulled her into me and held her until the tears stopped again.

I turned on the shower and washed her before we got out.

I helped her into her nightgown and dressed myself. We crawled into the bed together. I held her until she fell asleep. We would go over to her brother's house, but I needed for her to rest before we did anything else.

Zora

"Hi baby," she smiled while opening her arms for a hug.

I quickly made my way into her embrace while she rubbed my back.

"Why didn't you tell me you were my mother?"

I looked into her beautiful blue eyes waiting for an answer.

She led me to our couch by my hand. I sat down next to her.

"I didn't tell you because it was not my place to tell you. James needed to tell you. I'm glad you finally know."

"Did you love me? Did you want me?"

"I loved you more than everything and everyone. I had dreamed about you before you were even conceived. I knew I had to keep trying until I had you. You completed me. You completed your father. He fussed over you all the time. I wanted to name you Seven because you completed me, but your dad thought we should keep with the tradition and name you after a strong woman and author," she smiled.

"Mama, I never got a chance to know you," I cried.

"Baby, you know me with your heart. You know my love. My love has always surrounded you. It will continue to surround you. Speaking of love, do you know the one thing that I wish I could have done differently?"

I nodded my head.

"I should have married James. He was the love of my life. Sorta like Ezekiel is to you. Let him love you, baby, you deserve it. BJ deserves it, and my little baby girl in your stomach deserves it. Become a family and love him. Protect your love like you protect your children. Forgive your father and your brothers. They did their best. Can you do that for me?"

"Yes, Mama," I continued to cry. "Will I ever see you again?"

"I don't know. You're the mama now. Surround your family with your love and watch them grow. I love you, Zora Neale Chambers."

"I love you too, Mama."

I sat straight up in the bed after my dream. My face was wet with tears, but things were very clear. I knew what I needed to do.

"Zeke," I softly nudged him.

He sat straight up in the bed, "What! What's wrong?"

"Yes," I smiled.

"What?" he knitted his brows together.

"Yes, yes, yes!" I smiled.

"Wait...yes? You're saying yes?"

"Yes!" I nodded while smiling.

"Wait, just to make sure I'm not dreaming. Yes, you will marry me?"

"Yes, I will marry you. Yes, I love you. Yes, I want your last name."

"I want to adopt Braeden and change his last name."

"You do?"

"Yes, I do. What do you think?"

"Yes, I want you to be Braeden's dad. Yes, I want his last name to be the same as ours. Yes, yes, yes."

"Yes, you will give me Cashew and Almond?"

"What?"

"After Peanut. I want Cashew and Almond."

"Now you're pushing it!" I laughed. "No, just kidding. I will give you whatever you want."

"Word?"

"Word," I smiled.

He jumped up from the bed. He grabbed something from his travel bag then came back over the bed.

"Let me do this the right way."

He got down on one knee and took my hand into his. I started crying immediately.

"Zora, I thought that I would never let a woman have my heart. At first, I fought the feelings I had for you. They came hard and fast, but it hurt too much to fight it. I was happiest when I heard your voice. I smiled more when I saw your face. You and BJ came into my life, took my heart and split it between the two of you. I didn't think love felt like this. I mean I actually feel it. I feel it when we are away from each other, and I fight to get back to you. I feel it when you innocently touch my arm or brush past me. I need you in my life forever. I can't promise that I won't mess up because I'm fairly certain that I will but I will be the best husband, friend, father and provider that I can for you BJ and Peanut, oh and Almond and Cashew. Zora, will you marry me?"

I fought through my tears to find my voice, "Yes, Ezekiel! I will marry you."

He popped open the box he was holding to display a beautiful Princess cut diamond ring that rotated in the box with a light under it. The light made the diamond sparkle brighter. He removed the ring and placed it on my finger.

"Zeke, this is not the same ring."

"I had to step my game up," he chuckled. "No for real, this one was being made. I was going to keep asking you until I broke you down and you said yes. I love you, Zora."

"I love you too."

"Prove it."

Ezekiel

I stood from my kneeled position. Zora pulled me to her by my waist and started working on untying my pajama pants.

She freed my erection and started to stroke it with her small soft hands. She flicked her tongue across the head to collect the precum that had leaked out.

"Damn, Z. I love it when you do that."

She looked up at me and did it again before taking as much as she could into her mouth. She used her hands to stroke the rest. My head is already spinning from her using the right amount of pressure and the noises she is making let me know she is enjoying pleasuring me. My knees almost buckled when I felt my head hit the back of her throat without her gagging. Damn, she's the best at this. I looked down to watch me disappear into her mouth and then reappear. I almost lost it when I saw my ring on her finger. She increased the pressure of her grip on me and the pressure of her sucking motion. I wanted to tell her that I was about to bust but I know it wouldn't have been any use. She was claiming this one as her own.

"Ugh!" I yelled as I released down her throat.

She stood from her kneeled position and pulled her nightgown over her head.

"Lie down."

She followed my directions. I pulled her toward the edge of the bed by her legs. I bent down to kiss her while entering her at the same time. I pulled all the way out and entered her again. This time making sure I was completely buried inside her. She put her hands on my waist trying to push away.

"No, don't run from me."

I moved both of her hands and held them above her head as I continued to deep stroke. She moved to free her hands then rested them on my ass encouraging me to go deeper. Just when I think I've got her she maneuvers and does something to try to make me come. I felt myself about to blow. I pulled out.

"Hands and knees!" She flipped over and assumed the position.

I could see her juices running from her.

"You're dripping baby. Is this all for me?"

"It's all your's, baby."

I lined myself up with her opening. I took a moment to enjoy the curve of her hips and the plumpness of her behind. I got excited when I realized she said yes. She is all mine.

"Tell me again," I said as I caressed her ass.

"This pussy is all your's ba..."

I plunged into her cutting off her sentence.

"Zeke!" she yelled my name.

"Come for me, baby."

I felt her vibrate all around me before I felt that grip from the inside and knew I was about to come right along with her.

AFTER OUR LOVEMAKING SESSION, I called Roman and asked him to bring BJ to us. I needed to talk to him.

I was a little nervous about having this conversation with BJ. I'm not sure why a four-year-old was making me nervous, but he was.

He arrived about thirty minutes later.

"Hey man. We need to have a talk."

"Okay."

BJ sat on the couch next to me. Zora was in the bedroom. I told her that this was another one of those conversations I needed to have with Braeden by myself.

"I asked your mommy to marry me. She said yes. Do you know what that means?"

"It means that you are going to be my mommy's husband like Uncle Blue is Tee Tee's husband. We will live together all the time."

This kid is so smart.

"Yes, that what it means. How do you feel about that?"

"I like it. Can we live at our house with the pool?"

"That's something that your mother and I will have to discuss," I chuckled. "I have a question for you. What would you think about me becoming your dad?"

"You want to be my daddy?"

"It would be my honor to be your daddy."

He jumped up and wrapped his arms around my neck.

"I want you to be my daddy. Would I be a Bluette man?"

"B, you're already a Bluette man, but yes your last name would be Bluette instead of Chambers."

"I can call you Daddy?"

"I would like it very much if you called me dad."

"Okay, Daddy."

I was not prepared for the rush of emotions I had hearing him call me Daddy. He hugged me while I let a couple tears fall.

"I love you, Braeden."

"I love you too, Daddy."

"You want to go and tell your Mommy?"

"Yes!" he sang.

He got down off the couch and ran to the bedroom, "Mommy! My Daddy said he's going to marry you and change my last name to Bluette!"

15

I SAID YES! I was so happy. Ezekiel is happy, and so is BJ. When I heard BJ call Ezekiel Daddy, it just felt right. It sounded correct. I'm so happy. Today has been the best day of my life. I got my family back. Found out that my mother loved me and I'm engaged to the love of my life.

Countee invited everyone over to his house, so Roman, Nette, and Paxton came with us. We pulled up to large iron gates. They opened as we pulled up to them. We drove down a long driveway until we arrived in front of a large white home that was a mixture of contemporary and traditional style. It was stunning.

Countee was standing at the front door waiting for us.

"Come in," he moved to the side so we all could enter.

"Chambers," Paxton nodded towards Countee.

"Bluette," Countee responded.

"You two know each other?" I asked.

"Yeah, Bluette and I served in the same Army unit for a while," Countee answered.

"Small world," Blue smiled.

"Very!" Paxton added.

We followed him into the heart of his home. My other brothers were already there. So was my dad.

"Everyone, these are Ezekiel's brothers, Roman and Paxton."

My dad walked over to them with his hand extended.

"Pastor Roman, nice to meet you."

"Same here, Reverend Chambers."

"I heard you say you served with my son?"

"Yes Sir, we served together briefly," Paxton responded.

"Thank you for your service." They shook hands.

My brothers came over and shook hands with the Bluette men also.

"Daddy, this is your grandson, BJ."

BJ walked up to my dad and said, "Hi Grandpa."

My Dad bent down. BJ wrapped his arms around my Dad's neck. My dad hugged him back.

"What does BJ stand for?"

"Braeden James," BJ responded proudly.

My dad looked at me with tears in his eyes. I smiled.

"Did you know that your name is my name?"

"It is?"

"Yes, well my name is James Braeden. People used to call me JB when I was your age."

"Wow, mommy my grandpa's name is the same as mine!"

"I know sweetheart. I named you after him."

"Grandpa, I go to school, and at school, I play with my friends. Their names are..."

"Whoa, Daddy don't let him suck you into that conversation! Let me introduce you to your other uncles first." I laughed.

I turned BJ's attention to my brothers.

"BJ, these are your uncles, my brothers."

"Oh, I like having uncles 'cause they learn me stuff."

"Teach you, B," Ezekiel corrected.

"Yeah," BJ slapped his forehead with his hand, "they teached me stuff."

Everyone chuckled.

"BJ this is my brother Countee. He's the oldest."

"Hi, Uncle Countee. I remember you."

"You do?"

"Yes, when we were at the park."

"You remember that, huh?"

Countee rubbed the back of his neck with his hand.

"What is he talking about Countee?" I asked.

"I found you in New York. I watched you and BJ at the park one day. I wanted to say something to you but like we discussed earlier, I didn't."

"Mommy, I told you I saw a man that looked like you."

"I thought you said I looked like a man! I started wearing lip gloss and earrings!"

Everyone laughed.

"How did you find me?"

"I own a Private Investigation and Security firm. I can find anyone. I came back to get these two. You'd moved by the time we got back to New York."

"You might have to give BJ a position. He blew your cover," Paxton laughed. "You slipping, Chambers?"

"Never that, Bluette." Countee rolled his eyes.

"I'm Amiri." BJ hugged him. "It's nice to meet you, Braeden."

"Thank you, Uncle Miri."

"This is Langston," I pointed to Langston.

"Hi BJ." They hugged.

"I have something I want to tell everyone since we are all together." I grabbed Ezekiel's hand. "I accepted Ezekiel's proposal. We're getting married!"

Zanetta shrieked. She ran over and hugged me. I showed her my ring.

"Wow, I didn't know circus clowns made enough to afford something like this!"

"Whatever Nette," Ezekiel laughed. "Reverend Chambers, I'd

already asked Zora once, and she said no. If I had known that you would be back in her life, I would have asked your permission first."

"It is because of you that I have my daughter back. For that, I will be eternally grateful. If she chooses you, then I do too. Just know that I missed someone hurting her once. That will never happen again."

"I got it, Sir. Thank you."

They hugged.

Countee had a ton of food cooked. We sat and enjoyed each other's company. I saw my dad laughing. I can't remember the last time I saw him laugh. BJ was glued to my dad's side the entire night.

BJ fell asleep, and all the men followed Countee to the back of his house to check out his gun range. Zanetta and I stayed in the house.

"So, when is the wedding? Before you answer that, can we take a moment to acknowledge that you are engaged to be married? Then we also have to acknowledge that we are going to have the same last name!"

"I know!"

We both squealed.

"I don't know when the wedding is, we haven't discussed it. We were too busy celebrating," I smiled, "but I want it to be soon."

"You better celebrate!" We slapped hands and laughed. "You don't want to wait until after Peanut is born?"

"No, I would do it right now if we could. I love him so much. I shouldn't have waited to say yes."

"What made you change your mind?"

"My mother. I dreamt about her, and she told me to let him love me."

"That was great advice."

"Yeah, I'm ready to build a life with my church boy."

Ezekiel

We stayed at Countee's house until late into the evening. Zora's brothers are all cool. Countee owns a PI and Security firm. Amiri is a Zookeeper. He takes care of the Polar Bear at the Saint Louis Zoo. Langston is a College Professor. He teaches African-American Literature. James (he told me to call him James instead of Reverend Chambers) asked all of us if we would come to his church on Sunday. Blue, Nette and Paxton had to get back to Houston so that Blue could be at our church, but Zora and I decided to stay.

Zora and I were sitting in our hotel room relaxing. BJ was spending the day with his grandpa James.

"Have you thought about the wedding?"

I was sitting up in the bed with my back against the headboard. She was between my legs with her back against my chest. I was rubbing lotion on her stomach.

"I was telling Nette that I want something small and intimate. I don't want a full production. What do you think?"

"I want whatever you want. We can spend a million or a thousand. I'm cool with either one."

"What if we plan something on the property that you took me to."

"That would work. When do you want to do it?"

"I want to do it as soon as we can get it planned."

I smiled. I was happy to hear her say that.

"What do you expect from me as your husband?"

She turned to face me.

"I expect for you to mean what you say. Tell the truth no matter what. Be open and honest about how you feel. Like, let me know if I'm not giving you enough attention or if I'm being too clingy. I expect for you to keep me first no matter how many little nuts I push out for you."

"Little nuts?" he laughed.

"You know what I mean, Peanut, Cashew, and Almond."

"I knew what you meant. Cause there is nothing little about the nuts you push out."

"Shut up Zeke. That's it for me. What about you? What do you expect from me?"

"I expect for you to continue to be great. I expect you to put a lot of energy into being the best Doctor you can be. I expect for you to always be honest with me. Let me know if I'm messing up because I will. I expect for you to stick it out with me even if things get real crazy. This is for life."

I nodded my understanding.

"What about cooking, cleaning, bills?"

"You keep an immaculate house now. I don't expect that to change. We can keep my housekeeper if you want. You cook when you can. I will cook too. I would like to have dinner as a family as much as possible. We always have Chef. She can prepare things that can be frozen. I will take care of the bills. I will expect for you to invest a portion of your salary, pay your tithes and some of it should go into a retirement fund. I am doing the same thing with mine. We can sit down with Paxton to work on that. My money is your money. You will have access to everything that I have."

"My money is your money too."

"My momma always said that a woman should have a little money that she keeps to the side for herself. I think that's a great idea."

"Where will we live?"

"Where do you want to live? We can stay at your house, or we can stay at mine. We can build something on the property. It's up to you."

"If we move into your house, can we still keep my house? It's my first big purchase. I don't want to sell it right now."

"We can keep it. We will figure out what we want to do with it later. We will work on getting Peanut's room together. We can turn that room next to our bedroom into your closet and office. Would you like that?"

"I would love that!"

"Good, then it's settled. We have another wedding to plan."

"We do!"

Ezekiel

"Good morning church!"

"Good morning!" The church responded.

"It's a good day to give God praise for all of his marvelous blessings, amen?"

"Amen," the church responded.

We were sitting in the front row of Pool of Siloam Church, James' church. All three of Zora's brothers came today. James had just taken the platform.

"I want to share some things with you today if that's alright."

The audience encouraged him to continue. Someone placed a stool next to him, and he sat down.

"When I accepted Christ into my life over twenty-five years ago, I gave up everything I knew to follow him. I came to him after having lost the love of my life and was left alone to raise four children on my own. I know a lot of you didn't know that detail. I never shared it with anyone because I wanted to start fresh. I married a girl from the church that I joined. She promised me that she would help me raise my children as her own and we began our life together. I didn't look back. I was called to ministry about two years after I became saved. I read, studied, researched and did everything I could to learn about God. I left the raising of my kids up to my wife because in my mind God and ministry came first.

After some time, I started this ministry. I started out with my wife and my kids as my members, and eventually, we grew. By the way, I am very proud to call myself your Pastor."

The crowd shouted out affirmations, and he continued.

"As this ministry grew, I spent more and more time with ministry and less and less quality time with my family. I missed some things, y'all. Some huge, very important, life altering things, with all of my children. From my oldest son Countee to my baby girl, Zora. The ministry became my mistress. I took better care of my mistress than I did my family. I am grateful that Yahweh is a God of second chances. All of my children are here with me today." He pointed to the front row.

The audience stood up and started clapping. After they finished their applause, he continued.

"I didn't think I would live to see the day that I had all of them together again under one roof let alone joining me on Sunday morning. I want to publicly apologize for putting ministry before you, all of you. I apologize for not protecting you, and I apologize for not being there when you needed me most."

I held Zora's hand a little tighter. Someone passed her a tissue to wipe the tears.

"I wanted to announce a couple of things to you today. First thing, I am a grandpa, and I have another one on the way. My baby girl and her fiancé, Ezekiel, are expecting my next grandchild in a few months."

The audience cheered.

"I was introduced to my first grandson the other day. Would you like to meet him?"

The audience cheered.

"BJ, come up here with Grandpa."

BJ climbed down out of his chair and joined James on stage. He picked him up as the audience clapped. They were wearing matching bowties from BJ's collection.

"Can you tell everyone your name?"

BJ put his mouth to the microphone and said, "You know my name, Grandpa. It's your name!" BJ looked at my dad confused.

"Well, the audience doesn't know your name. I wanted you to tell them," my dad responded.

"Oh, okay my name is Braeden James Cham...Bluette!"

My heart swelled hearing him use my last name.

The audience laughed.

"How old are you, Braeden?"

"I am four years old. My mommy says I'm going on fifty, but I think I'm going on five."

The audience laughed again.

"I like our bowties. Where did we get these from?"

"My bowtie collection."

"Your bowtie collection?"

"Yes, I am the COO of BJ's Bowties. It's a Bluette Men company."

"Oh, I see. What is the COO's job?"

"I help make sure the bowties get made. I pick out fabrics with my Tee Tee. My Uncle Paxton learned me how to be a businessman like him and my uncle Blue and my daddy."

The audience ooh'd and ahh'd while BJ spoke. He sat BJ on a stool next to his as he sat back down.

"As you can see, I have missed out on quite a bit of my grandson's life. He already owns a company."

The audience laughed.

"My next announcement is that today will be my last day as the Senior Pastor of Pool of Siloam."

Everyone gasped and spoke among themselves.

"I am retiring and leaving the church in the capable hands of Elder Moyses Daughton and his wife, Mila."

The new Pastor and his wife stood while everyone clapped.

James spoke to Zora and me and told us his decision to move to Houston. He had already spoken to the person that would be taking over his church. He said they'd discussed this happening even before he was reunited with Zora. After his reconciliation with her, he decided to move the date up. Zora told him that he could have her house since she and BJ would be moving into my house. That was all he needed to hear.

"Sheila and I are no longer together due to irreconcilable differences. I will be accompanying Baby Girl and her family back to

Houston. It has been an honor to serve as your Pastor. I truly love you all. Keep my family and me in your prayers, and I will keep you in mine."

He picked up BJ from his stool and walked down out of the pulpit. We all followed behind him while the church stood and clapped. Some people stepped out into the aisle to hug him while others waved and smiled.

Zora

"Hey Baby Girl, before you return to Houston, there is something else I need to discuss with you. Would you mind meeting me at my office?"

I was on the phone talking to Countee while Ezekiel and I were packing our luggage to head back to Houston.

"Zeke, Countee needs for us to stop by his office before we leave. Will we have time?"

"Yeah, we will have time."

"Cool. I will send one of my men to pick you up. He can take you to the airport after were done."

"Okay, see you in a few minutes."

Countee's employee met us at our hotel about thirty minutes later. He drove us to a glass office building and pulled into the parking garage. We followed him to Countee's office.

"What's up, BJ?" Countee pulled BJ in for a hug.

"Nothing Uncle Countee," BJ smiled.

"I have a room down the hall that has video games, books, and snacks. Would you like to see it?"

"Yes!" BJ sang.

"Baby Girl, is it okay if BJ hangs out with my assistant while we talk?"

"Yes, that's fine."

Countee's assistant took BJ's hand and led him to a room down the hall while Zeke and I followed Countee into his office.

"Have a seat," Countee pointed to the plush chairs in front of his desk. "I asked you to come here because there is one more thing you need to know."

I immediately had all sorts of thoughts run through my head. "Is my dad sick? Do I have another sibling?" I didn't know what to think.

"When I found you in New York, I also came across some people that you knew. One, in particular, I figured you would want this information on." Countee handed me a manila folder. "Open it."

I opened the folder and right on top of several pieces of paper was a picture of Bahir. I looked at the picture for a moment before I looked at Countee.

"This is Bahir, BJ's biological father."

I passed the picture to Ezekiel.

"I know. Look at the rest of the papers."

The first paper on the stack was Bahir's birth certificate.

"He was born in the United States? He told me he was born in Lebanon."

"No, he was born in Florida. He was adopted by a family that moved to Lebanon. His mother was too young to care for him, so she gave him up for adoption."

I looked at the next page in the stack. It was a list of names.

"What is this?"

"This is a list of his known associates. Most of those people are on the terrorist watch list, dead, or in jail."

"What do you mean? Bahir was a college student."

"Bahir Rezek was a college student, but he was associated with some bad people. Drugs, illegal gun sales, stolen goods and human trafficking."

"What? No, not Bahir. He was a mild tempered, corny type guy."

"He was a professional thief. He went for unique, rare and high-value items."

Countee gave me a stack of pictures.

"These are some of the things he has stolen."

There were pictures of paintings, jewelry, sculptures, and vases. I passed the pictures to Ezekiel.

"He wasn't flashy or anything. He didn't have nice clothes or shoes. He lived in a basement apartment!"

"For years, the authorities didn't know who he was. He could be out in public, and no one would ever suspect him because he was very good at keeping a low profile."

"Am I tripping or do you keep referring to him in past tense?"

He nodded to the folder. The next paper on the stack was an arrest record and mug shot.

"He went to California to break into someone's house that had a valuable painting. He was able to the get painting. He was even able to sell it, but he didn't realize that the person he robbed was a very connected person. The owner of the painting put a bounty on his head which is why he disappeared from New York. He ran back to France to try to hide out. He eventually had to turn himself into the French authorities to keep from getting murdered. He sent you that letter while he was en route to France."

"How did you know he sent me a letter?"

"I found the person that mailed it for him. He didn't want to mail it, out of fear that it would be traced to his location, so he paid someone to put it in the mail in New York."

"Where is he now?"

"Dead."

"Dead! I thought you said he turned himself into the French police?"

"He did, but they couldn't protect him. The person he stole from is a well-connected man. He has a far reach."

I was not prepared to hear that Bahir was dead. The weird thing is it didn't impact me at all. Hearing that news was like hearing my Facebook friend's cousin's brother's ex-boyfriend died. I felt sorry that someone lost their life, but I was so far removed from that person that I couldn't feel the sadness.

"Are you okay, Z?"

I looked at Ezekiel. I smiled.

"I'm good. I mourned Bahir a long time ago."

I closed the folder and handed it back to Countee.

"I wanted you to have this information, Baby Girl. I don't know what you'd planned on telling my nephew about his biological but now you know."

"I don't know what I planned on telling him."

"When the time comes, we will talk to him about it, together."

Ezekiel kissed my hand that he was holding.

We stood to leave.

Countee pulled me into a hug. I missed hugging my brothers.

"We are going to get Dad all packed up and down to Houston in a couple weeks. So I will see you soon. I love you Baby Girl."

"I love you too, Count."

Ezekiel

As soon as we returned to Houston, we started planning our wedding. I temporarily moved into Zora's house while they did construction on my house. I was building her closet and office like I promised. I wanted all of that completed before my family moved in. I wanted Nette to start designing Peanut's room, but Zora told me that we should probably wait until we are sure she's a girl. I'm positive she's a girl, but I will listen to her and wait until after the official ultrasound before we start the design.

James moved to Houston about two weeks after we left Saint Louis. He and Zora wanted to live closer to each other, so he found a condo a few miles from my house instead of living in Zora's house. He has settled in quickly. He spends as much time as he can with BJ which has been helpful since Zora and I have been planning our wedding. Blue and my dad told me the only words that I needed to say during the planning process were: 'I agree' and 'yes.' So, that's all I've been saying, and it's worked out well. James and Zora's brothers are footing the bill for the ceremony.

"Daddy, my grandpa James said that we are going to have fun while you and Mommy are away on your trip. He said we are going to go swimming, we are going to read books, go to Uncle Blue's church and other fun stuff."

It always makes me smile when my son calls me Dad. I love this little kid. We'd been together all day getting the final fitting for our suits and getting our hair done for the ceremony. Tomorrow is our wedding. Zora is spending the night at Nette's condo with my mother, Lady Grace, Nette and Olivia. Olivia has become part of the family. Paxton is feeling her, so the ladies have taken a special interest in her. My brothers and I haven't had a conversation about it yet, but it's cool to see him interested.

"That sounds like a lot of fun." I was helping BJ into his pajamas. "Are you ready to say your prayers?"

"Yes."

We got on our knees together.

"Hi, Jesus. It's BJ. Thank you for being my friend. Thank you for my mommy and my daddy. Thank you for baby Peanut even though she's still linkubating in my mommy's stomach. Thank you for my Tee Tee and my uncles. Thank you for my Grandpa and my Pop. Thank you for Grandma. That's all. Amen."

"Amen," I smiled and helped him into the bed. I kissed his cheek and closed his door.

My brothers were waiting for me in the living room.

"He's down?" Blue asked.

"Yeah, he's down."

"Man, who would have thought that we would be hanging out together the night before your wedding?" Paxton questioned.

"I know! I honestly didn't plan on ever being married now I can't picture my life without Zora. Do you remember when we were in Saint Louis and Nette said that I was going to meet someone?"

"I remember. She said it after her session at the conference, right?" Blue said.

"Yeah. Do you know that from that moment until I met Zora things were off? I slept with a couple women after she told me that and I was bored and uninterested. I mean I never attached feeling to sex anyway, but this feeling was one of indifference, almost. Like I could take it or leave it...preferably leave it. I kept trying to brush it off like it was age or maybe the women I'd chosen but in the back of my mind, I knew. I knew that someone was coming. The moment I saw Zora walk into Nette's apartment, I knew she was that someone. This is going to sound real corny, but it's like I was living in black and white. Zora and BJ add color to my life. They make me work harder to achieve my goals. I keep my word, so I don't disappoint them. Having her next to me helps me sleep at night. Waking up to her in the morning gives me the drive I need to get through the day. She is my passion."

"I'm happy and proud," Blue continued, "A man that finds a wife finds a treasure and obtains favor with the Lord. I know people quote that scripture all the time, but it's accurate. Congrats, little brother. You have chosen well."

We hugged.

"I agree. I remember Dad saying that Bluette men always know when they've found the one. I thought that maybe you had over-looked her all these years!" We laughed. "I'm glad Zora is the one. She and BJ have added color to all our lives. Congratulations, I'm proud to be your brother."

Paxton and I hugged.

"So now for the gift. This is from Pax and me."

Blue handed me a small box. I opened it. At first glance, it looked like a small black toy car with wheels. Upon further inspection, I realized it was Tesla key fob. I took it out the box and looked at my brothers.

"This is a fob for a Tesla?"

"Yeah but not just any Tesla, it's the model X with the falcon wing rear doors. We figured you would need space to get the kids in and out the back seat."

"It's being customized, but it will be ready when you get back from your honeymoon," Paxton said.

I stood and embraced both my brothers.

"Thank you."

"We took Zora's present to her before we came over here. Nette said she didn't want us ruining Zora's makeup the way you both tried to ruin her makeup at our wedding."

"What did you get her?"

"We purchased a building for her to house her free clinic in whenever she is ready to open it. Right now, it has a couple other businesses in it, so she will have an income coming in from it. We will manage it for her," Paxton explained.

"That's what's up! Thank you."

"So, are you ready?" Blue asked.

"In the words of the great boxing champ Jack Jenkins in *Harlem Nights*: Re, re, ready...hell yeah...I'm ready."

We all laughed as I gave my best impression of the stuttering boxing champion in the movie.

Zora

We kept the guest list for our wedding small. Family and close friends. I invited all the partners and their wives. My brothers came in from Saint Louis. Lyrica and Obasi flew in. Everyone that I loved was there to watch Ezekiel, and I take our public vows.

We actually got married a couple days after we returned from Saint Louis. The only people in attendance for that were BJ, Paxton, Olivia, Zanetta and Roman. I asked Paxton and Nette to sing. I was surprised when they both agreed without fighting me on it. They sang *Spend my Life with You* by Tamia and Eric Benèt. Roman played the acoustic guitar while they sang. After they sang, Roman performed the ceremony. We Facetimed my dad and Ezekiel's parents. I didn't want to wait for a wedding to become his wife.

The weather cooperated, and we had a beautiful outdoor

wedding. We put a tent on the property to hold the ceremony and another one to have the reception. Then we had smaller ones that we used as dressing rooms. My biggest worry was the bathroom situation but we found a company that supplied some of the cleanest portable restrooms I'd ever seen, and they came with attendants!

Bishop officiated, and my dad walked me down the aisle. I was being fitted for my dress up to the day of the wedding. My stomach was growing so fast. The same designer that made a dress for Nette's ceremony made mine. It had a sweetheart neckline and empire waistline. The bodice was covered in pearls and jewels. The full skirt was roomy enough for Peanut.

At the reception, Lyrica sang a song that she'd written especially for Zeke and me. She looked beautiful with her baby bump. She was a little further along than I was, but it looked like our stomachs were about the same size.

Paxton stood to get everyone's attention. The room became quiet.

"Ezekiel has always been the one in the family that did things his own way. Roman and I tried hard to stay within the lines, follow the rules but Zeke, not so much. Today Bro, we are proud of you and the decision you made to make Zora your wife. We love you, Zeke and Zora." He raised his glass. "To Zeke and Zora; we pray you have a lifetime of happiness and love."

Everyone repeated after him.

Ezekiel and I stood together.

"We want to thank everyone for being here with us and participating in this celebration with us. My wife and I..."

He smiled at me. I'm still getting used to being called wife, but I love it.

"have an announcement that we would like to share with everyone. We officially found out that Peanut is a girl. I would like to say to everyone that doubted me, 'I told you so.'"

Everyone laughed.

"I am so happy that this amazing, smart, gifted, beautiful, no-nonsense woman agreed to be my wife. I love you, sweetheart."

He quickly kissed me and passed me the microphone.

"When I first left home, I thought that life would always be a fight and a struggle. I thought that hard work would produce results, but I was convinced that I would never be happy. I thought that I was fine with that until I met my husband and experienced true happiness. I realized that with him in my life, not only was I happy but I didn't struggle. I didn't have to work as hard. I didn't have to be responsible for everything. He proved to me that I was worthy of being loved by someone other than my son. He picked up my son the very first day he met him and hasn't put him down since. His love for me helped me re-discover God's love for me. I fell in love with a church boy!"

THE END

EPILOGUE

Ezekiel

"HEY BABY, how did the test go?"

"Is this Mr. Bluette?"

I pulled my phone from my ear to look at the number. It was Zora's number, but this wasn't her voice.

"Who is this?"

"Hi, this is Mallory, I was at the testing site with your wife."

Zora had gone this morning to take a written test to monitor the progress of her residency. She spent hours studying for it.

"Why do you have my wife's phone?"

I could hear a lot of commotion in the background.

"She was coming out of the test, and her water broke. There are several doctors here with her, so she is in good hands. The ambulance is coming to take her to the hospital."

"Where is she? Is she okay? Can she talk?"

"Doctor Bluette, your husband is on the phone."

"Baby," Zora spoke into the phone, "my water broke, and these contractions are kicking my ahhhhh..."

I heard someone in the background telling her to breathe.

"Mr. Bluette?" Mallory was back on the phone. "Her contractions are not consistently five minutes apart, but since her water broke, we have to get her to the hospital."

I was running around the house making sure I had her overnight bag, my keys, my phone...where is my phone? I looked for about five minutes before I realized it was in my hand.

"I will meet you at the hospital."

"Okay."

I heard Zora yelling something in the background.

"Doctor Bluette said not to forget the gift for BJ."

"Tell her I have it."

I disconnected the call.

I called my mother.

"Mom, Peanut is coming. Zora's water broke at the testing center. She is on her way to the hospital."

"We are on our way baby. I will call everyone else. You just make sure you focus and get to your wife in one piece."

"Okay, BJ is with James, and I think Blue is at the studio..."

"Sweetheart, I got it. You just focus on the road and get to the hospital."

I arrived at the hospital just as the ambulance was pulling up with Zora inside. I ran over to make sure she was okay.

"Hey baby," she smiled, "look at all of this attention your daughter is getting already."

I smiled, "She's like her dad."

"Mmmmmmmmm," Zora gripped my hand.

"Breathe, Doctor Bluette..." one of the paramedics said as they wheeled her into one of the rooms.

A nurse came in and instructed Zora to change into the hospital gown. She had another contraction while we were getting her into the gown.

Doctor Ingram came into the room.

"Ezekiel, good to see you." He extended his hand.

I shook it before he turned his attention to Zora.

"I see Peanut is ready to make her entrance?"

"She is," Zora said out of breath.

"I'm going to check you to see how many centimeters you are dilated and then we will try to move you upstairs to your birthing room. If you are too far dilated, we are going to keep you down here and deliver her here, okay?"

Zora nodded.

Doctor Ingram checked her cervix.

"You're at about five and a half. Almost too far along for an epidural but we can try. They are going to move you upstairs. I will see you in a few okay?"

"Thank you, Doctor."

They quickly moved Zora to her birthing room. By the time they started her IV and hooked her to all of the monitors, the entire family was there. My mother had come into town a week ago because she wanted to make sure she was here when Zora went into labor. James arrived at the hospital with BJ. Blue and Zanetta were there with Paxton and Olivia.

Pax and Ollie have developed a friendship. At least that's what they are calling it. I'm cool with it. She is very sweet she seems to bring a level of calm to Paxton that I haven't seen in a long time.

My dad and Zora's brothers were all en route.

They were able to give Zora the epidural which helped with the pain. It was hard to watch her go through those contractions. She had one contraction before the epidural that caused her to cry. Paxton and Roman decided to leave the room. It was too much for them. I wanted to walk out with all them but since it was my baby she was birthing I had to stay.

James said, "I went through this with your mother. I can't do it again."

He left and took BJ.

By the time she was dilated enough to push, everyone had arrived.

My wife did such a phenomenal job birthing our daughter. My mother, Zanetta, and Olivia were all in the room. The men never did return. After only three strong pushes, I heard the beautiful sound of my first daughter's voice. She had strong, healthy lungs.

"Do you want to cut the cord, Dad?"

I took the scissors from Doctor Ingram and cut the umbilical cord.

Zahria Vashti Bluette weighed eight pounds and four ounces. She was twenty-two and a half inches long.

BJ came into the room to see his little sister.

I handed him the gift that Zora and I had picked out for him.

"Look BJ, this is a gift from Zahria to you."

People told us that we should give BJ a gift and tell him it's from the baby. That would help with him feeling left out with all the attention that the baby would be receiving.

He took the neatly wrapped present and ripped the paper off. It was a t-shirt that read, "I'm the BIG brother."

He loved it. He immediately took to the role of big brother and protector. If someone was holding Zahria, BJ was sitting right next to them.

Zora

I passed my test even though I had contractions the entire time I was taking the test! I thought they were Braxton Hicks contractions until I finished the test and my water broke. I feel like I should have received extra points for breathing through contractions and getting the answers correct.

MOMMA GRACE STAYED with me for the first few weeks after Zahria came home. I don't know what I would have done without her. Zahria doesn't have blonde hair or blue eyes, but she looks just like her dad. He is so in love with this little girl.

My family and I traveled with my Dad to meet my mother's family. I have several cousins who have blue eyes. BJ played with his cousins while my mother's cousins and aunts told me stories about her. I visited her grave and told her thank you for loving me.

The length of my residency has been extended because I needed to take time off after having Zahria. I don't mind though. I'm not in any rush. I'm still seeing patients at the practice and learning from Doctor Miller.

I didn't think love would find me but it did. I am so happy to be Ezekiel's Passion.

THEN

Paxton

"What does your family think you did in the military?"

I was sitting across from Countee at his office in Saint Louis.

"IT specialist."

"IT!" He burst out laughing. "Do you even know how to turn on a computer?"

I narrowed my eyes at him.

"Does Zora really know what happened to BJ's biological?"

"She knows that he's dead."

"Does she know who killed him?"

He sat back in his chair, "What do you need?"

"I may have a problem. There's a woman..."

"That's always where the problems begin."

"My woman. I need to make sure her past stays in the past."

"You want to get the team together again?"

"I may need them. I will let you know."

I stood.

"I hope she's worth it."

"She is. She's my tranquility...my peace."

THANK YOU!

To my BETA readers and my proofreader.

My family for giving me space to create.

Thanks, Te' for the use of your character and your product. You Rock!

Check out Isaiah Noble and his siblings in *The Nobles of Sweet Rapids* series by Te' Russ. http://a.co/1tpTWHs

Thank you, Yahweh! You are my source!

I am most like God when I am creating!

Also by
Bailey West

I'm most like God
when I am creating.

The Bluette Men Series

Blue's Beauty
Ezekiel's Passion
Paxton's Peace

The Valentine Law Series

Serving Time
Free Indeed
Trusting the Process

Lessons In Love Series
Inn Love

LET'S KEEP IN TOUCH

www.facebook.com/groups/baileyscoterie/
Instagram.com/authorbaileyw

Made in the USA
Middletown, DE
12 November 2019

78256508R00176